"Do you realize the position you've put me in?"

"It's not bad enough that you jump bail and I cover for you. Now I'm withholding evidence from the police." The fact that Clancy hadn't asked him to protect her, that he'd done it all on his own, only made it worse. "I just compromised myself and my career, put my P.I. license on the line for you," Jake told her, laying it on a little strong.

"Let's not forget why you're really here." She glared at him. "To get the goods on me, isn't that what you said?"

She looked ashen. Shaken. Scared. Not at all like a criminal.

Before he could consider how stupid it was, he pulled Clancy into his arms. She resisted at first, but slowly he felt her soften in his embrace. He tried to focus on the case, not on the wonderfully feminine feel of the woman he held.

Jake growled at himself in disgust. He wanted to kiss her, protect and shelter her. But he couldn't let anything get in the way of the truth. Not even Clancy.

D0051245

Dear Reader,

They're rugged, they're strong and they're *wanted!* Whether sheriff, undercover cop or officer of the court, these men are trained to keep the peace, to uphold the law. But what happens when they meet the one woman who gets to know the man *behind* the badge?

Twelve of these men are on the loose...and only Harlequin Intrigue brings them to you—one per month, in the LAWMAN series. This month, meet hotshot P.I. Jake Hawkins as he takes on a most challenging client—a sleepwalker!

Author B.J. Daniels knows firsthand about sleepwalking—she's gone on those nocturnal excursions since childhood. And B.J.'s set this story in her home state of Montana, at one of her favorite lakes. Readers may contact B.J. at P.O. Box 183, Bozeman, Montana 59771.

Be sure you don't miss a single LAWMAN... because there's nothing sexier than the strong arms of the law!

Regards,

Debra Matteucci
Senior Editor & Editorial Coordinator
Harlequin Books
300 East 42nd Street
New York, NY 10017

Hotshot P. I.
B. J. Daniels

Harlequin Books

TORONTO • NEW YORK • LONDON
AMSTERDAM • PARIS • SYDNEY • HAMBURG
STOCKHOLM • ATHENS • TOKYO • MILAN
MADRID • WARSAW • BUDAPEST • AUCKLAND

To the man I share my life, my love and my dreams with:
PARKER WILLIAM HEINLEIN

ISBN 0-373-22417-6

HOTSHOT P.I.

Copyright © 1997 by Barbara Johnson Smith

Printed in U.S.A.

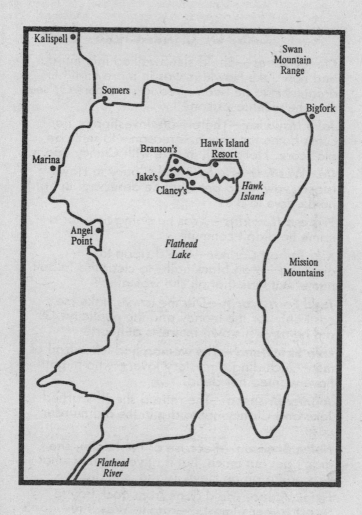

Kalispell

Swan
Mountain
Range

Somers

Bigfork

Marina

Branson's   Hawk Island
                   Resort
Jake's
Clancy's   *Hawk*
                  Island

Angel
Point

Flathead
Lake

Mission
Mountains

Flathead
River

CAST OF CHARACTERS

Clancy Jones—She'd sleepwalked into murder and now Jake Hawkins was in more than her dreams. Had he been hired to save her? Or see that she went to prison?

Jake Hawkins—The private investigator had come home for only one reason—to settle an old score. Not to fall in love with Clancy again.

Dex Westfall—He followed Clancy to Hawk Island, vowing to get what he deserved. But did he deserve to die?

Warren Hawkins—Was he doing time for a crime he didn't commit?

Kiki Talbott Conner—She'd stoop to anything—even blackmail—to clear the Talbott name. But was that all she was after?

Tadd Farnsworth—Did the lawyer take the case only for the money and the publicity? Or did he have his own interests at heart?

Lola Strickland—The woman had left a trail of men—including a mystery lover—who might have wanted her dead.

Johnny Branson—The retired sheriff warned Jake and Clancy not to dig in the old murder case.

Helen Branson—Because of her health, she didn't get out much. But if anyone knew what was going on on Hawk Island, she did.

Frank Ames—He'd gone from dock boy to resort owner almost overnight. Was it just good luck? Or bad luck for someone else?

Prologue

Clancy didn't know what had awakened her. She blinked, confused by the moonlight streaming across the third-story balcony, even more confused to find herself standing at the narrow log railing, staring down at Flathead Lake.

Waves lapped at the dock in the small bay below the island lodge. Clancy's heart rate accelerated along with her growing apprehension as she realized what was so terribly wrong.

The view. She shouldn't have been able to see the bay from this angle on her bedroom balcony. Behind her, the door to her family's lake lodge stood open. Past it, furniture huddled under sheets like ghosts. A corner of one sheet flapped softly in the night breeze. Clancy stared at the room, frantically trying to orient herself in a place haunted with childhood memories. The garret on the third floor—a room that hadn't been used in years for anything more than storage.

The early June breeze stirred the sheets and ran like a chill across her skin. She looked down, surprised to find she wore nothing but her nightgown. Her feet were bare—except for the sand. It was happening all over again! Fear raced ahead of her thoughts. Where had she been? What had she done *this* time? With growing panic, Clancy became aware of something heavy clutched in the fingers of her left hand.

A bronze sculpture of a cowboy, one of the first she'd ever made. It had been on the mantel downstairs. She shuddered as she realized how she and it must have gotten up here.

She hadn't sleepwalked in years. But the terror of waking up not knowing where she was or where she'd been wasn't something she'd forgotten from her childhood. She remembered with horror the last time she'd walked in her sleep. The night of the fire.

Clancy turned, wanting only to get back to her bedroom on the other side of the lodge, and realized she wasn't alone. Her heart slammed against her ribs. She fought back a scream as the moonlight spilled across the garret. Someone was on the couch. Sprawled, legs out at an odd angle. She stepped into the room, flipping the light switch. And stopped.

The bronze slipped from her fingers, hitting the hardwood floor with a thud, as she recognized the boots. Bright red cowboy boots. With wet sand on them. Just like her feet. Her heart thumped like a drum, filling the silence of the room.

Dex Westfall lay on the couch. His dark hair, normally coiffed to perfection, was now matted to the side of his head. Blood, once the color of his boots, stained the sheet covering the couch. His eyes stared, vacant, empty.

Clancy stumbled back, suddenly aware of the stickiness on her fingers. She stared at her left hand, her terror accelerating. How had she gotten blood on her? Her gaze leaped to the cowboy sculpture lying on the floor. Her heart rate rocketed, her pulse now a deafening roar in her ears. She didn't need anyone to tell her that the dark stain on the bronze was Dex's blood or that her former boyfriend was dead.

It was happening again. Only this time, her worst nightmare had come true. She'd killed someone in her sleep.

Chapter One

Ignoring the overdressed stranger on the dock, Jake Hawkins loaded the cooler full of groceries into his twenty-five-foot fishing boat, then reached for his tackle box and new rod and reel resting at the woman's high-heeled feet. He noted with no small amount of satisfaction that she'd finally gotten the message. Beneath the huge hat, she pursed her thin, lipstick-red lips and stripped off the large designer sunglasses to give him the full effect of her icy baby blues. The look she gave him shot off more sparks than all the diamonds weighing down her body.

He smiled to himself. From the moment he'd found her waiting for him on the dock beside his boat, there hadn't been anything about Mrs. Randolph L. Conners that he liked—from her wealthy smugness to her condescending certainty that he was about to go to work for her. And he especially didn't appreciate being bothered on his day off. It was Monday and he was going fishing for a few days. And nothing was going to keep that from happening.

"Like I said, I don't baby-sit heiresses," he repeated as he turned away from the Galveston skyline to take a whiff of the gulf breeze. "Especially heiresses who have just murdered their boyfriends." The gulf shimmered in the morning sun, beckoning him. He couldn't wait to hear his twin 150-horsepower engines rumbling as he crossed the water, the wind in his face.

"I don't think you understand, Mr. Hawkins," Mrs. Conners said, enunciating each word carefully. "I'm not hiring you to baby-sit. I'm hiring you to see that my niece is exonerated."

Jake pushed back his Houston Astros cap and laughed. She wasn't hiring him at all. He didn't have the time or the inclination. Not even the money could entice him right now. Not when he had a well-deserved fishing trip planned. "You need a good lawyer, not a private investigator. But I can give you a few names—"

"I already have the best lawyers money can buy," she said, sounding pained that she had to explain everything to him. "I need someone with your...talents."

He prided himself on what he called his hunches, and right now one was riding up his spine like a centipede wearing spiked heels. While his hunches were seldom wrong, he hoped this one was; he had a bad feeling that somehow he was going to end up working for this woman.

"My talents?" he repeated, also hoping he was wrong about where she was headed. He shook his head as if he didn't get it.

Exasperation gave her a pinched look that reminded him of one of those mean little hairless dogs. "I want you to prove my niece's innocence, Mr. Hawkins. Whatever you have to do. Whatever it costs. My niece will not be convicted of murder."

Jake jumped from the boat to the dock with a thud. "If you think you can hire me to tamper with evidence..." He found himself looming over her, his blood pressure up and running.

She tilted her head back ever so slightly until he could see her eyes shaded beneath the hat. If she felt even a little bit intimidated, it didn't show; her gaze glittered with brittle-hard certainty. "You misunderstood my intentions."

"Like hell I misunderstood," Jake said, locking his gaze on the woman. "If your niece is guilty, then she deserves to do time. And from what you've told me—"

"You are wrong, Mr. Hawkins," she said, her voice as hard and gritty as gravel. "My niece is a Talbott. A Talbott does not go to prison."

Talbott? He felt a jolt of recognition shoot through him. He squinted at her, telling himself Talbott was a fairly common name. Not that it mattered, he reminded himself; he wasn't going to take this case. But still he couldn't shake off the rotten feeling tap-dancing at the back of his head.

"Do you understand what I'm saying, Mr. Hawkins?"

He understood perfectly. The niece was an embarrassment and too good for prison. He couldn't believe the gall of this woman. And now she wanted someone to go in and clean up the mess. At any price. Well, she'd picked the wrong man. "Like I said, I can't help you. It's my day off and I'm going fishing."

Jake flung his duffel bag into the boat, hoping Mrs. Randolph L. Conners would take the hint. But he wasn't averse to throwing her into the gulf if he had to.

She squared her shoulders, straightening her expensive suit. "I'm sure after you've given it some thought you'll change your mind, Mr. Hawkins."

He pointed to the shore. "Don't count on it."

She smiled. "We'll see."

Fighting to control his temper, Jake watched her walk away. He hated having someone raise his blood pressure, especially this early in the morning and on his day off.

As he went to untie the boat, he noticed the envelope on the bow, underneath the cellular phone the woman had surreptitiously left to hold it down in the light sea breeze. The envelope was creamy white; the address engraved. He slipped it from under the phone, not surprised to find his name hand-printed on the clean white surface or the paper smelling of her expensive perfume.

He figured the envelope would be full of old family money, but it felt a little too light. Maybe she'd written him a check. Jake ripped open the envelope, planning to do the same with the check.

But it didn't contain a voucher of any kind. Nor were there any crisp large bills inside. Instead, there was a single sheet of paper, folded neatly. On the sheet were printed the words: Deer Lodge. September 30. 9:00 a.m.

At the bottom was her neatly signed signature: Kiki Talbott Conners.

Kiki Talbott. He should have known. With a curse, Jake crumpled the paper and threw it into the water, feeling his plans crumple with it. The phone began to ring. He looked out across the gulf, suddenly reminded of a photograph that used to sit on the mantel of his family's Flathead Lake lodge in Montana. Memories flooded him. Bittersweet memories that he'd spent ten years trying to forget. He picked up the phone.

"I've left you a ticket and triple your normal first week's salary at the airport," Kiki informed him in her no-nonsense tone. "Your flight leaves in less than two hours. You'll have to hurry."

"And where exactly is it you think I'm going?" Jake asked, anger making his words as hard as stones.

"Montana. You can buy anything you need when you get there," she continued. "Of course, I will reimburse you for all expenses."

"Montana?" Jake swore and pushed back his baseball cap, dread making his body ache as if he had a bad case of flu. "I think you'd better tell me just which niece of yours we're talking about." He held his breath, waiting for the other shoe to drop.

Sea gulls squawked overhead; the gulf breeze tickled the sandy blond hair curling at his neck.

"Clancy Jones. Her mother was a Talbott. Her father was—"

Jake let out an oath. "I know who her parents were, for hell's sake. And I know who *she* is! You don't seriously believe that I'm going to help *her?*"

Kiki's tone was coldly calm. "Mr. Hawkins, you're very good at what you do. One of the best. That's why I've hired you. That's why you're going to do whatever you have to do to get my niece exonerated—in spite of your...former connections with her.''

Jake walked over to his duffel bag and, cradling the phone against his shoulder, dug through his clothing. ''Lady, the only reason you're *hiring* me is because you have something to hold over my head, and you damn well know it.''

Jake thought he heard a hint of emotion in her voice when she finally spoke. ''Please understand, I will do whatever I have to do to protect my niece. Including helping you on September 30. Or hurting you. And believe me, I'm in a very good position to do either.''

Jake carefully lifted the .38 nestled in its worn shoulder holster from the duffel bag. He wondered if Kiki had any idea what kind of man she'd just hired. Or how big a mistake she'd just made.

''How do I know you'll hold up your end of the bargain?'' he asked, glad she wasn't still on the dock, afraid of what he might have done.

She let out a long, impatient sigh. ''I'm a Talbott, Mr. Hawkins. Please don't confuse us with the Joneses. Our word is our bond.''

''Right.''

''One more thing, Mr. Hawkins,'' she said, dropping her voice. ''Because of your less-than-amiable association with my niece, I might offer you a tip as to how to best handle her—''

''Look, Kiki,'' Jake said as he snugged the .38 to his ribs. ''I have a little tip for you. You can force me to take this job, although it's not the smartest thing you ever did. And you can force me to take your money and waste my time trying to find evidence that your niece isn't guilty of murder. But you can't tell me how to do my job.''

''Now, Mr. Hawkins—''

''The truth is, Kiki, you can only buy so much with your kind of blackmail. And you've already bought more than you can handle.''

Chapter Two

Awakened from a troubled sleep, Jake rolled over, forgetting where he was, and banged his head on the balcony railing. That rude awakening and the once-familiar view reminded him exactly where he was. As soon as he'd landed, he'd rented a boat to get to Hawk Island and his family's lodge. And he was there because of Clancy Jones.

Having no intentions of staying long, he'd just rolled his sleeping bag out on the balcony, wishing he was on the deck of his boat. The truth was he couldn't stand the thought of sleeping inside the lodge. It felt too musty and confining, brought back too many memories.

He'd gone to sleep cursing Clancy, while glaring through the railing at the only other dwelling on this side of the rugged island—an almost identical log lodge nestled in the pines across the small bay.

A single light had shone in one of the rooms on the second floor of Clancy's lodge until the wee hours. He'd seen an occasional shadow and wondered if she was alone. Angry that he couldn't sleep, either, he'd speculated on what she might be doing still up. Working in her studio? Or trying to sleep and not think, like him?

At one point, he'd considered going over to see her, getting it over with. But it was late, and he told himself waiting until morning was the best plan. He'd finally dozed off, only to be dragged from sleep by a loud noise, which did little to improve his disposition.

As he stared across the moonlit bay, trying to figure out what had awakened him, a movement jarred his attention into focus. Something was thrashing around in the water off the end of Clancy's dock. He saw what appeared to be a head surface, heard the choked cry before it disappeared again. Clancy?

Shedding his bedroll, Jake leaped from the end of the balcony, dropped onto the beach and took off at a run. He saw the head materialize again, dark against the silvery surface of the water, heard the cry for help and pushed his legs harder. All the time his mind raced ahead of him; the swimmer couldn't be Clancy. She swam like a trout and was much too smart to be swimming—drowning—at this hour of the night.

He sprinted down the weathered dock to the end as the person emerged once again—yards beyond his reach. Having no time to consider the consequences, he dove in. The sudden shock of the cold water brought him wide awake; he surfaced, gasping for breath. Just ahead of him he could see the swimmer start to disappear under the dark water again. He swam hard and reached out to grab the only thing he could. Hair. It was long enough he could bury his hand in it.

But to his surprise, the swimmer pulled him under with a force that almost made him lose his grip. Immediately he realized his mistake. The silly fool was struggling, fighting him, and he remembered why he'd never considered the lifeguarding profession. Too dangerous. At least in the private eye business you knew who you were dealing with: murderers, crooks, cheaters and liars. Not some novice in over her head in deep water, panicked to senseless desperation and determined to take you down with her.

Jake got a tighter hold on the hair and a grip on one flaying arm, and with all his strength kicked toward the moonlit surface. At first nothing happened, then they both rose in a rush, the swimmer choking and coughing as they surfaced. Jake used a no-nonsense half nelson to drag the person to the dock and, none too gently, hoisted the obviously feminine body onto the worn boards. He felt a moment of relief. This woman, whoever she was, wasn't Clancy. Not with *that* body. Her wet clothing molded to her curves—dangerously enticing, fully developed curves.

She leaned over the edge of the dock, fighting for breath, her dripping shoulder-length hair in her face. Slowly, she raised her gaze, sending a shock wave through him.

Clancy? Even under the wet mop of blond hair, even in the shimmering silver of the moonlight, there was no doubt about that face. Her hair was longer. Not quite as blond. But that face. That cute little nose. That slightly puckered, almost pouty mouth. That wide-eyed, curious deep brown gaze. If anything, she was more beautiful than he remembered. And certainly more…filled out. And in all the right places. That adorable seventeen-year-old tomboy he'd known was now one hell of a good-looking woman.

But he wasn't sure what shocked him the most. Seeing the change in her after all these years. Or realizing she was the swimmer he'd had to rescue. What had happened to the Clancy he used to know, the one who was much too smart to swim alone in the middle of the night?

"What the hell were you doing swimming at this hour?" he demanded, anger following his relief that Clancy was all right. He needed her alive, he told himself. His relief had nothing to do with any old feelings from their past, he assured himself, ignoring the flashes of memories of the two of them as kids. They'd been so close—best pals. More than that. Kindred spirits. The truth was, he'd thought he was in love with her.

"Swimming?" she said, choking. "You think I was swimming?" She coughed, then leaned back, her gaze settling on him with suspicion. "Someone tried to drown me."

"Wait a minute," he said, holding up his hands. "I was

the one who fished you out of the drink." He felt something cold sprint up his spine as he looked into her eyes.

"Someone grabbed me and—" Clancy glanced around in obvious confusion, her eyes wild with fear. "You dragged me out?"

"Yeah." Jake studied her for a moment, wondering how long it would take her to acknowledge that she knew him. "About this *someone* who tried to drown you...you might notice there seems to be just the two of us on this whole side of the island." He glanced toward the still water, then at the empty shoreline, then at her again.

"Thank you for helping me," she whispered, still looking disoriented. And more than a little scared.

He'd known seeing her again was going to trigger a lot of old emotions, emotions he couldn't afford. He quickly reminded himself that Clancy hadn't only perjured herself on the witness stand and helped send his father to prison ten years ago, now she was facing a murder rap of her own. Forget that cute kid he used to build sand castles with on the beach and catch trout with off the end of this dock. Someone had bludgeoned Dex Westfall to death, and from what Kiki had told him, the police thought that someone was Dex's girlfriend, Clancy Jones.

"So what were you doing out here on the dock at this time of the night?" he asked, unable to keep the reproach out of his voice. He was wet and tired and didn't appreciate being awakened in the middle of the night. Especially by this woman.

"I heard someone...calling me." She sounded dubious.

Welcome to the club. "Someone calling you?" He glanced at the still water beyond the dock. The pines etched a dark, ragged line against the night sky. Then he looked over at her again. "Someone called you, so you walked down to see what they wanted in the middle of the night?" Perfectly logical.

He saw her look toward her lodge, her eyes widening. He followed her gaze, surprised to see that not a single lamp glowed in any of the windows. She hadn't turned on a light before coming down to the dock?

"I suppose you didn't recognize the voice calling you or see the person who pulled you into the water?" he asked, not even trying to hide his disbelief. He could read most people as easily as he could the cover of a tabloid from across the floor of a good-sized minimart. Clancy Jones was lying through her teeth, but for the life of him, he couldn't imagine why. He reminded himself that lying seemed to come easy for her.

"Whether you believe it or not, someone tried to drown me," she said, her voice breaking. She didn't sound any more convinced than he was, but she *was* scared. He could see it in her movements as she got to her feet, nervously tugging her wet clothing away from her body.

For the first time, he realized she wasn't dressed for a night swim. She wore a T-shirt and a pair of leggings. Both were wet and molded to her body. An amazing body, Jake grudgingly admitted. Her feet were bare, and she still wore her watch and a single gold bracelet. Both looked expensive. He ignored the voice of reason that questioned why she would have gone swimming wearing an expensive watch, why Jake had had to pull so hard to bring her to the surface. The questions wedged themselves in the back of his brain, a reluctant sliver of doubt.

"Right," Jake said. "And where is that someone now?"

When he raised his gaze to her face, he saw that she was staring at him again. Squinting, actually, as if the moonlight was too bright.

"Who are you, anyway, and what are you doing here?" she demanded.

He tried not to let it hurt his feelings. Why should she recognize him or even remember him? She'd only spent the first seventeen years of her life living right next door to him, spending most every waking moment with him from the time she could walk. And it wasn't as if he wanted to believe he'd made an impression on her just because she had on him. True, there'd been that kiss, the first for both of them, on this very dock, and she'd said she loved him, but hey—

"Jake Hawkins," he said, surprised at the hurt and anger he heard in his tone. And the bitterness. "Not that there's any reason you should remember *me*. But perhaps you haven't forgotten my father. Surely you recall that your testimony sent him to prison ten years ago."

"Jake." It came out a whisper. She seemed to wobble a little as she squinted harder at him. "It's been so long…you sound so different…and—"

He rolled his eyes. "Forget it." For a moment, he just glared at her, mad, irritable and just plain out of sorts. He shifted his gaze to the lake. Lights flickered on the mainland. The air smelled of fish and pines. He should have been at sea, drifting with the night clouds, catching stripers and sailfish. He should have been at peace, breathing salt air, not standing on a dock in the wee hours of the morning with a woman who'd forced him to remember things he'd only wanted to forget. A woman, who unlike him, seemed to have put at least some of that past behind her.

"Why now?" she asked quietly. "After all this time?"

Fueled on a mixture of hurt and anger, he answered, "Your Aunt Kiki sent me to save your butt."

"What?" The surprise on Clancy's face was worth the flight to Montana. It was almost worth missing his fishing trip. "You met my Aunt Kiki?"

"The Wicked Witch of the East herself." He'd never completely believed the stories Clancy had told after one of her required trips back East each spring to visit her rich aunt. He did now. "She's everything you said she was. And then some."

"I don't understand," Clancy said, frowning. "Why would Aunt Kiki send *you?*"

"Probably because I'm a private investigator and your aunt thinks her money and I can dig up evidence that will keep you out of prison." Even as he said it, he realized it didn't make that much sense to him, either. He had a hunch, one he was holding off like a bad cold. He told himself not to look a gift horse in the mouth. Kiki had provided him with the perfect opportunity. Why question it?

Clancy met his gaze; tears glistened in her eyes. "I see."

He realized she did see at least part of it: one of the only reasons he was here was because Aunt Kiki had procured his services. He thought it would give him more satisfaction than it did to hurt her. What had she expected? That he'd come back and forget what she'd done, forgive her? Not likely.

"It's unfortunate that you've wasted your time," she said, her words so faint, he almost missed them.

Wasted his time? What was she saying, that she killed Dex Westfall, that she was guilty?

She straightened, her glance shifting from her bare feet to his face. "The last thing I need right now is...*you* helping me."

He stared at her. "It's not like you have a lot of choice in the matter. I doubt there's a line of private investigators knocking down your door to take *this* case."

She let out a small laugh; her hand fluttered for a moment in the air between them. "Jake, we both know you're not here to save me. Admit it, you'd love nothing better than to see me behind bars."

He started to admit it, but she didn't give him the chance.

"What was my aunt thinking?" With a dismissive shake of her head, she turned and headed down the dock toward shore. "Consider yourself fired."

"Wait a minute!" he called after her. "You can't get rid of me just like that."

She didn't even turn around.

Jake stood on the dock, shaking his head in disbelief as he watched her stride toward her lodge. Fired? He'd never been fired in his life. Especially by some woman who didn't have the good sense not to go swimming in the middle of the night. A woman who had the audacity to make up a story about an attacker calling her down to the dock to drown her— Jake glared at Clancy's ramrod back as she retreated up the beach. Once a liar, always a liar, he thought.

"Fine," he called after her. "Fire me. Say hello to my father when you get to prison."

Her lodge door slammed, leaving him standing alone in the moonlight. He cursed and started toward his own lodge. Matching her angry strides, he stomped down the beach but quickly slowed to a limp. The bottoms of his feet hurt like the devil from racing across sand, rocks and rough wood to save a woman who didn't even recognize him. He cursed himself for not only his unappreciated heroics, but also for that moment of weakness he'd had when he first saw Clancy again. For just that instant, he'd actually cared. How could he have forgotten, if for even a moment, the part she'd played in helping send his father to prison? He assured himself he wouldn't forget again.

CLANCY FELL BACK AGAINST the door she'd just slammed and tried to stop shaking. She'd promised herself she wasn't going to fall apart; she'd already cried too many tears and it had accomplished nothing. But just when she thought things couldn't get any worse—Jake appeared.

She hugged herself to hold down the shudders that welled up inside her. Confusion clouded her thoughts. Someone *had* called her down to the dock and tried to drown her. Or had they? She closed her eyes, searching through the darkness of her memory, fighting desperately to remember. Could it have been just a bad dream? But it had seemed so *real*. The hand coming out of the water, grabbing her ankle, pulling her into the water. Once she hit the water, she'd been wide awake. But had there really been someone else in the water trying to drag her under? Or had it been Jake fighting to bring her to the surface? It had happened so fast. And yet she remembered the voice. It had been familiar. Jake's voice?

Her eyes flew open at the thought. No, it hadn't been Jake's. His voice had a hint of a southern drawl.

Jake. A rush of emotions assailed her. Memories, as sweet as the warm scent of summer. Regrets that made her heart ache. She'd never expected to ever see him again. Never expected to have these old feelings come back with such force. Then to find him on her dock tonight. And now of all times.

She moved to the table to retrieve her glasses, anxious to be able to see clearly again, wishing she'd had them on earlier. Or at least had her contacts in. All she'd gotten was a blurred impression of Jake. Medium height and muscular. She smiled, remembering the boy she'd grown up with, the boy she'd fallen so desperately in love with.

She thought about the betrayed, angry look he'd given her that day at the courthouse ten years ago. Tonight, she'd heard that same anger and bitterness in his voice. He still blamed her for his father going to prison. And now he'd come to Montana to help her? She couldn't possibly let herself believe that.

But Jake had saved her life tonight, hadn't he? Clancy shivered, remembering the dark water and the hands pulling her under. Or had they been Jake's hands trying to pull her toward the surface? If there had been an attacker, where had he gone so quickly?

She shivered, hugging herself tighter. Right now she needed a hot bath and dry clothing. She didn't want to think about the fact that she'd walked in her sleep again; she particularly didn't want to think what could have happened if Jake hadn't been there.

She hurried upstairs, anxious to get out of her wet, cold clothing. But as she disrobed and stepped into the hot shower, exhaustion pulled at her, making her thoughts as clouded as the steam that rose around her.

She yearned to be warm and dry. To wrap herself in one of her mother's old quilts. To curl up in front of the fireplace. To forget everything. And sleep. She closed her eyes and leaned back against the shower wall.

JAKE QUICKLY SHOWERED and changed into warm, dry clothing, hoping it would soothe his anger and frustration. It had done neither by the time he dialed the private number Kiki had left for him at the Kalispell, Montana, airport along with another cellular phone. She'd evidently anticipated that he'd chuck the first one into the gulf, which he had. It bothered him that Kiki thought she knew him so well.

Kiki Talbott Conners answered on the fifth ring. With more than a little satisfaction, he realized he'd awakened her from a sound sleep.

"What time is it?" she groaned.

Way past *his* bedtime, he knew that. His eyes felt as if they had sand in them. "A quarter after three."

"In the morning?"

"That could explain why it's still dark out." He could just imagine her in a huge satin bed at the Bigfork condo she'd rented, surrounded by plump pillows and pampered poodles. "Your niece and I just got reacquainted."

"At *three* in the morning?" Kiki demanded, grogginess turning quickly to surliness.

He walked to the window. "It's a long story." It looked as though all the lights in Clancy's lodge were on. What was she doing still up, he wondered. And why all the lights? What was she afraid of? Surely she wasn't buying into her own lies about a mysterious killer who came out of the water like a shark from *Jaws*. "Let me cut to the chase. Your niece doesn't want me on this case."

"That surprises you?" Kiki asked, adding an audible "humph." "Perhaps she thinks you harbor a grudge against her."

Kiki's words snapped his attention back like a short rubber band. "Of course I have a grudge against her. And for a damned good reason." He raked his fingers through his hair, remembering what Clancy had said on the dock, *What could my aunt have been thinking?* Exactly what Jake wanted to know. "Which brings me to the reason I called. Knowing that, why in the hell did you want me up here?"

A faint tinkling sound broke the silence. She was pouring herself a drink. He felt as if he was going to need one, too. Kiki had enough money to buy the best private investigator in the galaxy. And if she wanted evidence tampered with, she could have bought that, too. For a price. But not from Jake Hawkins. So why hire a man who had every reason *not* to help her niece?

"The reason I hired you is the same reason you're not going to quit," she said simply.

He wanted to tell her just how wrong she was but that damned hunch of his was doing the lambada across the back of his neck to a little ditty called "Here Comes Heartache."

He heard her take a sip of her drink, taking her time. "Come on, Jake," she said impatiently. "You know the reason."

"Blackmail." He had a bad feeling that Kiki knew all the blackmail in the world couldn't make him do something he didn't want to do. He had his own personal reason for being here, and his hunch machine told him Kiki knew that, had known it all along. So what the hell had she hired him for?

Kiki sighed deeply. "Jake, we both know why you're in Montana, and it has nothing to do with blackmail."

He couldn't believe he was playing this game with her. "Why don't you spell it out for me, Kiki." He held his breath, afraid she was about to validate the strongest hunch he'd ever had.

"You're in Montana because you think Clancy's the key to proving your father's innocence."

Bingo. Jake squeezed the phone and closed his eyes. Clancy *was* the key. Had always been the key. She'd lied on the witness stand to protect her own father and let Jake's go to prison. And now Jake had Clancy where he wanted her. He'd taken this case for one reason only: to get the truth. And as certain as the coming sunrise, he'd do whatever he had to do to get it out of her.

He stared across the bay at Clancy's. "My motives for being here don't worry you?" he asked Kiki incredulously.

"No," she answered in that tone he'd come to despise. "I've seen how deep your loyalty runs. Unlike your mother. She could never forgive your father for disgracing her. She moved the two of you to Texas. She never visited him in prison. She forgot Warren Hawkins as if he'd never existed." Kiki sounded so damned sure of herself. "You, on the other hand, can't let go of the past. You believe in your father's innocence and would do *anything* to prove it. The same way you can't let Clancy go to prison for a murder she didn't commit."

"I wouldn't be so sure of that," he said, moving away from the window. Kiki thought he was a crusader for injustice? He wanted to laugh. Didn't she realize it was Clancy who'd done him the injustice? The woman was a liar; she'd proven that tonight. How could Kiki be so convinced Clancy hadn't killed this Dex Westfall guy? Blind loyalty? He'd once felt that for Clancy, and look what she'd done to him and his family. No, he suspected with Kiki it was simply a matter of saving the Talbott name.

"I'm quite sure of you," Kiki said, her tone downright haughty.

He wanted to tell her what a fool she was. After all these years, she'd just offered him the perfect opportunity to get what he wanted. The truth. And revenge at the same time. "What makes you think you know me so well?"

Kiki let out a long sigh. "I heard about how wonderful you were for years, Jake Hawkins. Did you forget that for a long time, my niece foolishly thought she was in love with you?"

Kiki hung up before he could respond. Not that he had a response for that one, anyway.

CLANCY'S EYES POPPED OPEN at the sound of the phone ringing and realized she'd dozed off standing in the shower! Panic came in hot pursuit of the realization. What if she'd fallen into one of her deep sleeps and sleepwalked again—this time totally naked?

Whatever it took, she had to stay awake. She cranked the shower handle and let out a shriek as the cold water made her skin ache. But just as she was being revived, the phone began to ring. She quickly turned off the water and reached for a towel.

Dripping, she hurried to the phone and picked up the receiver. "Hello." She could hear breathing at the other end of the line. "Hello?" There was no answer. Just what sounded like soft, labored breathing. "What do you want?" she demanded. No answer. Clancy slammed down the phone. A prank call. Someone who'd read about her in the paper. She'd get her number changed. Maybe even get an unlisted number.

She sat on the edge of the bed, suddenly too tired to move. The soft warmth beneath her beckoned her to crawl in, to cover her head and escape for a few hours in sleep. She stood and headed back to the shower, not about to make the same mistake she'd made earlier. After spending two nights in jail, she'd been running scared and not thinking clearly. She'd been so desperate she'd called her aunt Kiki who'd pulled strings and got her out right after the late afternoon bail hearing Monday. Clancy's plan had been to go to Bozeman and Dex's apartment as soon as she got out on bail. She'd come straight to the lodge to pick up a change of clothing. Unfortunately, after she'd hurriedly packed and started to leave, she'd spotted the flicker of a flashlight at the Hawkins' lodge and spotted the blue outboard tied at the dock. She'd assumed the county attorney had put a deputy on her.

She knew she was only out on bail because of Aunt Kiki and her money. She figured maybe the county attorney had gone along with the bail to please Kiki but had put a deputy on her to cover his political posterior.

So Clancy had foolishly sat by the window to wait him out—not knowing it was just Jake Hawkins, not some deputy, watching her. And she'd fallen asleep and sleepwalked.

She stepped back into the shower and let the icy cold water beat her body wide awake. She didn't dare let that happen again. Nor could she afford to wait until morning to leave. Although she didn't relish the idea of crossing the lake in the dead of night, Jake had left her no option. She'd wait until she could be relatively sure he was asleep, then she'd take her boat to the mainland marina where she kept her car. From there she'd drive to Bozeman, go to Dex's apartment and— She wasn't sure what she'd find there, but hopefully something that would prove she was innocent.

Sometimes she could almost forget about the upcoming trial. Almost pretend none of this was really happening. Then she'd get a flash of Dex Westfall sprawled on the couch in the garret. Murdered. And her standing over him with the murder weapon in her hand. One of her own sculptures.

Her heart told her she hadn't killed him. But reason argued: how do you know you didn't? You were asleep. And look at all the evidence against you.

Exhaustion tugged at her, beckoning her to the one place where she didn't have to think. Sweet slumber. But with sweet slumber came somnambulism, and she feared her nocturnal wanderings. Look what had happened tonight. What *had* happened tonight? She wasn't even sure. Her hands shook as she pulled on a pair of jeans and a T-shirt.

She clung to only one hope. That somehow she could prove her innocence. And the only place she knew to start was with Dex. She had to find out everything there was to know about him, including why he'd ended up dead in her garret.

She told herself going to Bozeman, to another county, wasn't really violating her bail. And anyway, she'd be back before anyone even knew she was missing. If she was lucky. But she'd take extra clothing, just in case. In case she found out something that would prove she had killed him and she decided to make a run for it?

Clancy was coming down the stairs, her hair wrapped in the towel turban-style, when she heard the pounding at her back door.

"Clancy, I know you're still up," Jake called. "You might as well open the door."

She pulled the towel off her head, shook out her hair and used the tip of the damp towel to clean her glasses. Maybe he was coming to tell her he was leaving, going back to wherever her aunt had found him. Hadn't she wished for the opportunity to really see him before he left?

If only her other wishes were granted that easily, she thought as she opened the door to find him standing on her step. He'd changed out of his wet jeans; he wore chinos and a white T-shirt that accented his broad shoulders and his tanned, muscular arms. A Houston Astros cap was snugged down on his sandy blond head; his hair curled at the nape of his neck still wet from a shower. His clean, spicy smell engulfed her.

"It's late," she said, but he didn't seem to be paying any attention. He was staring at her as if he'd never seen her before. The same way she was staring at him.

Her earlier impression of Jake hadn't done him justice. He'd been cute at nineteen; now he was strikingly good-looking. Strong features. A full, sensual mouth. Expressive gray eyes. A man with character. He had the kind of face she'd love to sculpt. A mixture of toughness and tenderness.

"You wear glasses," he said simply, sounding pleased.

She didn't tell him she'd worn glasses since she was fifteen—just not around him when she was a girl. "I can't see much without them."

He smiled then. "That's nice." He leaned one broad shoulder against the jamb.

She wasn't sure what she wanted him to say. Goodbye? Or maybe that he was sorry he'd hurt her. Or even that he understood she'd only done what she had to at the trial. "It's late," she repeated.

"Yeah," he said, the smile dissolving as if he'd suddenly remembered why he'd come over. "It's about your case."

She stared at him, telling herself she shouldn't be surprised. "I thought I fired you."

His frown deepened. "Your aunt hired me, and she's the only one who can fire me. And trust me, as much trouble as she's gone to to get me here, there isn't much chance of that happening."

Clancy could only assume her Aunt Kiki had lost her mind.

"So now that we have that settled…" He glanced past her into the lodge.

"Yes, I guess that settles everything." She yawned openly, not that the Jake Hawkins she used to know could take a hint.

"Except for one thing," Jake said, his voice deadly soft. "I had a fishing trip planned that your aunt interrupted to get me up here." He held up his hand to silence her before she could tell him what he could do with his fishing trip.

"Let me give it to you straight. I'm here for only one reason—to get the goods on you," he said, his gaze hard as his body looked.

She swallowed, the cold hatred in his voice making her heart ache, her eyes burn with tears. Only stubborn determination kept her from crying. She wasn't about to let him see how much he'd hurt her ten years ago, how much he could still hurt her.

"I'm going to find evidence I can use against you," he said. "And then you're going to tell me the truth about what you really saw the night of the resort fire, the night Lola Strickland was murdered."

Clancy started to tell him she *had* told the truth, but she knew it would be a waste of breath. He hadn't believed her at the trial, why would he believe her now?

She looked into his eyes, wondering what had happened to the boy she'd loved, the boy who had loved her. She saw nothing in all that gray but bitterness. But instead of hating him, her heart broke as she thought of all the years he'd suffered. Because of his father. Because of her. Jake should have trusted her. He should have known she wouldn't lie, she wouldn't hurt him or his father, and she wouldn't have thrown away their love without a fight, the way Jake had.

"In the meantime," Jake said, "you and I are going to be inseparable until you're acquitted—or sent to prison."

She bit back a curse. "You're making prison look better all the time."

His gaze met hers. "I think I know why you lied about my father, but no matter the reason, you're going to admit it to me. And very soon." He touched the brim of his baseball cap. "See you in the morning."

She slammed the door and dropped into a chair at the table, feeling incredibly tired and despondent. Aunt Kiki had brought Jake back knowing how he felt about Clancy, knowing how she'd once felt about him. That old familiar ache seized her heart in a death grip. How Clancy *still* felt about him.

Tears welled up in her eyes and spilled down over her cheeks, bitter on her tongue. She wiped at them. She still loved him. Through all the hurt, she'd never stopped loving him. Could never stop loving him. But like him, she felt betrayed. And angry with him for not trusting her. She knew she'd have to draw on that anger to keep Jake from knowing how she felt about him—and using it against her.

Emotional exhaustion and lack of solid sleep stole at her strength. She leaned her head on her arms and closed her eyes, telling herself she'd rest for a while, just until she could be sure Jake was asleep. Crossing the lake at night seemed less dangerous now. Much less dangerous than facing Jake Hawkins. If there was more incriminating evidence out there against her, Jake would find it.

She wished with all her heart that she could turn back the clock, back before the night of the fire and Lola's murder, back when Jake loved her. She closed her eyes. And saw Jake come sauntering up the sandy beach, sixteen and suntanned, that grin she loved on his handsome face. And she ran out to meet him, as carefree as the breeze that rippled the surface of the lake.

CLANCY OPENED HER EYES, shocked to find the sun streaming in through her bedroom window. Even more shocked to find herself curled in the middle of her bed, the quilt rough with sand from her bare feet. She lay perfectly still, her mind frantically trying to recall when she'd come to bed. No memory.

That's when she noticed her left hand clenched into a fist, as if she held something that might try to escape. With dread, she slowly uncurled her fingers. There in her palm lay a single tiny blue bead.

Her heart pounded. There was nothing unusual or unique about the bead. Except Clancy knew where it had come from. With a tremor of terror she remembered Friday night when Dex had called and demanded she meet him at the Hawk Island Café on the other side of the island.

He'd been holding a necklace of colored beads when she'd walked up to him. The outdoor café was empty that late at night and that early in the season. Dex sat at a table in a flickering pool of light from the Japanese lanterns strung overhead. She had looked at the necklace with growing dread, thinking it was another present, wishing she hadn't agreed to meet him.

He must have seen the expression on her face, because he gave a bitter laugh as she took a seat across from him.

"Don't worry, it's not for you," he'd said, holding up the string of beads for her to see. With a jolt she realized she'd seen it somewhere before. The tiny beads were pale blue. A handmade ceramic heart hung from the center of the necklace. It was painted navy with a smaller pink heart in the middle.

"Where did you get that?" Clancy asked, trying to remember where she'd seen it before.

"It's part of my mother's legacy," Dex said.

His mother? "What are you doing here?" Clancy demanded, wishing she'd never come, wondering how he'd even known where to find her. She'd never told him about the family's lake lodge. When she'd broken it off with him in Bozeman, she'd thought she'd never see him again. She felt a chill as she watched him hold the necklace up to the light and smile.

"What do you want, Dex?" Clancy asked with dread.

His eyes narrowed as he glared at her. "You're part of that legacy, Clancy."

She felt her fear level rise. How could she not have seen this side of him from the very start? "I thought we'd agreed not to see each other again."

"*We* agreed?" He reached across the table and grabbed her arm, squeezing it until she cried out in pain.

"Leave me alone, Dex. I'm warning you—"

He squeezed harder. "If you think you've seen the last of me you're—" He looked past her, seeing something that made his eyes widen. He released her arm almost involuntarily. She turned to look but saw nothing in the darkness beyond the café.

He lowered his voice. "I'm not leaving this island, Clancy. Not until I get what I deserve." He'd hurried off, leaving her sitting, head reeling, wondering what he'd seen in the darkness that seemed to frighten him. And what Dex thought he deserved.

Just hours later, he'd turned up dead in her garret.

Now she stared at the tiny bead in her palm, knowing this had to be one of the beads from the necklace. Apprehension rippled through her as she stared at her sandy feet. Something had triggered her night wanderings again. And she couldn't seem to stop them. Now she'd returned from sleepwalking with a single bead from a broken strand. When had it been broken? And where had she found this one blue bead? Even more frightening, how had she known where to look?

She slid her legs over the side of the bed and staggered into the bathroom. As she dropped the bead into the toilet and flushed, she watched it disappear with growing terror. She couldn't keep kidding herself. Like the broken string of tiny blue beads, her life was coming unraveled.

Chapter Three

Clancy glanced warily across the bay at Jake Hawkins's lodge. The shades were drawn; she could catch no sign of movement behind them. The blue outboard was still moored at his dock, a boat she assumed he'd rented to get to the island. She looked at her watch, surprised to find it was earlier than she'd thought. Then she turned her gaze again to Jake's lodge across the small bay. The coast looked clear. She picked up the overnight bag and her purse and opened the back door, expecting Jake to suddenly appear and block her escape.

As she stepped out onto the small back porch, she glanced apprehensively behind the lodge. While she found no one hiding in the lilac bushes that brushed the back side of the building, she did see something that stopped her cold. Slowly she put down her purse and overnight bag and moved toward the first lilac bush. Some of the branches along the lodge side of the bush had been broken. They hadn't been yesterday afternoon when she'd returned from jail. She was sure of it. She'd stopped on the porch to dig out her key and picked up the sweet scent of the lilacs, now in full bloom. And she wondered where she'd be this time next year when they bloomed. In prison?

Clancy brushed back the branches, not surprised to find the grass beneath the kitchen window crushed where someone had stood, looking in. Through the glass Clancy could see her coffee cup at the table, the chair pushed back from where she'd sat last night. Someone had stood on this very spot, watching her!

She crashed her way out of the lilacs as if the person was at her heels. Scooping up her purse and overnight bag, she rushed down the beach toward her dock. Who had been at the window? The same person who'd called her down to the dock and tried to drown her? It hadn't been a dream, her mind screamed. No more than the crushed grass beneath the window.

With relief she passed the old boathouse, and Jake didn't jump out of the shadows to stop her. All that stretched ahead now was the dock and her boat waiting beside it. The sun danced on the slick surface of the lake, golden. The tall pines shimmered, a silky green at the edge of the water. She took a calming breath. The air smelled of so many familiar, rich scents. Safe scents she'd grown up with. But she was no longer safe. From Jake. From the phantom in the lake. From the real live person who'd stood looking in her window. As long as she kept sleepwalking, she wasn't even safe from herself.

She reached the dock without incident and started down it, walking as quickly and quietly as possible. A sudden flash of memory tormented her. A hand coming out of the water. Grabbing her ankle. Pulling her. She walked faster, fear dogging her steps.

Just a few feet ahead she could see her boat, a yellow-and-white inboard-outboard; a coat of dew on the top and windshield glistened in the morning sunlight. Once she reached it and started the engine, Jake wouldn't be able to stop her. The thought buoyed her spirits.

She shot a parting glance toward his lodge. Jake must still be asleep. He'd been so adamant about shadowing her every step last night, this seemed almost too easy. She smiled to herself, imagining his surprise when he woke and found her gone, as she untied the bow and started to swing her overnight bag into the hull.

"Good morning!"

Clancy jumped, nearly tumbling backward off the dock. She swallowed a startled cry, pretending she wasn't trying to get away and his catching her wasn't a problem. Jake grinned up at her from the bottom of her boat, where he lay sprawled on a sleeping bag, his arms behind his head.

"Going somewhere?" he asked, raising an eyebrow at the overnight bag still clutched in her hand.

She cursed under her breath.

"If you're set on a life of crime, Ms. Jones, you're going to have to be more devious," he said, getting to his feet. "And jumping bail." He wagged his head at her. "Bad idea."

Clancy groaned. This man was the most irritating— She took a breath, trying to still her anger as well as the silly sudden flutter of her heart as he vaulted effortlessly from the boat to join her on the dock.

"Level with me, Clancy," he said, his voice as soft and deep as his gray eyes.

The sound sent a tiny vibration through her, igniting memories of the chemistry between the two of them as teenagers. She wondered if it was still there and hastily brushed that errant thought away.

Having to deal with this man on top of everything else was too much, she told herself. She didn't have the time or energy for this. Nor did she need the constant reminder of what she'd lost ten years ago—or how much more she had to lose now.

"Where are you going so early in the morning?" he asked as he stalked toward her, backing her against the edge of the dock, trapping her.

Clancy had to tilt her chin back to meet his gaze. He'd cornered her in more ways than one. And she acknowledged that it wasn't going to be easy to get rid of him. But getting rid of him was exactly what she had to do if she held any hope of clearing herself.

"If you must know," she said, coming up with the first

plausible explanation that popped into her head, "I'm going to see my lawyer."

Jake pushed back his baseball cap. "Good, I need to see your lawyer, too."

She shot him a look. "You're going like *that?*"

He glanced down at his rumpled chinos and T-shirt, then looked up at her as he rubbed his blond, stubbled jaw. "It kind of makes me look dangerous, don't you think? Like a man who has nothing to lose?" He gave her a slow, almost calculated smile. "And anyway, what choice do I have? If I were to shower, I'd barely have the water turned on before you'd be hightailing it to wherever you're in such a hurry to get to."

That was exactly what she had in mind. She wished he didn't know her so well.

He stepped back to allow her room to get into the boat. "But I'm à reasonable man. I'll even let you drive your boat."

"You're so thoughtful," she said, but didn't move. Outwardly, she gritted her teeth and fumed. Inwardly, she plotted. She would dump Jake. And soon. She had to. She just didn't know how yet.

WHEN CLANCY DIDN'T make a move to get into the boat, Jake swung back in and offered her a hand. He'd hoped his disposition would improve with daylight. It hadn't. If anything, the late-night adventure, his phone conversation with Kiki and trying to sleep in the bottom of a cold boat with his clothes on had left him even more irascible. Add to that, the gall of Clancy thinking she could get away from him this morning.

He'd been on this case less than twenty-four hours, and he felt as if he'd been beaten up by somebody twice his size. He didn't like the feeling he was being manipulated by not one, but two females. Kiki had hired him for reasons he could no more fathom than he could walk on water. And Clancy. At one time he thought he'd known her better than he knew himself. But that was years ago and a lot of water under the bridge. For all he knew, she was a killer. Let her rot in prison for all he cared.

You've become a cold-hearted bastard, haven't you, Hawkins. Reluctantly, he admitted it was true. Something had died inside him that day at the trial. He'd lost Clancy, and he'd lost his father. Only, Clancy had voluntarily chosen to leave; his father hadn't.

He watched her flick a glance at his outstretched hand but make no move toward it or the boat. Instead, she brushed her hair back with her fingers and looked toward shore as if she were thinking of making a break for it. Silently, he dared her to try. So help him, he'd take her over his knee and—

"Clancy," Jake said softly. "There're a few things you should know. One, I hate being lied to. Two, these dirty little secrets of yours? I'm going to know them all before I catch a plane back to Texas, and you can bet the farm on that." He extended his hand again. "And three, if you try to run again, I'll track you down no matter where you go, and you won't like it when I find you."

He flashed her a smile. But to his surprise, she took his hand, stepped into the boat and came right up to him. If he'd thought he could intimidate her, he'd been wrong. Her gaze met his, challenging him, daring him to take her on.

"Jake, there're a few things *you* should know," she said as softly as he had. "One, I don't have the time or energy to lie to you. Two, I have no intention of helping you send me to prison. And three—" her smile deepened "—I'm going to ditch you just as soon as I possibly can." She moved past him to slide behind the wheel. An instant later she started the boat.

Jake smiled to himself as he took a seat next to her. He'd forgotten how much he'd liked Clancy Jones's spunk as a kid. He was glad to see it was one of the things that hadn't changed about her. Unfortunately, it didn't alter the fact that she'd lied about his father or that she was lying to him right now about not jumping bail. If she wanted to play hard ball, he'd play, too. But he doubted she was going to like his rules.

THEY PICKED UP the expensive bright red Mustang convertible he'd rented with Kiki's money at the mainland marina. The marina was one of several his father and Clancy's had owned as partners. Jake saw Clancy raise an eyebrow as she climbed into the car's leather seat and realized he'd dropped another notch or two in her estimation.

"Doesn't it bother you to take my aunt's money on the pretense of helping me?" Clancy asked.

"No," Jake replied, angry to discover that what she thought of him mattered.

"I thought you hate being lied to," she said. "Or do you overlook it when you're lying to yourself?"

He floored the gas pedal, sending gravel flying as he headed into town. Beside him, Clancy smiled. Jake cursed. What an impossible woman! He'd expected her to still be that cute little tomboy he'd grown up with, someone he thought he could handle—not some beautiful woman who knew how to push all his buttons. He swore to himself. What had made him think this job was going to be easy?

She smiled, seemingly amused. "You're certainly wide awake this morning. I don't remember you being such a morning person."

He didn't want to be reminded of their past or of the foolish, love-struck nineteen-year-old he'd been. Not that he was about to let that past distract or dissuade him from what he'd come to Montana to do. He'd come to settle an old score, and he had no intention of taking any trips down memory lane along the way.

"I'm *forced* to be wide awake at all hours around you," he said as he pulled out into the traffic and headed for the office complex. "Want to tell me why you were about to jump bail? Or do you want me to guess?"

"Guess," she said, looking out the side window.

"Look, why don't you just level with me. I'm going to find out, anyway."

She glanced over at him, and to his surprise, her eyes glistened with tears. "What if you're wrong, Hawkins? What if I didn't lie about your father?"

He felt a sharp stab at his heart, followed instantly by an unexpected desire to take her in his arms and comfort her. What was it about this woman that made him feel protective? Had always made him feel that way?

He shoved away the desire, the same way he'd shoved her away ten years ago. "You lied and we both know why."

She shook her head and looked away.

"You could tell me the truth now and save us both a lot of grief," he said, letting the old rancor replace any warmer feelings he might have had for her.

"And save you the satisfaction of blackmailing it out of me?" She shook her head. "Not a chance, Hawkins. Let's find out just how good a private eye you really are."

Jake drove toward Kalispell, furious that she could still get to him. He blamed it on that silly childhood crush he'd had on her. He'd opened up, letting her get closer than any other person in his life. Now he bitterly regretted having done that. It made him vulnerable. And it gave her the upper hand.

Okay, so she wasn't going to make it easy. She was going to make it pure hell. But what she didn't seem to realize was that he'd already been to hell and back because of her. And it was payback time.

CLANCY BREATHED A SIGH of relief when Jake finally pulled up in front of Lake Center, a large old hotel that had been made into an office complex. All she wanted to do was to get out of the close confines of the car and put some distance between the two of them. With a little luck, a lot of distance.

But as she started to open her door, he grabbed her arm.

She pretended she didn't feel the jolt from his fingertips that seared her bare skin.

"I wish I didn't know you so well, Clancy," he said, sounding as though he meant it. "Whatever's on that conniving mind of yours, forget it. We're going to see your lawyer and find out what evidence they have against you."

She gave him what she hoped was one of her most innocent looks. "All right. But I'm starved. Why don't I go get us some breakfast at that café up the block and bring it back. What can I get you?"

He laughed as he opened his door and got out. She stepped out of the convertible, only to find him waiting for her. She watched him lock the car, her overnight bag in the rear seat. Then he linked his arm with hers and steered her toward the building's front entrance.

She didn't resist the gentle strength of his persuasive hold on her. It wouldn't have done her any good if she had. But while she also wouldn't admit it under Sodium Pentothal, she liked the feel of his skin against hers; she liked his touch, as dangerous as it was to her future, to her heart. And she glimpsed something in his expression that made her wonder if he wasn't as immune to her touch as he wanted her to believe.

"Geez, Jones," he said as they headed for the elevator. "Breakfast? A bit too predictable and not very imaginative. But a nice try, nonetheless."

Too predictable, huh? Not imaginative enough for him? Well, she'd see what she could do about that.

Jake studied Clancy as they stepped into the elevator and she pushed the third-floor button. She'd been like a kid in church, squirming in her seat on the way into town, glancing at her watch every few moments, tapping her toe to a nonexistent tune. She reminded him of a woman about to jump off a ledge. Actually, more like a woman about to jump bail, he corrected himself.

As the elevator climbed slowly to the third floor, Jake

wondered what Clancy would have done this morning if he hadn't been there to stop her? With the depth of her bank account, she could probably disappear without too much trouble. At least for a while. But why run? Unless she was guilty of Westfall's murder and knew she was headed for prison.

But wouldn't a woman who planned to disappear forever take more than a small suitcase—or nothing at all—and buy what she needed when she got there?

The elevator doors thumped open, and it suddenly occurred to him that there might be a man—a man other than Westfall—in Clancy's life. That could explain the small suitcase. Jake realized he knew nothing about the nature of Clancy's relationship with the deceased. Kiki had said Clancy had dated Dex. But that didn't mean Dex was the only man, now, did it? Clancy could have dozens of men on the string.

"You don't mind if I step into the ladies' room a moment to freshen up, do you?" Clancy asked, breaking into his thoughts.

He grinned at her, hoping it hid his true feelings. "I'd hate to see you any fresher than you already are, but hey, it's all right with me since I'm coming along. Not that I don't trust you."

She scowled. "You can't seriously plan to spend every waking moment with me?"

"Every waking—and sleeping—moment." He took her elbow as they headed down the hall.

"That might be a bigger job than you think," she said cryptically. "And I suppose you want me to believe you're doing this for my own good, right?"

He held open the door to the ladies' room for her. "How can you doubt it?"

She shot him a drop-dead look.

"The truth, Jones, will set you free," he said, and smiled.

"Or send me to prison for life." She took only a quick

glance into the rest room before she added, "I think you're right. I'm fresh enough."

As he let the door close, Clancy took his arm and smiled up at him as if he'd actually done something that pleased her. One side of her mouth crooked up a little, her brown eyes glinted with mischief, and just the hint of a dimple dented her left cheek at the corner of her lips. Jake had forgotten her smile could pack such a wallop. It hit him in the chest, taking away his breath and knocking him off guard.

He stumbled. Her smile deepened; humor glinted in her gaze. If he'd had any doubt before, he didn't now. She knew damned well the effect she was having on him, and she loved it. This was war. And for a moment, he wished there was another way, other than all-out war, to settle things between them.

He stared at her, wishing he could find the answers he needed in that face of hers. If only he could look into those brown eyes and know everything he wanted to about her. Like why she'd lied about his father. If she'd killed her boyfriend. Where she'd been going this morning in such a hurry. Why she'd betrayed him.

Instead, all he got were more questions from that adorable face of hers. And more suspicions.

She brushed against him as she stepped past, the silkiness of her skin sparking responses in him he didn't want to be feeling. Her scent filled him, branding his senses. He watched the provocative sway of her hips as she walked away from him. He assured himself he could handle this woman, that it would be a pleasure giving her some of her own medicine.

But that little voice of reason that kept him honest suggested the best thing he could do would be to get this case over with, pry the truth out of Clancy and head back to Texas lickety-split.

He swore softly to himself as he opened the door to the office with the sign that read Attorney Tadd Farnsworth, and watched Clancy waltz through, her bottom filling out her jeans in a way that should have been against the law. Clancy played him like a cheap guitar, but made him feel like he was a fine Gibson. Jake promised himself he'd have her dancing to his tune—and soon.

Chapter Four

"Jake? Jake Hawkins?" the handsome, prematurely gray-haired man said, coming around his large desk. "I didn't know you were back in town." Tadd Farnsworth's smile was as quick as his handshake and just as slick.

"I didn't know I had to check in at the border," Jake said, taking the attorney's outstretched hand.

"And Clancy," Tadd said.

Jake thought Tadd held her hand a little too long, his look a little too sympathetic and seductive.

Jake told himself he would have liked Tadd Farnsworth if the man hadn't been the prosecuting attorney who sent his father to prison. But he knew that wasn't true. At one time Tadd had been a regular at the island resort, always sporting a fast new boat, always a hit at the parties Jake's mother threw at the lake lodge. Jake remembered only too well how taken his mother had been with Tadd. That was plenty reason to make Jake dislike the man.

Seeing the way Clancy smiled at Tadd, Jake could see that even ten years older, Tadd still had a way with women. He decided he liked him even less.

"I was sorry about your mother, Jake" Tadd said as he returned to his chair behind his desk. "I heard she passed away a few months ago. My condolences."

"Oh, Jake," Clancy said. "I didn't know. I'm so sorry."

Jake nodded and took a chair beside Clancy. He didn't

want to talk about his mother. Especially with Tadd. Nor did he want to talk about his father. He pulled his business card from his wallet and tossed it on the desk. "I'm here on the Dex Westfall case."

Tadd picked up the card. His eyes widened. "I'd heard Kiki had brought in some hotshot private eye." He laughed. "I'll be damned. So you're a P.I." He shook his head. "Interesting, her choice of investigators, wouldn't you say?"

No kidding. "I'd like to see what evidence you've got so far."

Tadd nodded. "Sure you wouldn't like some coffee? Or maybe a stiff drink?" His smile slipped a little as he looked from Jake to Clancy and back. "You're not going to like this case."

"There isn't much about it I've liked so far," Jake said. Clancy mumbled something under her breath and looked at her watch.

"Don't worry. This won't take long," Jake assured her.

"Do I look worried?" she asked with wide-eyed innocence.

The attorney excused himself and returned a few minutes later with a large manila envelope. He placed it on the desk in front of Jake and returned to his seat without saying a word.

Jake opened the flap, pulled out a stack of papers and flipped through them. He let out an oath without even realizing it.

"Told you you weren't going to like it," Tadd said.

The case against Clancy was overwhelming.

"I think I will take that coffee," Jake said to Tadd.

Jake sat stunned as Tadd buzzed his secretary. It had been one thing telling himself the woman who betrayed him was a killer. It was quite another to realize it might actually be true.

"Why didn't the sheriff just hang her on the spot?" Jake asked Tadd after he took a sip of the coffee the attorney handed him, happily discovering it to be heavily laced with bourbon.

"Would have a hundred years ago. If she'd been a man." Tadd chuckled. "Instead, she's a woman. And a Talbott to boot." He shot Clancy a smile to say he was just kidding, but with one look from her, it died on his lips.

Jake wondered if she realized that she'd be cooling her heels in a cell right now if it wasn't for Aunt Kiki's money and the illustrious Talbott name. Not to mention what Kiki must be paying Tadd. Jake wouldn't be surprised if Kiki wasn't also making a large donation to the Tadd Farnsworth for County Attorney campaign for added incentive.

Jake thumbed through the rest of the evidence, including a list of Dex Westfall's belongings from the murder scene: a bloody western snap-front shirt, a pair of jeans and red cowboy boots. No socks. No underwear. Jake raised an eyebrow. Had Dex gotten dressed in a hurry for some reason? Or was that his usual attire? Jake made a mental note to ask Clancy.

There was also a list of items found at the cabin Dex had rented at the Hawk Island Resort, including Dex's wallet, watch, keys and some loose change.

"He didn't have his wallet or keys on him the night of his murder?" Jake asked Tadd, suspecting even more that for some reason Dex Westfall had dressed in a hurry.

"I guess he didn't need them," Tadd said. "No place to spend money and he sure couldn't drive anywhere. He probably took one of the island trails to Ms. Jones's."

"You don't know how he got there?" Jake asked, surprised.

"Does it matter?" Tadd said. "He got there. We know that."

Everything mattered, Jake thought. What Dex hadn't done was drive. There were no cars or roads on Hawk Island. That left two other options: he could go by boat around the island to Clancy's. Or he could take one of the many mountain trails. Because the sheriff hadn't found a boat at the scene didn't mean Dex hadn't had someone drop him off. And that meant maybe he'd planned to have that same someone pick him up again.

Dex was last seen with Clancy after the resort café closed on Friday night. That meant there wouldn't have been any place on the island for Dex to spend money. But Jake still thought it odd Dex hadn't taken his wallet. Most guys would grab their wallet, keys and watch out of habit. Some things you just felt naked without. Like underwear.

The wallet, according to the report, contained less than thirty dollars. He glanced through the photocopy of the items—a Montana driver's license, a few credit cards. Jake frowned. No photographs. Not even one of Clancy, the guy's girlfriend. No family photos. No receipts or junk like most people carried in their wallets. No mementos.

Dex Westfall's belongings reminded Jake of a new subdivision. No feeling of history. Everything of Dex's had been marked on the sheriff's list as in new condition. Jake found himself wondering just who the hell this guy was and what Clancy had seen in him as he glanced at Westfall's driver's license photo again. The guy was almost too good-looking. Jake had never figured Clancy for that type, but then, he reminded himself, he didn't know Clancy anymore. He looked over at her. For instance, what was she thinking about right now? He realized how little he knew about her. It worried him. A lot.

Taking out his notebook, Jake jotted down Dex's social security number and address from his driver's license, and took down the credit card numbers. He put everything back in the envelope and looked up at Tadd.

"What do you know about this guy?" Jake asked.

Tadd shrugged. "No more than what's here, and we won't know until his next of kin are notified." Jake noted Clancy's sudden rapt attention and wondered why this subject would interest her when nothing else about her case had.

"There's one other thing," Tadd said. Jake felt the bad

news coming even before Tadd opened his mouth. "You should know the sheriff has two witnesses who overheard Westfall and Clancy arguing at the marina café the evening Dex Westfall was murdered. Both said they heard Clancy threaten Dex."

Jake groaned inwardly.

"One is a waitress at the marina café," Tadd continued. "The other is Frank Ames. You remember him?"

Yeah, Jake remembered the tall, pimply-faced kid six years his senior. Frank had always had a major chip on his shoulder, one that Jake had more than once wanted to knock off. Jake's father had given Frank a job at the resort, wanting to help him. But Frank's hostile unfriendliness had forced Warren Hawkins to let him go, making Frank Ames all the more bitter.

"Frank owns the resort now," Tadd said. "Maybe you'd heard."

"No, I hadn't." Jake hadn't heard anything about Hawk Island since the day he promised his mother he'd never say his father's name in her presence again. It had been the day they left Flathead Lake, right after Warren Hawkins had been convicted of embezzlement, arson and one count of deliberate homicide. They'd left town on the whipping tail of a scandal that had rocked the tiny community. Kiki had been right; his mother had insisted they leave without stopping at the Montana State prison in Deer Lodge to see his father even one last time.

Jake had kept his promise to her; he'd never mentioned his father's name. But several times a year he'd visited Warren Hawkins in prison. Jake had wanted to reopen his father's case and do some investigating on his own, but Warren had asked him not to. Jake had left it alone, not wanting to hurt his mother any more than she had been.

But now she was gone. And he was back in Montana thanks to Aunt Kiki. Back on Flathead Lake. And that hunch of his was knocking at the back of his brain, demanding to be let in. Demanding that he follow it, no matter where it might lead. Clancy was his ticket as surely as Tadd Farnsworth was a born politician. It was just going to be harder to get the truth out of Clancy than he'd first thought.

"Can I get a copy of this and the autopsy report?" Jake asked, tapping the envelope with his finger.

Tadd nodded.

"Give me call when it's ready." He gave Tadd the number from the cellular phone Kiki had given him.

"Here's my home number," Tadd said as he took out a business card and wrote on the back. He handed it to Jake. "In case you come up with something." He sounded more than a little doubtful that would happen.

Tadd pushed his intercom button and instructed his secretary to make Jake a copy of the Dex Westfall case, including the latest on Clancy's sleepwalking defense.

"What?" Jake snapped, telling himself he must have heard wrong. He glanced over at Clancy; she met his gaze for an instant, then looked away, her body suddenly tense. Jake cursed under his breath. What else had Clancy and her aunt failed to tell him?

"I guess you didn't know," Tadd said, smiling sympathetically at Jake. "Clancy was sleepwalking the night Dex Westfall was killed. That's why she doesn't remember what happened."

Jake stumbled to his feet, feeling the weight of the world settle around his shoulders. He took Clancy's elbow and steered her out into the hall.

"Sleepwalking?" he demanded the moment the door closed behind them. He couldn't believe what a chump he was. Even when she'd lied on the stand, he'd figured she only did it to protect her own father. If Tadd was opting for a Twinkie defense like sleepwalking, it meant only one thing: Clancy'd killed Dex Westfall and she damn well knew it.

"Sleepwalking?" Jake demanded again, trying to keep his voice down.

"I guess I shouldn't expect you to believe me," Clancy

said, jerking her elbow free of his grip. She started down the hall, but he grabbed her shoulder and whirled her around to face him.

He let his gaze rake roughly over her, telling himself not to be fooled by that face of hers with its cute little button of a nose or the crocodile tears in those big brown eyes. He pulled her into the first alcove and blocked her retreat with his body. "Another murder and you just happened to be sleepwalking *again?*"

Clancy found her gaze locked spellbound with his. There was something commanding about him. He demanded her attention, and ever since she was a girl, she'd been unable to deny him. She looked into his eyes; they darkened like thunderheads banked out over the lake. Everything about him, from his eyes to the hard line of his body, warned her of the storm he was about to bring into her life. Jake Hawkins was a dangerous man, one she'd be a fool to trifle with.

"I walk in my sleep. I have ever since I was a child."

He stared at her, suspicion deep in his expression. "Sure you have."

She wanted to slap his smug face. "I assume you've never walked in your sleep."

"No." He made that one word say it all.

She reminded herself that people who'd never sleepwalked didn't understand, couldn't understand. But she wanted Jake to, needed Jake to.

"It's frightening, because when you wake up you don't know how you got there. You don't recall getting up. Suddenly you are just somewhere else, and you don't remember anything. Not even where you've been." She met his gaze. "Or what you've done."

"How come I never heard about you sleepwalking when we were kids?"

She glanced away. "I was…ashamed. Wandering around at night in my pajamas, not knowing what I was doing. It was something I didn't want anyone to know about."

Jake nodded, eyeing her intently. "And you're trying to tell me that the night Dex Westfall was murdered you were walking around in your pj's, sound asleep, and you don't remember killing him? Not that you didn't kill him, but that you don't remember because you were sacked out?"

"I'm trying to tell you the truth," she said angrily, and wondered why she was even bothering. "Sleepwalking isn't something I have control over. It just…happens. Like last night."

"Last night?" He dragged his fingers through his hair. "You mean last night on the dock when you were sure someone pulled you into the lake and tried to drown you? Now you're telling me that you were asleep?"

She didn't like his tone. "I was walking in my sleep." She took a breath and looked away. He'd never given her the chance to explain ten years ago; he'd just assumed she'd lied on the stand and he'd cut her off without a word. Without a goodbye. "Just like I was the night of the fire."

"How convenient that you were asleep at the murder you committed," Jake said, bitterness oozing from his every word. He slammed a palm to the wall on each side of her. "And how inconvenient for my father that you just happened to wake up in time to see him kill Lola Strickland."

"Yes." She ducked under his arm and ran down the hall, blinded by tears and regrets. Behind her, she heard him. The sound was a low, pained howl, the cry of a wounded animal. It tore at her heart. She wanted to take him in her arms, to comfort him. But nothing she could do or say would do that. She'd told the jury the truth. She didn't know what else had happened that night at Hawk Island Resort because she'd been asleep—walking, but sound asleep. Sleepwalking had always been her private shame. A frightening weakness that was best kept a secret. Until the night Lola Strickland was murdered. Now that horrible memory had come back to haunt her—just the way her sleepwalking had come back.

Jake slammed a fist into the wall, too stunned to chase

after her. Sleepwalking? She'd been sleepwalking the night of Lola's murder *and* the night Dex Westfall was killed in her garret? And last night on the dock? His brain tried to assimilate this information but couldn't.

That's why her story had sounded like a lie. Could she really not remember anything? Was that why there'd been so many holes in her story? Because she'd been asleep? His mind refused to accept it. Just as it had ten years ago. She was lying. Again. Sleepwalking! Again.

He charged after her, only to run headlong into a group of students on some kind of career day. The teacher tried to gather her flock, but they scattered like errant chicks. Jake forced his way through to reach the elevator door just as it closed. He watched the numbers overhead to make sure Clancy was headed down before he took off at a run for the stairs. She didn't really think she could get away from him, did she?

He burst out of the stairwell and into the main lobby as the elevator doors were closing again. He raced over to them, slapping the doors open and startling the only occupants, an elderly couple.

"Sorry," he said. "I was looking for a blond woman. About five six. Cute." Incredibly sexy. And innocent-looking. He started to make a curvaceous outline with his hands, but stopped himself. "Nice figure. Wearing a navy shirt, jeans and sandals?"

They both gave him a knowing smile. The elderly woman pointed across the hall to a door marked Women. "She seemed a little upset," the woman said, clearly blaming him.

"Thanks." As the elevator doors closed again, Jake made a beeline for the bathroom, cursing himself for letting Clancy out of his sight for even an instant.

He stormed through the doorway, propelled by a flammable fuel of high-grade anger. "If you think I'm going to believe this latest story of yours—" he said, taking up the conversation right where they'd left off.

His voice echoed off the tiled walls. A half-dozen women looked up, startled. Clancy wasn't at either of the two sinks powdering her nose. That left only the row of four stalls.

"Sir, you're in the wrong rest room," one woman politely informed him as if he didn't know.

He politely informed her that he didn't care, then he leaned down to look for Clancy's sandaled feet in the occupied stalls. No Clancy. The last stall appeared empty; someone had put a handmade Out of Order sign on it.

Most of the women had the good sense to flee from the room, though they did it in high indignation, telling him in no uncertain terms what they thought of his behavior.

You want to see bad behavior, he thought to himself, *wait until I get my hands on Clancy.* A couple of women stayed to give him grief. He ignored them, waiting for the stalls to empty out. As he glanced around the room, he assessed the situation. There was only one door. Clancy hadn't had time to come back out.

Jake waited for the last woman to exit. As she stomped past, he noticed that the summer breeze coming through the open window at the end of the room smelled sweet with the scent of freshly mown grass. Jake could hear the sound of a lawnmower buzzing just outside at ground level. In front of the window, someone had upended a trash can.

Jake cursed himself and his stupidity as he pushed open each stall door on his way to the window. All the stalls were now empty, just as he knew they would be. And on the corner of the metal window frame was a small scrap of navy blue material that perfectly matched the shirt Clancy had been wearing.

Damn her hide, she'd given him the slip.

Chapter Five

Clancy caught the first flight out of Kalispell. She thought she'd feel safe once the plane was in the air. Instead, she couldn't shake the feeling that someone was after her. And not just Jake Hawkins.

She glanced around at the other passengers but saw no one she knew. No one even appeared remotely interested in her. As the plane banked to the east, she looked out the window and told herself she had to calm down and think clearly. Her life depended on it. And yet she'd never felt more afraid, more alone.

Except for one other time in her life. The night of the resort fire. The night Lola Strickland was murdered. Clancy closed her eyes and tried to fight back the painful memories. But the memories came, edged with one penetrating truth: she'd walked in her sleep that night, just as she had the night Dex Westfall died.

It had been late that night ten years ago when she'd come down the stairs, awakened by the sound of her parents arguing. Her parents never argued. Until that moment, she'd led an idyllic life on the island. The only dark spot in her whole childhood had been her required yearly visits back East to see Aunt Kiki and get a little culture so she didn't grow up a wild heathen. Clancy had hated the visits, the stiff, prissy dresses, the long, boring lessons in social graces, her aunt's endless lectures on the value of money and the Talbott name.

But it was her aunt's low opinion of Clancy's father that made her call Kiki the Wicked Witch of the East. Kiki had always thought her sister had married beneath the family name when she'd married Clarence Jones. Clancy idolized her father.

Clancy had stopped on the stairs when she heard her father's voice saying that he couldn't go to the police, wouldn't go to the police. Warren was his best friend.

But her mother had argued that Warren was stealing from the businesses and had been for some time. Clancy felt a sick, sinking feeling, knowing that their lives had suddenly changed and would never be the same again.

When her father left by boat to meet Warren at the resort, Clancy followed by land, afraid for her father for reasons she couldn't explain then or now.

But when she reached the resort office, she could hear her father and Warren inside and decided to wait in one of the boats tied at the dock. She'd fallen asleep.

Later, she'd woken only to find that she'd walked in her sleep. To this day, she had no idea where she'd been or what she might have seen. All she remembered was waking to find herself standing outside the office.

Her father's boat was gone. Inside the office she could hear voices raised in anger. From the shadows, she watched in horror as Warren Hawkins struggled with Lola Strickland. Lola stumbled backward into an adjoining room. Both figures disappeared for a few moments, then Warren emerged at a run. Behind him the office burst into flame, and within seconds the fire consumed the building.

Just thinking about that night brought back the incredible regret. Lola's death and Warren Hawkins's arrest ended the life she and Jake had known on Hawk Island. Jake and his mother left Flathead; Jake left hating Clancy. Clancy's parents had moved to Alaska to start over. They'd lost everything. Kiki purchased the lodge at Clancy's pleading.

Clancy had foolishly hoped her family would some day be reunited there. Two years later her parents were killed in a small plane crash outside of Fairbanks.

Clancy didn't come back to the boarded-up lodge for years and then only occasionally. At first the bad memories were just too painful. Then the good memories started to surface again.

She opened her eyes and looked out the plane window. She'd had such hopes when she'd returned. Had she made a mistake coming back? Was there a curse on the island and her? Some debt not yet paid?

She felt a chill as she thought of Jake. He'd believed his father's version of what happened that night. Warren Hawkins testified during the trial that he knew nothing about the missing money. After Clarence Jones left, he'd gotten out the books to go over them. Warren was in charge of that part of the businesses in the partnership with Clarence, but he'd turned a lot of the responsibility over to Lola, he'd said.

Warren said he'd heard someone in the adjoining office. When he'd gone to check, he saw two suitcases outside the door and found Lola cleaning out the safe.

He'd tried to stop her. Lola had poured gasoline around the office, obviously planning to cover her tracks. In their struggle, she must have lit the gas. The room burst into flames. That's when Warren swears he saw someone move in the shadows; someone else was in the office by the back door. When he ran out, Lola was still alive. He thought she was right behind him.

Warren said the other person in the office that night must have taken the money from the safe, because it wasn't found in the debris from the fire and Lola certainly didn't get away with it. That person must have also murdered Lola. In the autopsy it was found that Lola had died from a head wound—not from the fire. That made Warren look all the more guilty.

In the end, the jury didn't believe there was another person in the office that night. Nor did they believe Lola set the fire. It looked too much like Warren had embezzled money from the businesses and tried to cover his misdeeds with the fire. Lola, who was leaving the island, just happened along at the wrong time. All of the joint businesses' books were destroyed in the fire. Warren couldn't prove his innocence. Nor could the police prove his guilt.

Clancy's testimony had clinched it. Warren was convicted of embezzlement, arson and deliberate homicide. He got sixty years at the state prison at Deer Lodge.

And because of Clancy's testimony, Jake had walked out of her life without a word. The hurt from that still made her heart ache. And now— Now he'd come back. For revenge.

Just what she needed, Clancy thought as the plane descended into Gallatin Field outside of Bozeman. An old boyfriend with a grudge on top of all her other troubles.

At the airport, Clancy rented a car and drove the eight miles into Bozeman to Dex's condo. She felt as if time were running out. Jake wouldn't be far behind her, she knew that. And he'd be furious. Boy, was that putting it mildly.

But she hoped that by the time he tracked her to the airport, discovered she'd flown to Bozeman and rented a car, it would be too late for him to stop her. By then she'd have searched Dex's place and hopefully found something that would help her case. Though she couldn't imagine what.

There was also the possibility that Jake would go straight to the county attorney. By the time she reached Bozeman, the police could be looking for her, as well.

Either way, she needed to get this over with as quickly as possible.

Dex owned a condo on the southside of town, set back against a hill overlooking Sourdough Creek. Clancy parked and sat in the car for a moment, watching the quiet street. No other vehicles cruised by. She told herself she was just being paranoid. No one was after her. Except Jake. And maybe the entire Bozeman police. And possibly the person who'd tried to drown her last night.

She picked up her purse from the seat and got out, closing the car door behind her. As she walked toward the front door of the condo, she searched the street. A florist's van passed by; the driver never even looked her way. She could only hope the spare key was where it had been the last time Dex locked himself out. Carefully, she slid the large flowerpot slightly to one side. Nothing but dust. She pushed it a little farther and was relieved to see the key.

Quickly she scooped it up, slipped it into the lock and turned. The door swung open.

Clancy stepped into the high-dollar condo, wondering whether the police had already been here, whether they'd already searched the place and found something that would further incriminate her. The cluttered condo didn't surprise her as much as the man who came out of the kitchen.

"Excuse me," he said, sounding annoyed and a little frightened by her intrusion. He was short, with rumpled dark hair and sunless pale skin, and he was wearing nothing but shorts. "How did you get in here?"

Her first thought was that the condo had been sold. Her second was that Dex had a roommate she hadn't known about. A roommate who was looking more than a little anxious.

"I'm a friend of Dex Westfall's," she said quickly, not sure that was exactly accurate, but it beat the alternative. That she was the woman the police had arrested for Dex's murder.

"Dex Westfall," the man said, shaking his head. Had he heard Dex was dead? She felt her heart rate accelerate. Worse yet, had he heard about her arrest? "I suppose he gave you a key."

She shook her head, wondering how she was going to explain what she was doing here. "I used the one under the flowerpot."

He swatted the air with the pancake turner in his hand. "Did Dex tell everyone where to find the key to my condo?"

"*Your* condo?" Clancy thought she must have heard him wrong.

"Dex Westfall was only house-sitting for me for a few months," he said, his tone increasing in both volume and irritation. "I come home to find he's run up my phone bill and failed to pay the utility bills, and now the police want to talk to me about God knows wh—" Behind the man, smoke curled out of the kitchen. He spun around and charged out of the room.

Pans clanged into the sink. A kitchen fan came on. A few moments later, he stalked back into the living room.

"Look," he said, his face flushed. "The guy's a deadbeat. Just give me the key and tell Dex I don't want to see him or any more of his girlfriends around here, all right?"

He didn't know Dex was dead. "The police called you?"

"I got a message on my machine," the man said. "I haven't had time to call them back." He seemed to resent her questions, but also seemed resigned to answer them. No doubt he felt sorry for a woman stupid enough to fall for Dex Westfall. "I just got back yesterday from Australia. I haven't even had time to unpack yet." He held out his hand for the key.

Clancy noticed the stack of newspapers by the door. Magazines and junk mail were piled high on a telephone table by the door. "Did Dex leave any personal items here?" she asked as she handed over the key. "He has something that belongs to me."

The man rolled his eyes. "Dex isn't completely stupid. He packed up and got out just before I returned home. Did you check his apartment?"

She stared at him. "His apartment?"

"You don't get it, do you," he said, his face growing redder. "Dex Westfall is a lying sleazeball. You aren't the first woman to show up looking for him. Or the last, I'm sure.''

No, she *hadn't* got it. She realized how little she knew about the man she'd dated. The man she was now accused of murdering. ''Where is his apartment?'' Her voice came out a trembly whisper.

He reached over to snatch a scrap of paper and a pen from the phone table and scribbled something on it. ''If you loaned him money, forget it. I'm sure it's long gone. Just like I would imagine he is. This is the address he gave me.''

Clancy took the piece of paper. It had a northside apartment address on it.

''If you should catch up to him, tell Dex— Never mind, it wouldn't do any good,'' the man said disgustedly.

She figured he'd find out just how right he was as soon as he returned his calls.

He moved past her to open the front door. ''Good luck,'' he said as she stepped outside, then he closed and locked the door behind her.

Clancy stumbled to the rental car and sat for a moment, too shaken to drive. She remembered the first time Dex had brought her to see his new condo. *His* new condo. He'd told her what a great deal he got on it. He'd insinuated that he'd purchased it with their future in mind and even talked about how easy it would be to build on a studio for her.

He'd been lying through his teeth. To impress her? Or con her? But out of what?

She started the car, anxious to get to Dex's apartment. Maybe the police didn't know about it yet. Maybe he'd left something that would help her.

Dex Westfall's apartment turned out to be a basement rental in an old run-down part of town. Clancy circled the block and, not taking any chances, parked behind the house. A short, worn path led from the alley to the basement entrance. Clancy stepped down the crumbling steps and peered through a dirty window into what looked like the furnace room.

"Can I help you?" The voice was elderly and shrill, with an irritated edge to it.

Clancy spun around to find a wrinkled woman; her pink curlers clung haphazardly to her washed-out gray hair. Her eyes were narrowed and mean.

"I'm looking for Dex," Clancy said, adding what she hoped was a friendly smile.

"Humph! Isn't everybody." The woman jammed her small fists down on her hips and glared at Clancy. "And just what do you want with him?"

"I'm his...sister," she said quickly. "I'm worried about him."

"His sister?" The woman eyed her. "Not much resemblance that I can see."

"Different fathers," Clancy said, caught up in her whopper.

The woman puckered her lipstick-cracked lips. "He owes me rent."

Clancy opened her purse. "How much?"

It took all of Clancy's charm, most of her cash and more flagrant falsehoods to get into the apartment. To her surprised delight, it didn't sound as though the police had been there yet. But then, they had their killer; they weren't looking for clues in Bozeman. Or maybe they'd only gotten as far as the condo, because that was the only address they had for Dex.

"Last thing he said to me was that he'd be back with enough money to buy this house and me with it," the woman said with a huff. "I've seen his kind before. Fancy dresser. Full of himself. Full of bull, that's what he was." She looked up at Clancy as she unlocked the apartment door. "Too bad you can't pick your relatives, huh? Don't take anything." With that, she left, her worn slippers shuffling up the cracked concrete steps.

Clancy closed the door and turned to look at Dex Westfall's apartment. Under the golden glare of a single bulb overhead, the cramped studio apartment looked seedy at best. An old couch hunkered against a dark paneled wall next to an overstuffed worn chair and a small kitchen table and two metal folding chairs. A blanket was neatly folded at one end of the couch. Dex's bed?

An old, hump-shouldered refrigerator kicked on in the kitchen area of the room, clanging a little before it settled into a tired, noisy thrum. Clancy reminded herself that she didn't have much time. Jake would be after her. And by now the man at the condo could have called the police back.

But still she didn't move. She stared at the apartment, trying to connect it with the man she'd known. Or thought she'd known.

On the makeshift counter next to the fridge was a sink and a hot plate. Not far from it stood a tall, homemade pine closet, a bent wire hanger caught in its door. Past it, through a narrow doorway, she could make out a toilet, shower stall and a bathroom window, trash and dead weeds blown in on the outside.

This was the kind of cheap apartment college kids rented while they attended Montana State University. They hung posters on the paneled walls, had loud parties and spent most of their time playing hackysack over at the park or studying at the library. There was no way that Dex Westfall had ever lived here. There had to be a mistake. Even if Dex was short of money—

She reached to free the coat hanger from the closet door. The last thing she expected to find was any of Dex's clothing inside— She'd been right. All of his clothes were gone. But what she saw sent a shock of horror through her.

The wall at the back of the empty closet was covered with papers and pictures, all thumbtacked to the wood. One photograph in particular caught her attention. She shoved back the half-dozen bent metal hangers dangling from the galvanized pipe rod. It was a photo of a young woman.

Clancy moved closer, panic making her movements stiff, unsure. The photograph was of her. Next to it was a ten-year-old newspaper article about Lola Strickland's murder and Warren Hawkins's trial. Clancy's testimony had been highlighted.

Her heart slammed against her ribs as she saw that the entire back of the closet was covered with articles about the trial and that summer. She felt her legs quake beneath her and all her blood seemed to rush to her head. She reeled and caught herself, grabbing the closet for support. A photograph fluttered to the floor. Mechanically, she reached to pick it up.

It was a shot of her in a dark green suit coming out of the gallery where she used to work in downtown Bozeman. She stared at the photo. It was a candid shot, taken from the other side of Main Street. She squinted as something in the picture caught her eye. A silver spot on the jacket's lapel. The pin her Grandmother Jones had left her when she died. Clancy drew the snapshot closer. She remembered that day! It was the last time she'd worn the pin. She'd gone to lunch and when she returned to work, the pin was gone. Lost. She'd run an ad in the paper, but the pin never turned up.

Her heart began to pound harder. It was the same day she'd met Dex. After lunch that afternoon. She'd been so upset about losing her Grandmother Jones's pin. And this man had walked into the gallery, looking for a sculpture. He didn't know the artist's name, just the artist's work. And he had to have the sculpture.

Clancy had been startled by Dex's good looks, his charm, his passion for an artwork he'd only glimpsed in a gallery window. And even more startled and pleased when the artist's work he was dying to purchase turned out to be her own.

Clancy gripped the photograph tighter. Dex had purchased one of her most unusual—and most expensive—sculptures. Then he'd asked her out for dinner that night, telling her he wanted to know more about the artist who did such magnificent work. And unlike her usual cautious self, she'd accepted.

Tears rushed to her eyes, fed by fear rather than regret. Fear and a fresh sense of panic. Dex had taken this picture of her *before* he'd come into the gallery, *before* he'd pretended he hadn't known the name of the artist he was searching for, *before* he'd ever met her.

Her pulse thundered, drowning out the thrum of the refrigerator, drowning out everything but one single thought: Dex Westfall had known her! From that very first day. He'd known who she was. From the newspaper articles about the trial. He'd known. And he'd come after her.

Clancy clung to the edge of the closet. Why her? She let the photograph drop. It drifted to the bottom of the closet, where it lay staring up at her. A play program lay beside it. A play Clancy had attended. Just days before Lola's death.

A thud overhead pulled Clancy back. Pretty soon the landlady would be down here, wondering what was keeping Clancy so long. But Clancy continued to stare at the pictures and newspaper articles, shocked by Dex's deception.

Carefully she moved away from the makeshift closet. The hangers rattled softly behind her. She glanced toward the small, dusty ground-level window over the sink, that feeling that she was being watched even stronger than at the airport. She shivered, urging herself to finish her search and get out of there.

The rusted bathroom cabinet was empty. So was the chest of drawers she found tucked back in the corner. It seemed obvious that when Dex had left, he'd had no intention of coming back. He'd pretty much taken everything. Except for his wall of mementos. A shudder of apprehension rocked her as she stood before the closet again. Why had he thought he wouldn't need them anymore?

That's when she spotted the letter. The letter she'd written him, warning him not to contact her again. He'd tacked it on the closet wall, still in its envelope. She reached for it at the same time she heard the creak of the door opening behind her. Clancy grabbed the envelope, folding it in her hand as she turned, and smiled to greet the nosy landlady.

But the dark silhouette that filled the doorway was much larger than the landlady and much more threatening.

"Jumping bail *and* destroying evidence?" Jake asked, that touch of a southern drawl doing little to take the edge off the anger in his voice. He stepped to her side in two effortless strides and, grasping her wrist, plucked the letter from her hand. "You're just damned and determined to go to prison, aren't you, Clancy Jones?"

Chapter Six

Jake hadn't thought past finding Clancy. Hadn't thought of anything but catching her. And now that he had, he stood scowling at her, uncertain as to what to do with her. Several thoughts crossed his mind, surprising him in both content and fervor. "I ought to—"

Clancy stepped back as he advanced on her, stumbling against the open door of what looked like a homemade closet.

Jake stopped dead when he saw the bulletin board Dex had constructed on the back wall and recognized the subject. "What the—?" He swore under his breath, that hunch of his doing the Charleston in a bright red sequined outfit.

He shot a questioning look at Clancy and noticed how pale she'd turned and realized it wasn't even his doing. "Would you like to tell me what's going on?"

She didn't get a chance to answer. Car doors slammed out front. A moment later, someone pounded on the front door of the house overhead. The screen door creaked open and a woman's high-pitched, irritated voice demanded, "Don't tell me Westfall is in trouble with the law, too."

"Cops." Jake swore and glanced around for a way out. He grabbed Clancy's arm and shoved her toward the bathroom. "I know how fond you are of climbing out windows." He popped open the bathroom window, pushing aside the garbage and weeds, and hoisted Clancy up and out. A few moments later, he was through the window himself and leading Clancy down the path behind the house.

"Is that your car?" Jake asked, hardly waiting for her affirmative response before he asked for the keys, opened the passenger door and shoved her inside. He climbed into the driver's seat, quickly started the car and pulled away.

"Where's your—"

"Parked up the block," he said. "Don't worry, I'll call the rental agency to pick it up." His second rental car on this case was the least of his worries.

A few safe blocks later, he threw on the brakes, startling her, startling himself, at the depth of his anger with her.

"Do you realize the position you've just put me in?" he demanded, unable to keep from yelling. "It's not bad enough that you jump bail and I cover for you. Now I'm withholding evidence from the police on top of it."

"I didn't ask you to cover for me," she said. "You might recall, I fired you."

He narrowed his gaze at her. "Thank you for reminding me of that. I'd almost forgotten." The fact that she hadn't asked him to protect her, that he'd done it all on his own, only made it worse. Far worse. And to add insult to injury, she didn't even appreciate his heroic gesture. He reminded himself she hadn't appreciated it last night, either. One of them was a damned slow learner.

"I just compromised myself and my career, put my P.I. license on the line for you," Jake told her, laying it on a little strong.

She didn't look impressed. "Let's not forget why you're really here." She glared at him. "To get the goods on me, isn't that what you said?"

"I don't remember you being like this," he snapped, forgetting he didn't want to be reminded of their past. He didn't want anything to weaken his resolve, and thinking about the two of them back then definitely made him weak sometimes. "You've grown into an amazingly irritating woman."

"Thank you," Clancy shot back.

Irritating. Conniving. Underhanded. Devious. Sneaky. All traits of a criminal mind, he noted. A murderer's mind. Why else had she jumped bail to get this damned letter? Wasn't that what really had him upset? That the reason for that mountain of evidence against Clancy was because she'd killed Dex Westfall.

He jerked the letter from his pocket where he'd shoved it before the impromptu climb out the window. "Is this what you didn't want the police to find?"

She started to say something, but he cut her off with a slash of his hand through the air between them. He pulled the letter from the envelope and quickly read it. There was no doubt it would be damaging in court. Clancy had dumped Dex in the letter, warning him not to contact her, to leave her alone. It sounded angry. And Jake couldn't help but wonder what the guy had done to prompt this letter. Was Dex the reason she'd quit her job at the gallery and moved back to Hawk Island? Jake suspected he was.

But the letter wasn't damaging enough to jump bail, to chance getting caught by the police, to climb out two windows in one day and race halfway across the state with the cops—and him—close at her heels.

No, Jake thought, glancing over at Clancy, nor did she look much like a criminal. She looked ashen. Shaken. Scared. He remembered the collection on Dex's back closet wall. "I take it you didn't know he had all that stuff on you?"

She bit her lip and shook her head.

Jake considered how he would have reacted to finding a closet wall covered with his life, complete with candid photographs. He thought about the guy tacking all that stuff up; Dex Westfall had to have been one weird bastard.

"He was obviously obsessed with you." Jake could understand that. "What is it you think he wanted?"

She shook her head. "He planned our first meeting." Her voice broke. "From the very beginning, he planned it all. But why?'' She started trembling as if the summer day had suddenly turned ice cold. He felt a chill himself. But fear was a much safer emotion than what he felt as he watched Clancy try desperately not to cry.

That was the thing about the Clancy he'd loved, he recalled. All tomboy tough on the outside but tender and soft on the inside. Before he could consider how stupid it was, he pulled her into his arms. She resisted at first, her body stiff, almost brittle. He pulled her to him, gently rubbing his hand up and down her back. Slowly he felt her soften in his embrace, felt her let the tears out, her face buried in his shoulder. Her back warmed under his hand. He could feel her heart pounding next to his. He concentrated on the rhythmic rubbing of her back, forcing his thoughts to focus on Dex Westfall, a man he was beginning to hate, instead of the soft, wonderfully feminine feel of the woman in his arms.

The crying stopped; so did the trembling. She pulled away. He sat for a moment, less surprised by the sharp jab of desire he felt after having her in his arms than his longing to kiss away her tears, to protect and shelter her.

He growled at himself in disgust. Lust he understood. Clancy was one hot-looking woman. But anything beyond that would mess up his head—and his whole reason for being here. Just as she'd pointed out. He wasn't going to let anything change that.

He started the car, wondering about Dex's relationship with Clancy. In his business, he'd heard a lot of hard-luck stories from women who'd been screwed over by men. This was one story he wasn't anxious to hear. He had a feeling he was going to want to have killed the guy himself. ''Let's get some coffee.''

''HOW DID YOU FIND ME?'' Clancy asked, cradling the coffee mug in her hands. He'd picked a truck stop just outside of Bozeman. Clancy looked small and vulnerable in the pea green upholstered booth, but some of her color had come back and she seemed a little less shaky.

"I added up a few things," he said, eyeing her over his coffee. At first, he'd been too furious to figure out anything. The fact that she'd run made her look guilty as hell. Not that everything else hadn't already made her look that way. The fact that she'd outsmarted him didn't help matters in the least.

But then he'd calmed down enough to replay it all in his head. From when he'd first seen her, hurrying toward the boat, anxious to get somewhere. The small amount of clothing she'd packed. He'd gone through the suitcase she'd left in the back of his rental car, hoping to find an address or phone number inside. No such luck. Instead, there was only what looked like enough clothes for an overnight stay. She hadn't planned to go far or for very long. An extra pair of jeans, a sweatshirt, one change of underwear, and a toothbrush and toothpaste.

Nor had she planned to go anywhere fancy. He happily threw out the boyfriend theory. No sexy nightgown. He added the fact that she'd seemed terribly anxious all morning, worried. She'd needed to get somewhere and in a hurry.

In the end, he'd felt a little better. Because unless he missed his guess, he knew where'd he'd find her.

"I placed a couple of calls, found out you'd taken a plane to Bozeman," Jake said simply. "It was just a matter of getting Dex's home address."

She looked up, surprised. "How did you—"

He smiled. "You'd be surprised what a motivated P.I. can find out. And I was *very* motivated after your devious departure."

"So, was it imaginative enough for you?"

He saw the beginning of a smile on her lovely face. "You want me to admit that you outsmarted me, don't you." He wagged his head at her. "All right, Jones, you got me. You happy now?"

Clancy smiled, her face transformed, sunshine after a storm. "You *are* good at your job, Jake."

He returned her smile, recognizing a reluctant compliment when he heard one. "It's what I get paid for." He hadn't meant to say that.

Her smiled faded. "Yes, I haven't forgotten that," she said, looking into her cup. "Or what really motivates you."

They finished their coffee, then he drove them to the airport where the small plane he'd chartered was waiting. He stopped for a moment to speak to the pilot, then ushered Clancy onto the plane. "I couldn't help but overhear. I didn't know you had your pilot's license," Clancy said as they boarded the plane.

"There are a lot of things you don't know about me, Clancy."

She was starting to realize just how true that was, she thought, hugging herself as if the afternoon had gone cold. Jake's arms around her had left an imprint, one she didn't want to forget. How could he have such compassion for her when at the same time he held such hatred for her? He'd just possibly postponed her going back to jail, and at the same time, risked his license and a brush with the law. She wondered if he even understood himself.

Still, she had been glad to see him when he showed up at Dex's. She'd needed someone desperately, and there was Jake. Just like old times. She'd almost run into his arms. Almost forgotten the bad blood between them.

"Thank you for helping me," she said, meaning it. "Again."

He mumbled something under his breath, then motioned to the empty plane. "Sit anywhere you like."

She headed for a window seat near the wing. Jake disappeared into the cockpit to speak to the pilot. A few moments later the plane began to taxi out to the runway. She was fumbling with the seat belt when Jake took a seat beside her. "I guess all of this sleuthing has made me a little nervous," she said, all thumbs. He took the seat belt strap from her and with practiced smoothness locked it into place.

"Try not to worry," he said, buckling up his own.

She clenched her hands together, her nerves a steady vibration running through her body like the whine of the plane engine as it readied for takeoff. The engine revved and the plane roared down the runway.

She looked out the window at the endless blue sky instead of at Jake's bottomless gray eyes. Only a few clouds huddled over the Tobacco Root Mountains. The rich green valley floor raced to the foothills and the pines. Below her, rivers ran to meet at Three Forks, the Jefferson, Gallatin and Madison converging to form the Missouri.

"Tell me about Dex Westfall."

She snapped back around in surprise, having momentarily forgotten the trouble she was in, both with the law and Jake Hawkins. "To help you put me in prison?"

Through the window across the aisle, the sun glistened, blinding white off the plane's wing as the pilot banked toward Flathead Lake and home.

"Come on, Clancy, you know I don't want to see you go to prison." He almost sounded like he meant it.

"Right. You'd much rather see me hang."

Jake pulled off his cap and raked his fingers through his hair. "Look, I'm still going to get the truth out of you, but in order to do that, I need to find something that proves your innocence. I don't see any way I can do that without your help." He slapped the cap back on his sandy blond head. "The way I see it, that puts us on the same team."

"Not hardly." She locked her gaze with his, wishing for the look she'd seen earlier, wishing for the old Jake, the one she'd once trusted with her life, the one who'd trusted her. "I'm fighting for my life, Jake. You're fighting for redemption. You want me to tell you that you were right, that I'm a liar, and that I betrayed you and your father." His jaw tensed, his gray eyes darkened. "You want me to tell you that you didn't make a mistake ten years ago. Well,

I'm sorry, Jake. You're wasting your time if that's all you came to Montana for. I didn't lie. And you'll have to judge just how large a mistake you made.''

Jake stared at her for a long moment, then, unsnapping his seat belt, he stalked off to the front of the plane without a word.

Clancy sat stunned, surprised by what she'd said to him, surprised even more by her raw anger. She felt the same way she had the last day of the trial when Jake had pushed himself to his feet, his gaze finding hers just before he walked out of the courtroom—and her life.

That day she'd expected him to come back. She'd been wrong. Today, she told herself she was smarter: she didn't expect him to come back for the rest of the flight. He'd said he wanted the truth, but look how he reacted to it. She cursed him for the coward he was and had worked herself up into a pretty good mad by the time he returned. She probably would have shared a few more choice words with him, but those words died on her lips when she saw what he'd brought her.

''I had the pilot pick us up a little something,'' he said, handing her a soda, a bologna sandwich and barbecue potato chips. Her childhood favorites; he'd remembered. ''I figured you haven't had any more to eat today than I have.''

All she could think to say was ''Thanks.'' She hadn't realized just how hungry she was until that moment. She took a bite, aware of his gaze on her as he sat down with an identical lunch, just as they had a zillion times as kids.

They ate in silence, Clancy intent on her sandwich right down to the last bite. ''I feel like a prisoner on death row eating my last meal.''

''Clancy.''

The way Jake said her name made her catch her breath. That single, simple word broke down the barriers she'd built around her heart. She could forget the past. She could forgive. If only he loved her again.

''Yes, Jake?'' she asked softly, wiping the last of the

bread crumbs from her lips. When he didn't answer, she glanced over at him, half hoping, half afraid.

She found his gaze soft, his eyes a rich light silver. She wasn't sure, but his expression seemed as hopeful as she knew hers must be. Did he want to believe in her? Was there a chance he could forget vengeance and remember what they'd shared before the trial and really help her?

In the length of a heartbeat, whatever she'd witnessed in his expression died. It blew out like a fledgling fire in a strong wind. "Jake." It came out a plea.

He shook his head, the moment lost, then looked past her to the plane window. "I forgot how incredible the sunsets can be in this part of the country."

Clancy turned to the scene outside, disappointed that he'd decided not to say whatever had been on his mind just then. The sunset was indeed spectacular. She couldn't remember the last time she'd seen anything so beautiful. Slivers of sunlight pierced the clouds like daggers of gold. The growing darkness dipped the peaks in deep purple while the dying sun painted the sky with a pallet of pinks.

The sight stirred something in her, giving her a feeling of strength and renewed hope. The sandwich helped, too. So did the truce, however uneasy, between them.

"I don't know what I can tell you about Dex Westfall," Clancy said after a moment. She didn't kid herself that Jake was on her side. But she needed his help. It was that simple.

"Dex planned our first meeting," she said, feeling a shudder at the memory of the bulletin board on the back of the closet. She told Jake about the day in late February when Dex came into the gallery pretending to look for the artist of a sculpture in the window.

Jake raised a brow when she told him she'd accepted a dinner date that very evening with a man who was a total stranger. She couldn't tell Jake that she'd been starved for a man in her life after Jake left her, but had never found one who even made her heart pitter, let alone patter.

"Dex was charming. He said and did all the right things." He'd swept her off her feet. At first.

But he never made her ache inside for him. Never made her deliriously happy at just the sight of him. Never made her want more. Like Jake had. Nor had his kisses ever made her feel the way nineteen-year-old Jake Hawkins's had. Nor had the kisses of any other man she'd dated.

"We dated for a few months," she said. "I never knew that much about him. He didn't like to talk about his past. All he told me was that he was raised in eastern Montana, on a farm. His parents were very poor, and once he got away from there, he'd never gone back."

"Why do you think he wanted to meet you?"

Dex had led her to believe he was as lonesome as she was. "He said he'd been looking for me all his life. At least that part was true." She grimaced at how gullible she'd been. "He told me he loved me."

"No kiddin'?"

She narrowed her gaze at Jake. "That surprises you?"

"On the contrary, in case you haven't looked in a mirror lately, you're not a bad-looking woman."

His compliment, although not eloquent by any means, warmed her nonetheless.

"What about you? Were you in love with him?" He balled up his sandwich wrapper and didn't look at her.

Did it bother Jake that she might have loved another man? Well, he needn't worry; there'd only been one love in her life, was still only one.

"I was flattered by the attention," she admitted honestly. "At first." At what point had the attention become too much?

"What made you finally write him off?" Jake asked.

She bit her lip. She'd literally written him off, and Jake had the incriminating letter in his pocket to prove it, not that the sheriff needed more evidence to convict her. "I just didn't want to see him anymore."

"So you were running from Dex when you went back to the island to live?" Jake asked.

She knew it had been more than that. Dex had frightened her in a way she couldn't even explain. But she'd also wanted to go home. She'd wanted to go back to a time when she'd felt safe. And loved. And that time had been on Hawk Island. "It felt like it was time to go home," she said.

Jake said nothing.

She'd had an uneasy feeling about Dex that she hadn't been able to throw. Now she realized she'd been right not to trust him. She felt almost a sense of relief to have her misgivings about Dex confirmed. Unfortunately, all that insight came too late. Dex was dead. And she'd be going to trial soon for his murder.

"Do you think he thought you had money?" Jake asked.

She'd considered that. "What money? I'm a struggling artist."

"Hardly," Jake said. "I've seen your work in galleries in Texas."

"I do all right, but not well enough for a man to want me for my money. And my parents lost everything after...what happened."

Jake winced. "And they blamed my father, I'm sure."

"No," she said with conviction. "They were horribly saddened by what happened to Warren." She looked over at him. "You lost your father to prison, but you can still see him. I lost both of my parents."

Jake looked away.

"The only thing I own is the lodge at the lake, thanks to Aunt Kiki," she said, then had a thought. "Unless he figured he could get his hands on Aunt Kiki's money."

Jake shook his head, seemingly happier that the conversation had returned to the case. "Kiki would have been a long shot. You're not her only heir."

She nodded, biting at her lip. "I still don't know what he wanted or why he came to Hawk Island." She looked out the window. The dying sun rimmed the mountains with gold. A deep purple filled the valleys and spilled over into the foothills. "That's why I went to Bozeman, to try and find out. Not to get that letter."

"Tell me about the night Dex showed up at the island."

She hugged herself against the memories of that night and related to Jake how Dex had called, insistent that he had to see her. She'd agreed to meet him at the café just to get it over with. Jake frowned when she told him how strangely Dex had been acting, talking about his mother, playing with that string of beads. Her legacy. "He said I was part of that legacy."

Jake's frown deepened.

She brushed her hair back from her face and took a calming breath. "I thought maybe he'd been drinking. He wasn't making any sense. Then he glanced past me into the darkness and saw something that…scared him."

"Something or *someone?*" Jake asked.

"I don't know, I turned, but whatever it was—if there was anything at all—was gone. Suddenly he became very agitated and said he had to go. He wasn't leaving the island until he got what he deserved."

"And maybe he got it," Jake said, his gaze intent on her face.

"I didn't kill him." She glanced away. At least she didn't believe in her heart that she'd killed him. "Why would I kill him in my sleep? What possible reason could I have had?"

Jake could think of a half-dozen reasons a woman might kill a man. And he figured a woman could think of at least six more without even being asleep. A woman who thought she could get away with murder because of her sleepwalking history could have any reason she wanted for killing Dex Westfall.

Well, Clancy might be able to dupe Tadd Farnsworth, who couldn't see beyond her shapely body and her aunt's money. But Jake Hawkins wasn't that easily fooled. He'd known Clancy. Maybe not as well as Dex had— Not wanting to continue with that line of thinking, he pulled a magazine out of the back of the seat in front of him and pretended interest in it he didn't feel.

After a few moments he looked over and realized the futility of his charade. Clancy was sound asleep. He stared at her beautiful face, peaceful in sleep, and wondered. Did she really sleepwalk? Did she kill Dex? Was it in her sleep?

He reached across the aisle for the manila envelope he'd tossed there earlier. He'd placed a call to the librarian while he was waiting to charter a plane. The envelope had arrived by courier shortly before his takeoff from the Kalispell airport. It contained photocopies of stories about sleepwalker murder cases. He'd been shocked by what he read on his plane ride to Bozeman.

Jake read case after case of what was known as homicidal somnambulism. One story, from medieval times, was about a woodcutter who thought he saw an intruder at the foot of his bed and, picking up an ax, killed his wife, who was asleep beside him.

The whole concept was too alien for Jake. Sleep-related violence. Out of the millions of Americans who had sleep disorders, only a small percentage became violent, picking up axes, guns or sculptures to kill while sound asleep.

He glanced over at Clancy, who was still sleeping peacefully, and tried to picture her. Her eyes would be open, her face bland. She'd be unresponsive to everything and everyone around her. In a hypnotic trance, functionally blind, the articles had said. She would pick up the sculpture, go up the stairs to the garret. Dex Westfall would be waiting for her up there. Who knew what for. And she would bludgeon him to death.

Her brain would be awake enough to allow her to do all of this while the rest of her mind would remain unconscious to everything that was happening. She would wake to find herself standing over Dex's body and be horrified at what she'd done.

Jake shook his head. How could Clancy have stayed asleep through such a violent act and then have total amnesia from the time of falling asleep until waking? It was much easier to imagine her killing her boyfriend in cold blood.

They were approaching the Kalispell airport when Clancy stirred and looked up at him wide-eyed. "I fell asleep?" She sounded horrified by the idea. "I didn't—"

"Sleepwalk?" he asked, tucking the manila envelope away. She really didn't think he bought this, did she? "No, you didn't leave your seat."

He had his own theory on Dex Westfall's murder. One he didn't like to admit, even to himself. "Dex was seeing other women, wasn't he?"

She seemed startled, and he told himself he should have felt like a louse, catching her off guard, half asleep. He didn't.

"Yes," she said quietly.

"A jury might read that as possible motive. The woman scorned. You know?"

Clancy shook her head. "It wasn't like that."

Right. "When did you find out about the other women?" he asked, already knowing the answer and realizing how damaging it was going to be in court.

"Right before I left Bozeman, I found a note from some woman. I don't doubt there were others. The man he house-sat for mentioned Dex's other girlfriends. But I just used that as an excuse to break off the relationship. I'd been trying to break up with him for several weeks."

Jake scoured a hand over his face. He needed a long, hot shower, a shave and a few hours of uninterrupted sleep in a real bed. "A note?"

"It was from some woman Dex had met in a bar."

"Some woman he'd—" He didn't have to finish; she anticipated this one.

"Some woman he'd been...intimate with," she admitted.

Jake groaned to himself. "Where is the note now?"

She shook her head.

The note would turn up, providing the prosecution with possible motive. Couple that with the letter in his pocket. "You wrote him a letter and broke it off right after that," Jake said, not even needing confirmation.

"Yes. Dex just wouldn't take no for an answer, so I thought if I wrote it down— Now I know he was after something else."

"Tell me about Friday night, the night you found Dex in the garret."

She shifted in her seat and looked out the window again. "I left him at the café and went home a little after ten," she said mechanically. Obviously she'd already recounted this story numerous times to the cops.

"Did you go by boat?" he asked.

"Yes." She seemed to be waiting for another question, but when none came, she continued. "I couldn't sleep. I went to my studio and worked for a while."

"Were you more angry or afraid?" Jake asked.

"What?" She sounded surprised by his question and not the least happy that he'd interrupted her again. She obviously wanted this over with as quickly as possible. "Why would you ask that?"

"I remember the year you started sculpting," he said, wishing he couldn't remember. "You used to work when you were upset."

"Both angry and afraid. I remember locking the doors. I never lock the doors at the lake."

"Then, you thought he might come over?"

"I guess I was worried that he might," she admitted.

"How do you think he got in? Did he have a key?" He felt her gaze burn his skin. "Did he come by boat or walk?"

"I didn't give him a key, if that's what you're asking." Her voice broke. "I don't know how he got there, what he was doing there, or how he got in. I don't know anything.

I went to bed around midnight, exhausted. The next thing I remember is waking up to find Dex dead." She shuddered and hugged herself against the memory.

Classic homicidal somnambulism. No memory. Confusion. Horror at having done it. Right. "The murder weapon was in your hand. How do you think it got there?"

She didn't answer. Jake glanced over at her. He knew that look. He remembered it only too well as a kid. He'd stepped over the line.

"You don't believe me," she said. "You don't believe anything I tell you."

He could hear the anger in her voice. And the hurt. He just didn't expect the hurt to affect him the way it did. Damn her. He couldn't afford these feelings.

"You think I killed him?" Her face was flushed, but he had no idea whether it was from anger or something else. Like guilt.

"*You* aren't even sure you didn't kill him," he pointed out carefully. Then he went a step further, telling himself he had no choice. "It could have been a crime of passion."

"Passion?" she cried.

Jake wanted to back off. But he had to get to Clancy somehow, he had to get at the truth. "Don't tell me it didn't hurt you. The guy screwed around on you. You thought he was the man of your dreams. You were in love with him. He turned out to be a jerk. A jerk who wouldn't leave you alone."

Her eyes flashed. "You're wrong." She glanced away. "I wasn't in love with him. I just wanted him to leave me alone." She raised her gaze to Jake's. He could feel the heat of it. "How can you possibly hope to find something that proves my innocence when you believe I'm a murderer?"

Good question. And one Jake had worried about himself. He studied her for a moment. "I don't know what to believe," he said honestly. "All I know for sure is that Dex Westfall is dead and the cops think—maybe with good reason—that you did it.'' He flicked the torn sleeve of her navy blouse. ''And all you've done is dupe me. For all I know I'll turn my back again and you'll be gone, maybe for good this time.''

''You're wrong, Hawkins. And I'm going to prove it, with or without your help.''

Jake looked over at her, admiring her determination if nothing else. He didn't even want to think about what Clancy had told him. Or the things she'd told him that she hadn't meant to. Dex Westfall had hurt her. He'd had other women. He'd played her for a fool from day one. And he wouldn't leave her alone. He'd even followed her to the island. And what had Clancy done about it?

Did he really believe she could kill someone? Not the girl he'd known. But what did he know about this woman? Nothing, he told himself. And he'd been in the P.I. business long enough to know that anyone could kill—given the right circumstances. And the fact that he knew Clancy had already lied at least once, didn't help her defense.

As the plane made its descent into Kalispell, Jake placed his hand over Clancy's. He came up with several good reasons for doing it. None of them had anything to do with any feelings he might have once had for her.

The night air smelled of Montana summer. It was warm with a gentle breeze that stirred Clancy's blond hair as they walked to the Mustang.

''Tell me something, Hawkins,'' Clancy said as he opened the passenger-side door for her. ''Has there ever been a case you couldn't solve?''

''No. And this one won't be my first.''

He watched her climb into the car and started to close the door, but stopped as something caught his eye. ''What did you do to your ankle?''

Chapter Seven

Clancy stared down at the scrape on her right ankle. Fear shot through her. "I don't know."

Jake touched his fingers to the discolored skin, tenderly, caressingly. She flinched.

"Does it hurt?" he asked, jerking back his fingers, obviously surprised by her response.

She shook her head, unable to speak. Hurt had nothing to do with her reaction to his touch. The pain of his fingers on her skin was a dull ache—far from her ankle.

"How did you get that?" he asked, frowning as he inspected the injury.

She flinched again, this time from a flash of memory. A hand coming out of the water. Grabbing her ankle. Pulling her—

"Last night," she whispered, staring out into the darkness. "On the dock when I was walking in my sleep—" She closed her eyes, trying to remember the moment when she'd awakened. It always felt like coming out of a fog with nothing ever very clear. Silver. A flicker of something silver coming out of the water. Then the hand and a sharp pain as the fingers reached out of the water and clamped around her ankle. Her eyes flew open. "He was wearing something silver on his wrist. It must have been a watch and it scraped my ankle."

Jake stared at her. "*Who* was wearing a watch?"

"The man who tried to drown me last night," she said, relieved she wasn't losing her mind. "When he grabbed my leg and pulled me into the water, his watchband must have skinned my ankle." She shivered, her relief short-lived. If it hadn't been a dream, if she wasn't crazy, then the scrape and the memory added up to something far worse. "Oh, Jake, I was right. Someone really *did* try to kill me."

Jake stared at Clancy, unsure how to respond. He realized she believed what she was saying, but the evidence was against it. If there had been someone else there last night, where had he gone? Wasn't it more likely that she'd scraped her ankle when she fell from the dock into the water? And the memory of the hand and the watch? Part of a dream. She'd said she was walking in her sleep. If a person could believe that. Jake operated on solid evidence, not even putting much stock in his hunches, no matter how right they ended up being, until he had tangible proof to go with them.

"You think I'm making this all up?" Clancy snapped. "Then, how do you explain the scrape?"

He knew sharing his explanation with her right now would do him more harm than good. "I can't." He barely got out of the way before she slammed him with the car door. He walked around to the driver's side and climbed in, wishing he could think of something to say that would cool her ire. Instead, he feared that anything he said right now would be wrong. So he kept silent, a male trait that he knew often only made her madder. But he'd risk it, he decided. It seemed the safest thing to do.

They drove with the windows down out past the lights of the city, past Christmas tree farms and tiny resorts until they were running along the shoreline of Flathead Lake.

Through the pines, Jake caught glimpses of the lake. It never failed to move him. The largest natural freshwater lake west of the Mississippi. The most beautiful. Incredibly clear by day. But by night, there was something haunting about it. Especially when the lights of the tiny communities nestled around it shimmered at its shoreline as they did now.

Jake felt a dangerous pull deep within him. A pull for this place. And the people in it. One in particular.

Out of the corner of his eye, he could see that Clancy still had a good mad going. She wouldn't even look in his direction. That was probably just as well, he thought, dragging himself back from places he couldn't afford to go.

The moment he pulled into the marina parking lot, Clancy had her door open and was halfway out of the car. "You wouldn't believe me even if you caught someone with a knife to my throat," she said, slamming the door behind her.

She was gone before he could get in a word. "Women." Jake grabbed her overnight bag out of the back and followed her down to the docks where they'd tied her boat that morning. It seemed like days ago now.

Music and the smell of fried foods filled the night air. A band at Charley's Saloon a few doors down cranked out country, while french fries sizzled in hot grease at the Burger Boat across the street. It was June, and the small resort community bustled with tourists and locals. Kids cruised the drag, honking, squealing tires, revving engines, yelling at friends. Summer on the lake. Jake felt a stab of envy, remembering when he and Clancy were kids.

Clancy was already in the boat, behind the wheel, waiting. Waiting, he realized, because he'd taken the key that morning. He grimaced. If he didn't have the key in his pocket, she'd have left him in a heartbeat.

He stopped on the dock for a moment, trying to figure out what he was going to say to her. In the distance he could make out the lights at Hawk Island Resort. They flickered on the water, beckoning him, drawing him back to the island just as Clancy had. He untied the boat and hopped in.

"It isn't that I think you're making anything up," he

said, sliding into the seat next to hers. Voices carried across the water, followed by laughter. "I believe you *believe* that's what happened."

"So you think I'm...what? Crazy?" She reached impatiently for the key, obviously annoyed that he'd taken it to begin with.

"I've never walked in my sleep, but I've had some doozy dreams where I couldn't tell reality from dreamland," he said, dropping the boat key into her hand. "They scared the hell out of me, they were so real."

Her fingers closed around the key. "But this *is* real, Jake. Someone is...after me." Her gaze shifted to the darkness beyond the shoreline. "This morning I found a place in the lilac bushes next to my kitchen window where someone had stood looking in. Someone's stalking me, just like Dex was. And I have no idea why." She flicked a look back at him. "You *do* think I'm crazy."

"No." That was the last thing he thought. "I think you're scared. And for a good reason." Someone *was* after her. Jake Hawkins. But he'd check under the lilacs. He was sure it had just been some kind of animal. "You're facing a murder rap. Anyone in your situation would be running a little scared."

Tears of frustration stung her eyes as she glared over at him, the skepticism in his tone still ringing in her ears. "You think that's all this is? I'm just running a little scared? There's a mountain of evidence that says I killed Dex Westfall. I can't sleep at night because my dreams force me to wander to places I don't want to go. Now someone is trying to kill me." She fumbled the key into the boat's ignition, her fingers trembling with anger, frustration, fear. "And you say you can understand why I'm running a *little* scared? Great, Jake. At least on top of all that you're not here to help send me to prison."

She turned the key, the motor rumbled to life, and she gave the boat full throttle, roaring out of the marina, ignoring the no-wake buoys.

They raced across the smooth, dark surface of the lake. The night air felt cool and sweet, the speed of the boat pleasurable. Jake sat silent, his face dark with a scowl that she knew meant she'd hit a nerve. It gave her some satisfaction. But she knew she'd be a fool to rely on Jake Hawkins for anything but more heartache.

She felt her anger slipping away as the early-summer night soothed her senses, the lake calming her as it always had. But nothing could chase away the fear at the edge of the darkness. Someone out there wanted her dead.

Clancy pointed the boat toward Hawk Island. The wind from the speed whipped her hair. She let it blow away her thoughts, let the steady throb of the motor lull her, promising her she had nothing to fear on such a beautiful summer night, on an island that was her home.

But as they rounded the end of the island, Clancy saw a light flickering in her lodge and knew differently. "Look!" she cried.

"What?" Jake asked, suddenly alert.

"A light in the garret. Didn't you see it?"

It was obvious he hadn't, but still, as she pulled back on the throttle, he reached over and shut off the running lights.

"Are you sure it wasn't just a reflection?" he asked.

She ground her teeth together. "It was a flashlight. Someone's in the garret."

"Don't go to the dock," Jake said. "Pull into the beach."

She did as he said, silenced by fear as she steered the boat to the nearest stretch of shoreline and cut the motor. She had seen a light. She wasn't starting to imagine things as Jake kept insinuating.

As they reached land, Jake jumped out and pulled the boat up on shore. Clouds hid the moon, pitching the narrow stretch of beach into darkness. Jake tied the boat to one of the pines that grew almost to the water's edge.

"I'm not leaving you here alone," Jake whispered as he

gave her a hand out of the boat. "Stay behind me, and if anything happens, get to cover."

Clancy followed Jake along the beach, hugging the rocky cliffs and the pines, her anger at him dissipating quickly. What would she have done if she'd come home alone? She'd sworn she wasn't going to rely on Jake, but right now she'd make an exception.

Water lapped at the shore as they crossed behind Jake's lodge. The light in the garret room had flickered like a firefly caught in a jar. What was someone doing in that room, the room where Dex had died? She felt a chill, although the summer night was exceptionally warm.

They were almost to her lodge when an owl let out a hoot. Clancy jumped, grabbing Jake's arm. He patiently unhooked her clawlike grip and motioned for her to stay low behind him.

They crept the last few yards in silence. Darkness draped the back of the lodge. Clancy held her breath as they climbed the steps and crossed the old wooden porch. The boards groaned under their weight.

"Is that your bike?" Jake whispered, motioning to the black mountain bike by the back door.

She nodded.

Jake tried the door. Locked. Clancy shook her head; she hadn't locked it. She could remember locking it only once in her life. And that night it hadn't kept Dex out, had it?

As she stood on tiptoe to reach above the door for the key, Jake groaned next to her. "Great place for a key. No one would ever look *there*."

Feeling Jake's reproachful gaze on her, she quietly slipped it into his waiting fingers and pressed against his back as he inserted the key in the lock. If he thought for a moment she was going to let him out of her sight, he was sadly mistaken. As she clung to him, she felt something hard. A gun.

The door creaked open. Jake drew the gun. Her heart

dropped to her knees as she realized the danger she was putting him in.

"No," she whispered. He stopped and she collided with his back.

"What?"

"I don't want you getting killed because of me."

"How thoughtful of you. Now, shut up."

He turned and started across the kitchen floor, with her right behind him. Something thudded, and Clancy let out a squeal before she realized the sound had just been Jake crashing into her microwave cart.

"Quiet!"

"Jake," she pleaded, suddenly more afraid for him than herself.

"Stay right behind me," he commanded as he headed up the stairs. "And be quiet."

Clancy held her breath, afraid to breathe, as they started up the stairs. She followed, her heart in her throat, her hand gripping a handful of Jake's shirt. They were almost to the top when she looked back. She let go of Jake. The front door stood partway open. Starlight slipped through the crack and splattered onto the living-room floor. Clancy reached for Jake but he was several steps ahead of her. A shadow moved into the light.

"Jake." It came out little more than a whisper.

The shadow turned into a dark figure in a hooded sweatshirt. It looked up at her. A startled, pained cry escaped her lips. She caught only a glimpse of the face beneath the hood. But it was enough. Clancy screamed.

The figure disappeared out the open door and into the darkness as quickly as it had appeared.

Clancy dropped to the stair, her gaze locked on the wedge of light still spilling in from the night.

"Clancy!" Jake cried, charging down the stairs to her. "What is it?"

She heard him groping for the light switch but couldn't

answer him. Instead, she stared after the intruder, too stunned to speak.

The living room was suddenly flooded with light.

"Are you all right?" Jake demanded, pulling her to her feet on the stairs. She fell into his arms. He held her tightly. "What happened?"

She stared over Jake's shoulder, her gaze fixed on the open doorway and the darkness beyond it. "I saw him."

"Who, Clancy?" Jake asked, pulling back to search her face.

She looked up. "Didn't you see him?" she asked, knowing he couldn't have. Pleading with him to say he had.

"Who did you see, Clancy?"

Her mouth opened but no words came out. She closed her eyes, willing away the image of the man in the dark hooded sweatshirt. "It was Dex Westfall. He's alive!"

Chapter Eight

Jake grabbed Clancy's shoulders and pulled her around to face him. "You saw Dex Westfall?" he demanded. He watched doubt flicker across her face. Worry settled in his stomach like a chunk of granite.

She tried to avoid his gaze. "I only got a glimpse so I can't be completely sure—"

"Clancy?" Jake asked, pleading.

She swallowed. Tears brimmed in her eyes. "It was Dex. I swear. It was Dex."

His grip tightened. "The *late* Dex Westfall?" He felt her flinch and let go of her, realizing he was hurting her. He led her down the stairs. The front door stood open.

"I know it sounds...crazy." She seemed to hesitate. "How could I have seen him when he's dead? I didn't get a really good look at him. He was wearing a dark gray hood that hid part of his face, but—" Her gaze flipped up to his, her eyes full of pleading. "It was him, Jake."

That rock of worry in his belly turned into a fifty-pound boulder. He went out on the deck and looked down the beach. Empty. He came back in and had barely closed the door when the breeze blew it open again, making them both jump. This time Jake closed the door and locked it.

"I know what you're thinking," she said, her voice barely a whisper.

Jake doubted she had any idea what he was thinking. He wasn't even sure himself.

"But I know what I saw," she said, the look in her eyes scaring the devil out of him. "It was Dex Westfall."

The cynical private eye side of him argued that Dex Westfall was dead; Clancy couldn't have seen him. She'd probably imagined it, or dreamed it, or she'd gone off the deep end.

But the man who'd fallen for her years ago made a good case that Clancy Jones had been one of the most rational, sensible and credible people he'd ever known. She might be a murderer, but he had his doubts that she was crazy.

"I'm telling you, Dex is alive," she cried. "Don't you see what this means? I didn't kill him."

Jake didn't want to burst her bubble, but it was time for a reality check. "If Dex isn't dead, then whose body did the sheriff find upstairs?"

Clancy blinked. Her face fell. She turned away from him to stare out the window. "I don't know. And no matter whose body it is, the sheriff thinks I killed him, right?"

That about sized it up. Jake knew how desperately Clancy wanted to believe she hadn't killed anyone. But the bottom line was someone had died in the garret upstairs and Clancy had had the murder weapon in her hand.

"If Dex is dead..." Her eyes turned dark with pain, her features drawn with fatigue. "Then his ghost has come back from the grave for me."

Jake glanced toward the darkness outside, his mind flashing on an image that freeze-dried his blood. The face of the woman his father had gone to prison for murdering. What if Lola Strickland's pretty face suddenly appeared outside his window one night? He shuddered at the thought. And reminded himself that no one came back from the grave. Not Lola. Not Dex.

He turned to lean with his back against the window, the last of the adrenaline ebbing. His body felt tired, his mind exhausted, as he settled his gaze on Clancy. Had someone been in the lodge tonight or had Clancy just imagined it? Like the person who'd tried to drown her last night?

"You first saw the light in the garret?" Jake asked after a moment. All he wanted to do was sit down, close his eyes, catch a few winks. He was too tired to think, too tired to try to figure out anything tonight. With effort, however, he pushed himself off the wall. "I'm going upstairs to take a look around. Why don't you—"

"I'm coming with you."

He looked at her, surprised she would willingly go back to the scene of the crime. "Look, I'm not wild about going up there. If I were in your shoes—"

"I'm coming with you," she repeated.

He nodded, recognizing that old familiar glint of persistence shining like a searchlight in her eyes and the stubborn way she stood when she wasn't about to budge an inch.

"There's nothing up there but old furniture," Clancy said as he led the way up the stairs to the third floor.

Old furniture. And bad memories.

The tiny room was indeed filled with furniture, Jake saw as he turned on the light and stepped through the open doorway. The single overhead light did little to illuminate the room. Shadows pooled everywhere. With the furniture covered in white sheets, the room had a ghostlike quality. Or maybe it was just the fact that Clancy believed Dex Westfall had come back from the dead that made it seem that way. It was enough to spook even nonbelievers, Jake thought.

The only bare piece of furniture was a couch in the corner under the eaves. The sheriff's department had obviously stripped it, taking the blood-stained sheet and cushion as evidence, but left behind the couch.

"I'm not sure this is a good idea," Jake said, turning to shield Clancy from the view.

"I have to do this," she said, her tone brooking no argument. "Besides, I'm the only one who knows if something is out of place up here."

He nodded and stepped out of her way. As he watched her walk into the room he thought to himself: here is a woman to be reckoned with.

With all the courage she had, Clancy looked toward the couch where she'd found the body. Her fingers flew to her lips to stifle the cry that rose from deep within her. Memories of that night flashed before her, flickering images of horror. She staggered. Jake reached for her.

She motioned him away. "I'm fine," she said, knowing that if he touched her now it would be her undoing. She hugged herself to still the trembling, her gaze scanning the room, trying to remember every detail.

Before the night of the murder, she couldn't remember the last time she was in this room. How could she know if something was missing? On top of that, Kiki had hired a cleaning crew after the sheriff's department finished taking prints and collecting evidence.

Clancy stared at the garret. Bits and pieces of memory floated back from Friday night.

Dex— Her gaze leaped back to the couch. It had been Dex, hadn't it? Something had made her think it was, but what? The bright red cowboy boots. The moment she saw them she'd known it was Dex because of those stupid boots he loved. But had she really looked that closely at his face? All that blood— She shook her head, frustrated at her inability to remember any more.

As she walked around the room, she quickly realized it was impossible to tell if an intruder had been here. But how desperately she would have liked to prove he had.

She pushed open the balcony doors and stepped out, immediately assaulted by a memory. She gripped the railing. "Oh."

"What?" Jake asked, joining her.

She shuddered as she stared out at the lake. "Friday night," she said as it came back to her. "I remember waking up on this balcony." She glanced down; her head spun just looking at the dizzying drop to the rocky beach below her. "What was I doing out here?"

Jake followed her gaze from the rocky beach below to the lake, sprawled to the horizon, a dark, silent pool, its slick, silken surface a reflection of the star-splattered sky overhead. He had no idea what Clancy had been doing out here. No idea what she had been doing in the tiny room beyond them just moments before Dex Westfall died. God, how he wished he did.

"I remember standing here not knowing where I was at first," she said. "The view was all wrong."

"What do you mean 'all wrong'?"

"I thought I was on my bedroom balcony." But it was next to her studio and at the east end of the lodge. She couldn't see this bay from it.

Turning slowly, she moved back through the open doorway as if she were still sleepwalking. "At first all I saw was the furniture. The white sheets were blowing in the breeze from the open doors and I realized I was in the garret."

Jake followed her, watching her face as she relived the night of the murder. She stopped, her gaze going to the couch. "Then I saw him in the corner." She looked down at her left hand. "I guess that's when I realized I had the sculpture in my hand. I dropped it on the floor. My feet—"

"What was wrong with your feet?" Jake asked.

"I must have been to the beach, because the tops of my bare feet still had sand on them." All of the shore around Flathead Lake consisted of small flat rocks—no sand. But Hawk Island had sandy beaches.

"What the hell were you doing on the beach at two-thirty in the morning?" he demanded, then shook his head. "I forgot. Sleepwalking."

If she heard the doubt in his tone, she didn't respond to it. "Dex's boots had sand on them, too."

"Maybe he followed you up here." An unpleasant

thought skittered past. "Or maybe you'd been on the beach together."

She stared at the stained arm of the couch as if there were things there she could see that he couldn't. From the horrified expression on her face, he was damned glad he couldn't see them.

"Where had I been that night?" Clancy asked, shifting her gaze to Jake. "I hadn't sleepwalked in years."

Not since the night of the resort fire, Jake thought bitterly. The night Clancy saw his father kill Lola Strickland. Or at least that's what Clancy would have him believe.

"Why would I suddenly start sleepwalking again after so many years?"

Jake wished he knew. He wished he could believe she sleepwalked at all. "What's the last thing you remember before you fell asleep?"

"I had been working late in my studio. I have, or I guess, that's *had* now, a show planned in August at a gallery in Bigfork. I was finishing up one of the pieces for the exhibit. As I headed up to bed, I couldn't help thinking about Dex, worrying about why he'd shown up here." She let out a long sigh. "That's the last I remember."

"Did Dex wear underwear?" Jake asked.

"What?"

"He wasn't wearing underwear the night he was murdered. Is that usual?"

"I would have no idea," Clancy said, turning away. "I didn't— I'm sure he wore underwear, but the subject never came up."

Jake smiled to himself, more pleased to hear that she had no idea than he should have been. "Unless I miss my guess, someone interrupted Dex that night, either from his beauty sleep or some other unclothed activity. He pulled on his jeans in a hurry and headed for your place."

"Who? Why?" Clancy asked.

"That's what we have to find out."

Framed in the balcony doorway, her hair shone golden,

her face a pale porcelain. It surprised him just how beautiful she looked standing there. How small and fragile. And so terribly defenseless. Protecting her seemed as natural as breathing and had ever since they were kids. He felt a pull so strong, the force threatened to draw him to her against his will.

"I think we'd better get some rest," Jake said, stepping past her to close the balcony doors. He could smell her scent as he passed. It made him weak. He took a deep breath of the night air and closed the doors. When he turned, he found Clancy standing at the top of the landing, staring down the stairs.

"I'll stay here in the lodge with you tonight," he said, surprising himself even more than her. "If that's all right with you," he added. "I need a good night's sleep, and that boat of yours isn't all that comfortable."

"You think I'm going to run off, Hawkins?" she asked, too tired to let his lack of trust do more than give her heart a twinge. The memory of Jake lying in the bottom of her boat, however, did offset the twinge some.

"I thought you could use some company," he said softly.

She studied his handsome features, trying to read motive in those bottomless gray eyes. The thought of staying alone tonight frightened her more than she wanted to admit. But was he suggesting staying here to watch over her? Or to keep her from jumping bail again? Did it even matter?

"I thought you didn't believe in ghosts," she said, reading nothing but concern in his eyes.

"I don't," he said. "Nor do I believe in taking chances until we know just what we're up against."

We're up against? Just hours ago, she'd warned herself not to rely on Jake Hawkins. But right now his words sounded better than a hot shower. After everything they'd been through today, couldn't she let herself rely on him for just one night? This whole day had made her realize what an incredibly strong, caring man Jake Hawkins was, just like the boy he'd been that she'd always loved so much. Only, she wasn't a girl anymore and he wasn't a boy. "You can take the spare bedroom. The sheets are in the hall closet. You know where that is."

He nodded. "Same place as my lodge."

He followed her down the stairs to the kitchen and, opening the refrigerator, pulled out two cold beers. He twisted the cap off one and handed it to her.

She took a sip, surprised at how good it tasted. "You don't believe Dex is alive and that he might be the one trying to kill me?"

His gaze, as warm and gentle as the summer night outside, brushed over her face. The kindness in his eyes made her want to cry. Slowly he twisted off the cap on his own beer. "The cops would know if it wasn't Dex's body," he said reasonably.

"Yeah, I guess so." She took a long draw on the beer. It tasted good. She leaned against the wall and closed her eyes. The beer made her drowsy.

"Why don't you go take a long, hot shower," Jake suggested. "I'll make sure everything's locked up for the night. Leave your door open."

"Thanks." She opened her eyes. His unruly sandy blond hair hung down on his forehead; the blond stubble at his jaw gave him a rugged, almost dangerous look that she found disarming. And appealing. Suddenly there seemed a million things she wanted to say to him, but she couldn't seem to sort them out. Nor did she trust her emotions. Not tonight. Maybe she'd tell him how much she appreciated him being here. Tomorrow. When she wasn't feeling so vulnerable. Or so tired. "Good night." She set her bottle on the table and turned to head for the stairs.

As she passed the telephone she noticed that the message light on the answering machine was flashing.

Clancy stepped over to it, hit rewind, then play. "Clancy?" Tadd Farnsworth's voice filled the room. "I didn't want to leave this on your machine, but I haven't been able to reach you and I wanted to be the one to tell you. The sheriff's having trouble getting a positive ID on the body you found in your garret. All he knows for sure is that the guy's name wasn't Dex Westfall. Dex Westfall never existed. At least not until five months ago.''

Chapter Nine

The color drained from Clancy's face. Jake watched her strength and sanity empty with it. He knew only too well what it was like having his world crumble under him, no longer sure what to believe, who to believe. Wasn't this what he'd wanted for Clancy? In that dark, malevolent part of his heart, hadn't he longed for her to suffer the way he had? And now she knew what it was like to have her life destroyed overnight. So why did he feel like dirt?

He watched Clancy try to dial Tadd's number. On her second attempt, Jake took the phone from her trembling hand and hung it up.

"I don't understand," she said, her voice breaking.

Jake understood. It was just as he'd suspected. The brand new clothes. The leased car. The new-subdivision feel. No roots. No Dex Westfall.

He also knew that if the sheriff didn't get a positive ID in the first twenty-four hours, it could take a while to put a name to their John Doe—if they ever did. Clancy might never know who died in her garret. Nor why the man had stalked her.

"I have to call Tadd," she said.

Jake shook his head. "You have to take a hot shower. I'll call Tadd. I'll come up when I'm through."

Clancy nodded, looking shell-shocked and terribly vulnerable. She stumbled toward him.

He felt a rush of tenderness for her. He pulled her into his arms, aware of her soft fullness, her wonderful warmth, her need so like his own. She raised her gaze to his, her eyes as dark as her lashes. The look in those eyes—

Without thinking, he dropped his mouth to hers, hungry to taste her, hungry to feel her body molded to his. He knew her kiss would taste of sunshine and summer. Her arms would offer comfort and sanctuary. That's what he needed tonight. That's all he needed.

But when his lips met hers, there was nothing safe or comforting about it. The kiss fired his blood, sending desire streaking through his veins at the speed of a grass fire. He became a part of the blaze, losing himself in the heat and the hurry. Losing himself in her. The realization burned to the bottom of his black heart.

With a silent curse, he pushed her away. "Go take your shower. I'll be up in a moment, to tell you what Tadd says."

She stood just looking at him. He felt like the bastard he was. But he'd better get used to it. He would see a lot more hurt in those brown eyes before he was through with her. When she turned and ran up the stairs, he had to kick down the urge to go after her. He slammed his fist against the wall and cursed Clancy for the love he'd seen in her eyes. It changed nothing between them.

He waited until he heard the water running upstairs before he dialed Tadd's home number. It was answered on the second ring.

"Where's Clancy?" Tadd demanded.

"Here, at her lodge," Jake said. "What's this about Westfall?"

"Fake ID, nothing matches up, not his name, social security number or prints," Tadd said.

No prints on file? Then he'd never been in the armed services or in trouble with the law, Jake figured.

"The sheriff's sent out flyers to all law enforcement

agencies across Montana and the Northwest. Maybe someone will recognize him."

"Clancy told me he grew up in eastern Montana, poor farming family. There might be some truth to it," Jake said. He'd found that people who lied often mixed in a little truth with their lies, just enough to hang themselves. He wondered if that was the case with Clancy. Would her lie about his father get her hung?

"I'll see that fliers get sent to the smaller towns back there," Tadd said.

"Anything new?" Jake needed to find out if Tadd had heard about Clancy's little trip to Bozeman.

"It looks like we might be dealing with some kind of nutcase." Tadd let out a long sigh. "The police in Bozeman found a closet wall full of background material on Clancy, including all that old stuff about your father's trial and Lola Strickland's murder. The landlady said Dex's sister had been there, paid his rent. Funny, but the sister's description sounded almost familiar." Bingo. "I thought Kiki hired you to keep Clancy in line."

"No," Jake said, his jaw tightening. "Kiki hired me to try to prove that Clancy didn't kill Dex Westfall—or whoever the hell he was."

Tadd didn't say anything for a moment. "How's Clancy holding up?"

"How do you think?" Jake snapped miserably. He hesitated, some old loyalty making him want to protect her. "Clancy thought someone was in the garret tonight."

"Someone broke into the lodge?" Tadd asked.

"Not exactly." Did he really believe there'd been anyone there earlier, especially someone who looked like Dex? "No sign of a break-in." In fact, the lodge had been locked, something Clancy said she hadn't done. Jake figured she'd just forgotten she'd locked it. Except for the front door, which had probably blown open.

"Was anything taken?" Tadd asked, sounding confused.

"We haven't searched the whole house, but it doesn't

look like he was your run-of-the-mill burglar. There're valuables sitting all over and they weren't touched." Jake assured himself he owed Clancy nothing but grief for what she'd done to him. Clancy's lawyer needed to know about everything, even if Jake didn't like the guy. "She swears the man she saw in the house was Dex Westfall."

"Right," Tadd said. He laughed, then must have realized Jake wasn't joking. "You aren't serious?"

"Dead serious."

"Come on, we might not know who he is, but we do know he's not up and walking around."

"At least some guy isn't up and walking around." Jake pulled off his baseball cap and raked a hand through his hair. He felt one of his bad feelings doing a little polka at the back of his neck. "Could you send me copies of that stuff tacked up on the guy's closet wall and one of those fliers?"

Obviously following Jake's line of thinking, Tadd let out an oath. "The guy she knew as Dex Westfall is dead. Clancy IDed him the night of the murder. He was her damned boyfriend. Don't try to tell me that maybe her boyfriend's alive and we have someone else on the slab in the morgue."

"Then it can't hurt for her to take another look."

Tadd groaned. "I'll get you a flier," he said, not sounding the least bit pleased. "Just try to keep her in the county in the meantime." He hung up.

Jake stood at the living-room window, staring out at the lake. He liked the quiet and the darkness. And the lake had always given him a sense of peace. Tonight it made him restless. Was the guy Clancy had known as Dex Westfall still out there? Or was it just Clancy's guilt making her see him everywhere she turned?

Long after he heard the shower stop running, Jake couldn't bring himself to go upstairs. His body felt leaden with fatigue. But the truth was, he didn't trust himself around Clancy tonight. It would be too easy to take her in his arms. Too easy to let her get to him. He felt a need for warmth tonight, and he'd seen the same need in Clancy's eyes. Along with love. It was the love that kept him from going upstairs.

He sat, put his head on the kitchen table and shut his mind to that kind of thinking. He thought of the past, letting the bitterness swell inside him.

THE HOT SHOWER did little to soothe Clancy. Her body ached with a need like none she'd ever known. She'd seen that same need in Jake's eyes. So why had he pushed her away? Because he wasn't about to make love to a woman he thought a liar? And a murderer?

And yet she came out of the bathroom half expecting to find Jake sitting on the edge of her bed, waiting for her. Half hoping. She reminded herself how much it had hurt when he'd walked away from her all those years ago. When would she ever learn?

She went to her dresser and, slipping off the silk robe, drew a long cotton nightgown over her head.

She couldn't trust her heart to Jake Hawkins ever again, but nor could she seem to stop it or her body from aching for him.

She lay on the bed, staring up at the ceiling, wishing there was some way she could prove to him she wasn't the woman he believed her to be. If only there were some way to show him that she would never have betrayed their love. Never.

She closed her eyes, too exhausted to worry about the goblins that waited for her on the edge of sleep.

JAKE JERKED AROUND at the sound of soft footfalls behind him. For a heart-stopping instant, all he saw was a ghost— a figure shrouded in white coming from the kitchen. "Clancy?" He hadn't heard her come downstairs, hadn't heard her come into the kitchen, and he realized he'd fallen asleep at the table.

She looked up but didn't seem surprised to find him sitting alone in the dark. As she stepped into the shaft of light that spilled down the stairs, he caught his breath. She looked so beautiful, her face shiny and squeaky clean from her shower, her blond hair still damp and dark, lying in tendrils against her cheek. The long white nightgown cupped her full breasts and floated around her slim ankles. His gaze fell on her inviting curves for a moment, then flicked down to her feet and the floor behind her. She was leaving sandy tracks on the hardwood floor.

"What were you doing outside?" Jake asked, his pulse suddenly thundering in his ears.

Her gaze shifted to him and he looked into her eyes. An icy wind wrapped around his neck like the hands of an assassin. "Clancy?" She didn't answer. She stared past him, through him. Then slowly she turned and headed up the stairs.

He hadn't believed her story about walking in her sleep. He still wasn't sure he did. He hurried after her, not knowing what he planned to do.

He found Clancy curled in the middle of her bed, her eyes closed, her breathing soft and rhythmic. As he stepped closer, he could see the sand still on her bare feet. She'd been outside on the beach. Doing what? He cursed himself. He'd have to keep a closer eye on her.

As he started to pull one corner of the comforter over her, he noticed her right hand balled tightly into a fist. It was the sand between her fingers that drew his attention.

Carefully, he touched her hand, expecting her to wake. She moaned softly in her sleep and her fingers opened like a flower to the sun. In her palm lay a single blue bead.

THE SUN CAME UP, filling the room with golden sunshine and warmth. Jake woke, sprawled in a chair at the foot of Clancy's bed. He sat up slowly, his body stiff and sore.

What he wouldn't give for a good night's sleep in a real bed. He'd opted for the chair, pulling it over in front of the doorway, because he didn't want to leave her alone again, even for a moment. He'd hoped the morning light would bring him some peace. Instead, he woke with the same haunting questions he'd gone to sleep with.

He studied Clancy's face. She looked so tranquil, he envied her restful sleep. His dreams had been filled with dark shadows lurking at the edge of his subconscious. He'd awakened at the slightest sound, a creak of a floorboard, the cry of an owl outside the window.

He couldn't shake the memory of Clancy sleepwalking. He'd never seen anyone do that before. It was weird. And spooky. He could understand why it frightened her so. He couldn't imagine waking up and finding sand on his feet and realizing he'd been somewhere and had no memory of leaving his bed. And yet a part of him was still skeptical, even though he'd seen it with his own eyes. Hadn't he?

He tiptoed out of the room and down the hall, anxious to get a hot shower, a shave and a change of clothes before Clancy woke.

He was dressed in jeans, toweling his hair dry, when she stuck her head into his bedroom doorway.

"Good morning," she said, and smiled tentatively. She wore jeans and a blue shirt the color of a summer sky. Her hair was pulled back with a ribbon, and there was a freshness about her, as if the sunshine coming through her window had renewed her spirit.

"How did you sleep?" he asked, tossing aside the towel to pull on a fresh shirt.

"Great. For a change." Her smile faltered. "Did you call Tadd? The last thing I remember, you were going to come up and tell me what he had to say. I must have fallen asleep."

"You were sacked out by the time I came up," he said truthfully. "I didn't have the heart to wake you."

He ran a hand through his hair, studying her. She didn't

seem to remember her little jaunt on the beach last night. Or maybe she was waiting for him to say something. Not a chance.

Last night he'd pocketed the bead, brushed the sand from her bed and covered her with the comforter. At the time, he'd wanted to protect her. But this morning, his suspicious mind wasn't ready to accept her sleepwalking. Not yet. If she'd staged it for his benefit, she'd made a fatal error. He suspected she no more sleepwalked than he did. And if he could prove it, he'd have her right where he wanted her. That kind of thinking made him feel more in control than remembering the way her lips had felt on his.

"Why don't I fill you in over breakfast." He smiled at her, noticing with regret that she'd resurrected the wall between them, her defenses safely back in place.

He told himself he should have taken advantage of the situation last night. What had made him think he might be vulnerable to her, a woman who'd betrayed him and still refused to admit that she'd perjured herself? He could have made love to her last night and maybe gotten to her and the truth. He promised himself he wouldn't pass up the opportunity if it presented itself again. *When* it presented itself again.

"What exactly did you say you were making us for breakfast?" he asked as he followed her down the stairs. He told himself sleeping with her would be a means to an end. Nothing more. And that the only reason he found himself looking forward to it, was because it would mean getting this case over with and returning to Texas.

CLANCY BUSIED HERSELF in the kitchen while Jake made a small fire in the woodstove to take the chill off the room. The sun hadn't reached that side of the lodge yet, and even though it was summer, it was still cool in the morning. As she listened to him whistling to himself as he stacked kindling in the stove, her heart cried out for the old Jake. Was there any of him left in this hard-nosed cynical private investigator?

"Buttermilk pancakes, my favorite," Jake said, taking a sniff over her shoulder. "Not with huckleberry syrup?"

She smiled at the pleading in his voice. "Of course."

He rolled his eyes toward heaven. "I may never leave here."

Clancy knew that wasn't true. She'd felt an urgency in him to get what he wanted from her and get out quickly. She wondered what would happen when he didn't succeed?

They ate in silence, Clancy watching in amusement as Jake scraped up the last of the syrup and pancake from his plate before pushing it away with a satisfied sigh. He'd always loved her pancakes.

"Fantastic," he said, giving her a smile that warmed her more than the sun now beginning to shine in through the kitchen window. The smile faded as his gaze met hers.

She knew what was coming. "Can I get you more pancakes?" she asked as she stood. She didn't want to think about Dex Westfall or the upcoming trial or who she thought she'd seen on the deck last night. In the light of day, she wanted to believe she'd been mistaken about the face looking anything like the man she'd known. She feared she was losing her mind; she didn't want Jake to tell her those fears were well founded. "It won't take but a moment to fry up a couple more."

"Clancy." He took her hand and pulled her back to the table. "We have to talk about it."

Resigned, she sat.

He filled her in quickly about the phony name and social security number. "Whoever he was, he was carrying a fake ID that said he was Dex Westfall."

"But no Dex Westfall ever existed." She wasn't surprised after finding out that he'd lied about the condo, lied about everything as far as she knew. "Then, who was the man—"

"The sheriff should know in a few days, and maybe then

we'll know what he wanted with you. I asked Tadd to send us the flier they're distributing. That way—''

"I'll know if the dead man is at least who I thought was Dex Westfall," she finished for him.

"Exactly. Meanwhile, we have work to do."

Work sounded good. She needed to do something. And the thought of doing it with Jake definitely had appeal. Especially since, as he'd said, she was running a little scared.

"I need to interview the two witnesses who overheard your conversation with Dex that night at the café," Jake said. "I was hoping you could tell me what you remember."

She leaned over her coffee cup and stared down into the black liquid.

"Tell me everything, no matter how trivial it seems," Jake instructed.

She nodded, remembering the summer night air, still remembering the sickening fried smells coming from the café. "Someone had been in the café working, cleaning the grill, I think. The air smelled of old grease. But the café was closed. There weren't any customers around. Dex was sitting at one of the tables on the deck. It was fairly dark."

"You're doing great," Jake encouraged her.

She drew a breath, letting it all come back. She told Jake again about the necklace, the legacy from Dex's mother, and how he had said Clancy was part of that legacy.

"What kind of necklace was this?" Jake asked.

Clancy looked up to find him watching her closely. "It was a string of beads like the hippies used to make and wear." She blinked. "Jake, how could there have been two witnesses who overheard the conversation? There wasn't anyone around."

"What about the person cleaning the grill?"

"Whoever was in the café couldn't have overheard us. We were sitting too far away."

"Did Dex give you any indication as to why he wanted to meet you?" Jake asked.

"No. I got the impression he had something he wanted to talk about, but whatever he'd seen in the darkness changed his mind." Clancy took a sip of the now-cool coffee. It tasted as bitter as the memory of Dex.

"What color was this string of beads?" Jake asked.

She looked up, surprised by his question. "Pale blue, with a tiny dark blue ceramic heart hanging from the center. Why?"

He shrugged. "Just wondering." He got up to take the dishes to the sink.

"The strange thing about the necklace was that I thought I'd seen it before," Clancy said, joining him. She shrugged and looked over to see Jake watching her. "I'm sure it doesn't matter. I just remembered something else. The clasp was broken."

"You think the beads are important in some way?" he asked.

"Maybe. The other night—" she picked up the dishrag, avoiding Jake's gaze "—I walked in my sleep again. When I woke up, I had one of the beads in my hand. I don't know where I found it. I just have a feeling that finding the rest of the beads might be a clue as to where Dex went that night."

Jake took the dishrag from her. He still didn't believe she walked in her sleep, she realized. She felt a hefty jolt of irritation. Why had she bothered to tell him?

"I'd like you to come with me to the resort," Jake said after a moment. "You'll have to wait in the boat while I talk to the witnesses."

Clancy told herself she shouldn't be hurt and angry at his lack of trust in her. "Let me see if I understand this: you'd like me to tag along so you can keep an eye on me, but stay out of the way so I don't hurt my case," she said, summing it up quite nicely, if she said so herself.

"I just don't want you staying alone. Or I could call your aunt Kiki to come over from her condo in Bigfork—"

"Don't even joke, Hawkins," she said. "Of course I want to tag along with you."

She didn't tell him that she had no intention of sitting by casually while he did all the investigating. Her life was at stake, and she had a couple of things she wanted to check out on her own.

He shoved back his Astros cap and grinned, probably thinking he'd won. That it was his favorite hat was no secret to her. It looked as if it was the first thing he put on in the morning and the last to be discarded at night, and had been for years. The bill was stained and faded from the elements. The once-white *H* had bled into the once-bright red star. Even the cloth-covered button on top was missing.

When she came back from brushing her teeth, she found him outside by the lilac bushes, hunkered down at the edge of the window. "Did you find anything?" she asked.

He shook his head as he straightened. She tried to hide her disappointment as she turned and headed toward the dock.

"How did you get into the private investigating business?" Clancy asked when they reached the boat.

"You want to drive?" Jake asked, holding up the key.

She gritted her teeth, reminded that every time they stopped anywhere he'd taken the key for safekeeping. "Why don't you drive," she said as sweetly as she could muster. "*You* have the key."

He either ignored her sarcasm or missed it. But something told her he hadn't missed it.

"When I first moved to Galveston I met this old private eye who fished off the same pier I did," Jake said as he pulled the boat away from the dock. "We became good friends. He taught me everything he knew about people and secrets." Jake pointed the boat out of the bay. "'Everyone has a secret,'" he used to say. 'All that separates murderers from ordinary people is that they have secrets they'd kill to keep.'" They rounded the end of the island, the sky as clear blue as the water was green. "He used to say I was a natural private eye. Cynical and determined. If someone has a secret, I'll find out what it is. Or die trying."

She felt his gaze on her and wished she hadn't asked.

Chapter Ten

To Jake's surprise, Hawk Island Resort looked much as it had when he and Clancy were kids. The store and café had been rebuilt on the same spot overlooking the marina. A row of six original cabins that hadn't burned still stood in the pines off to the right. Jake felt a rush of nostalgia, followed by nausea. There were too many memories here. Just as at his family's lodge.

Although it was early in the season, a few boats had already been moored in the bay when Jake eased into a slip at the docks. The air smelled of motor oil, gas and fish. "You want to wait here or at the café?" Jake asked.

"I'll stay here and catch some rays."

Clancy leaned back into the seat and closed her eyes. He studied her for a moment, wondering if it was safe to leave her alone. "I want to be able to see you at all times, Clancy. So I know you're all right." Then, feeling like the louse he was, he pulled and pocketed the boat key. Her eyes flickered open; he didn't like the look she gave him.

"I won't be long," he said, unable to think of anything to say in his defense. She mumbled something he figured he didn't want to hear, anyway, and headed up the pier.

At the outdoor sinks, a man cleaned fish from the full stringer of lake trout he'd caught. Jake was surprised when he saw who it was.

"Nice catch," Jake said, extending his hand to the man. "How have you been, Johnny?"

Johnny Branson looked up from his work. A smile crinkled his leathery face as he wiped his hand on his pants and took Jake's hand in his. "Jake Hawkins. I'd heard you were back."

Johnny was a large man with a full head of graying hair. He'd always reminded Jake of a Newfoundland puppy. Friendly. Loyal. And a little gangly. The former sheriff looked as though he'd lost some weight since Jake had last seen him. Johnny had been best friends with Jake's and Clancy's fathers since grade school. It had been Johnny who'd had to make the arrest and take Warren to jail. The strain of the trial had shown on Johnny, but the years since hadn't seemed to have been kind to him, either.

"I heard you retired right after the trial," Jake said.

Johnny nodded as he went back to cleaning his fish. "I'm a fishing guide now," he said, holding up a twenty-pound trout. "It suits me."

"Looks like business must be good," Jake said, not sure how to broach the subject on his mind. "I was hoping to talk to you while I'm back on the island. About my father's case."

Johnny didn't look up. "After ten years, can't be that much to say anymore, can there?"

He figured Johnny didn't want to drag up any of that old misery any more than he did. Johnny had taken his friend's conviction particularly hard.

"I was hoping you might be able to answer some questions I still have."

"That what brings you back?" Johnny asked, squinting past Jake to where Clancy waited in the boat. Idly, he rubbed the blade of his fish-gutting knife across one thumb pad.

"That and this mess with Clancy," Jake answered honestly. "I need to know if you thought my father was guilty."

"The jury thought Warren was, that's what mattered," Johnny said, cutting a clean slit up the fish's belly.

"I need to know what you thought. What you still think," Jake said. "Was justice served?"

"Life dispenses its own form of justice," he said as he ripped the guts from the large lake trout.

Jake shook his head. "I became a private investigator to ensure that justice gets done once in a while on earth. I'm too impatient to wait and let God set the record straight at the pearly gates." He met the man's gaze. "Just tell me if you think my father was an embezzler, murderer and arsonist."

Johnny chewed at his cheek for a moment as he looked out at the lake. "Sometimes people do things out of desperation, out of a feeling of helplessness and unhappiness."

He wanted to shake the big man and demand he answer his question, not dance around it. "Are you saying that's what happened to my father?" Jake asked, shocked by what sounded like an indictment against his father.

Johnny tossed the cleaned fish into the pile with the others. "I'm saying, leave it alone, son. No good comes from digging up the past."

The same thing Warren Hawkins had said to him. Jake walked away, heartsick and shaken. Not by Johnny's words as much as by the bitterness he'd heard in the man's voice. Was he really ready to find out the truth about his father? About Clancy? No matter how it came down?

As he walked up the steps to the resort store, he glanced to the right, to the west end of the island. The Branson home sat at the edge of the cliffs. A wide deck ran across the front with an elevator platform next to a long flight of wooden stairs that dropped to a dock at the water. Jake could make out a figure sitting near the edge of the deck. Johnny's wife Helen, her wheelchair glistening in the morning sunlight.

CLANCY WAITED UNTIL JAKE was out of sight before she made her move. She headed for the row of cabins against the hillside, having spotted a cleaning cart parked in front of number three.

Johnny Branson waved to her as he left in his boat. She was shocked by the change in him. He looked so much older and slighter than he'd been. She wondered if Warren Hawkins's trial hadn't made him age more rapidly. She was thinking about the trial and the effect it had had on them all as she took the trail to cabin three.

"Hello?" Clancy called, sticking her head into the cabin's open doorway. Like the other five cabins, number three was small, with twin beds against the knotty-pine wall and a marred night table and lamp between them. A girl of about fifteen looked up from her bed-making, the tail of a sheet in her hand.

"This cabin isn't ready yet," she said quickly. "Check-in isn't until noon."

Clancy smiled and stepped inside. "I don't need a cabin. Actually, I need to find out if one of your guests left anything behind."

The girl let go of the sheet and straightened, but she didn't look all that happy for the interruption. "If they did, it would be in lost'n found. I can show you."

"It would have been cabin six," Clancy said. "On Friday."

The girl stopped in her tracks and looked up, her eyes narrowing. "That was the guy who got murdered."

"So what was he like?" Clancy asked casually.

The girl rolled her eyes. "A major hunk. But kind of a real pain."

"Yeah?"

"He was always bossing me around, asking me to run here and there for him."

It was obvious she hadn't really minded. "What did he want you to do?"

"Get him things and take messages— Why are you asking about him, anyway?"

"It isn't every day there's a murder on the island."

"He didn't die here, you know," she said.

"That's what I heard. But he stayed here a day and a night, right?"

"Two nights," the girl said.

Two nights? Dex hadn't called her until the second day? "So he had you running errands for him," she said, knowing she had to tread softly. "I hope he tipped you well."

The girl shook her head. "That part stunk, too."

"Really? If he had you taking messages to people…"

The girl looked wary. "You with one of those weird newspapers?"

This time it was Clancy's turn to shake her head. "No, the truth is, I dated the guy for a while," she said truthfully.

"No kidding?" The girl looked at her with misguided respect.

"That's why I wondered if he left anything behind, a message or letter, maybe…for me."

The girl gave her a sympathetic look. "Sorry, when the police finally let me clean the cabin, I didn't find anything." She went back to her bed-making.

"What about the messages he had you take for him?" Clancy asked.

"It was just one. I took it to the marina and left it under a bait can beside the repair shop."

Interesting place to leave a message. "What night was this?"

"The first night. Thursday."

"Didn't you wonder who it was for?"

"It didn't have any writing on the envelope."

Clancy took a long shot. "Was the envelope sealed?"

The girl looked up and grinned. "Yeah. I couldn't make out anything, even holding it up to a light. I didn't dare open it."

Clancy laughed. "Thanks for your help." She had more

questions, but the girl was heading for her cart and another cabin and Clancy didn't want to press her luck. "Do you mind if I take a look around cabin six, just in case?"

JAKE FOUND FRANK AMES in the pumphouse behind the café, bent over, banging on a pipe, swearing.

"Frank?" Jake called over the racket.

He looked up, the wrench in his hand falling silent. Not much had changed about the tall, pimply-faced kid Jake had known. He was still thin, his narrow face pockmarked, his expression one of open hostility. "What do you want?"

"Just to ask you a few questions." He held out his business card. When Frank didn't bother to reach for it, Jake stuffed the card into Frank's shirt pocket.

Frank glared at him from dark, deep-set eyes that were just a little too close together. "Do I look like I have time to answer questions?" he demanded.

Jake had always wanted to knock that chip off Frank's shoulder. Only now, Jake's father wasn't here to keep him from doing it.

Frank must have realized that. "Hell," he said, pushing himself to his feet. "Make it snappy."

"You told the sheriff you overheard Clancy Jones talking to a man in the café Friday night," Jake said, disappointed Frank had given in so easily. He really wanted to thump that mean, nasty look off Frank's face.

"You know that or you wouldn't be here."

Jake smiled. He might get the opportunity to thump Frank yet. "What did you hear?"

"I already told the sheriff—"

"Tell me, Frank," Jake said between gritted teeth.

Frank slowly wiped the grease from his hands onto his worn jeans. "They were arguing about something."

"What?"

Frank shot him a contemptuous look. "How should I know?"

"You were listening to their conversation."

"I just happened to overhear Clancy threaten him, that's all."

"What exactly did she say?"

"I don't *exactly* remember." He shook his head at Jake's stupidity. "I got better things to do than memorize my customers' conversations."

Jake took a step toward Frank. "Try to remember."

"She said it was over between them. He said it was over when he said it was over. She said he was hurting her and he'd better leave her alone or else."

"Not bad for a conversation you can't remember," Jake said. "Where exactly were you when you overheard this conversation? I thought the café was closed."

He gave him a nasty sneer. "I was walking by."

Jake nodded. "This waitress who overheard this same conversation—"

"Liz Knowles. She's up at the café."

"Was she walking with you?"

"I think it's time for you to leave, Hawkins." Frank turned to go back to his plumbing problems.

"One more question. How was it you were able to buy this resort?"

Frank picked up a pipe wrench from behind the pump and hefted it into both hands. "I'm through answering questions. You don't own this place anymore. Your old man's behind bars, your girlfriend's a murderer, and you're nothing but some punk P.I. who doesn't know squat. So don't you come around here hassling me no more—or you'll regret it."

Jake smiled and pushed back his baseball cap. "One of these days I'm going to kick your ass, Frank. And that's a promise."

CLANCY KNEW THERE probably wasn't anything to find in cabin six, but she still had to look, and she hoped the cabin girl's curiosity would get the best of her.

Just as the girl had said, the cabin wasn't locked. Nor

did it look much different from number three. Except the beds were made. Clancy glanced around in all the corners, under the beds and behind the door. Nothing, just as she'd thought. Then she took a closer look, inspecting the cracks between the worn pine plank floor and the crevices between the floor and baseboard. No tiny blue beads.

Disappointed, she stood for a moment in the middle of the room, thinking about Dex. Where were the rest of the beads from the necklace? It was obvious the necklace hadn't been broken here. Some of the tiny beads would have gotten caught between the floorboards. Common sense told her she'd find the beads closer to home. They were near enough to the lodge that she'd walked to them in her sleep. But where? And what did the broken beads signify? Probably nothing. Her sleepwalking was often illogical, she reminded herself.

It made as little sense as Dex coming to Hawk Island. If it was to see her, then why hadn't he called her the first day? Why had he waited? And whom had he left a message for on the dock? As far as Clancy knew, Dex didn't know anyone up here but her.

"Find anything?" the girl asked from the doorway.

Clancy smiled to herself, glad she hadn't been wrong about the girl's curiosity. "Is it possible the message he wrote was for some woman he'd met here?" she asked, knowing that was more than a possibility.

The girl looked away.

Clancy knew she'd hit paydirt. "Dex always had a way with women."

The girl looked up, a smirk on her young face. "There was this one waitress."

Of course there was. "Which waitress?"

"Liz. Liz Knowles."

What a sleaze Dex had been! All the time he'd been dating her he'd been seeing other women. Then he'd come to Hawk Island supposedly to get her back and he was making time with one of the waitresses at the resort. Maybe she *had* killed him. "So the message from Dex was probably for her?"

The girl shook her head. "I passed Liz on my way down to the docks. She was already headed for his cabin."

"Maybe Liz just missed the message or picked it up later."

The girl brushed a speck of lint from her sweatshirt and, looking at the ground, shook her head. "Later I went to check. The message was gone. Liz hadn't left his cabin."

"Do you know if anyone else came to Dex's cabin that night?" Clancy asked on impulse.

"No." The girl looked disgusted, and Clancy realized her impulse had been right. The poor thing had hung around outside the cabin waiting for Liz to leave. All Clancy could think was how lucky the girl had been that Dex hadn't taken advantage of her schoolgirl crush.

But if the message hadn't been meant for Liz Knowles, then whom? Clancy felt a sudden chill as she remembered that night at the café when Dex had looked past her into the darkness and seen someone. Or something that had frightened him. She wondered what Dex had had to fear. And from whom. The person who killed him? "What about the night he was killed?"

"I had to work at the café. But I know Liz planned to go to his cabin that night."

Clancy remembered what Jake had said about Dex not having any underwear on when he was found dead. Liz Knowles might be the explanation for that. But if Jake's theory was right, who had interrupted the two?

"The only time he left the island was that first afternoon Thursday," the girl was saying.

Clancy's head snapped up. "He left the island?"

She nodded, looking unhappy. "He was all dressed up."

The girl obviously figured he'd had a date. She was probably right. "Do you know where he went?"

She shook her head.

Clancy had a thought. "He came back and *then* wrote the message you took to the dock that first night?"

She nodded, looking miserable. "He was in a really good mood."

THE FIRST THING JAKE noticed when he left the pumphouse and Frank was that Clancy was no longer in the boat. In fact, she was nowhere to be seen. He swore under his breath. This should not have come as a surprise. No, this was absolutely predictable. Anyone who knew Clancy would know better than to think she'd just sit idly by in the boat as he'd asked her. She'd never done anything he ever told her. Needless to say, that part of her hadn't changed a bit.

He spotted her finally by the cabins, talking to a cabin girl. Questioning a cabin girl, he corrected himself. Damn her hide. Well, at least he could see her, and she was all right. For the moment. He'd take this up with her when he finished interviewing Elizabeth Knowles.

The Hawk Island Resort café was actually little more than a grill that served burgers, hot dogs, fries and soft drinks. All the seating was outdoors at wooden tables under a canopy of pines and Japanese lanterns. Cheap plastic checked tablecloths flapped in the summer breeze. A woman in her early twenties in shorts and a tank top was busy putting out condiments.

"Lunch isn't served for another half hour," she said when she saw Jake. She had the harried, tight expression of a young woman who was already tired of her summer job and it was only early June.

"I'm looking for a waitress named Knowles."

She looked up.

He saw fear flicker in her eyes.

"I'm Elizabeth Knowles."

He asked her the same questions he had asked Frank. But got different answers.

"What makes you think they were arguing about

money?'' he asked, his interest piqued not only by the difference in how she and Frank related the conversation, but by this woman's obvious sympathy toward Dex.

Elizabeth shrugged. "He said she owed him money. But it sounded like she'd dumped him, too, and he was upset about that.''

Funny, but money had never come up in the conversation, according to Clancy. And Frank. Jake glanced around the café. "Where were they sitting?''

She pointed to a far table at the back edge of the deck flanked by two large pines.

"And where were you when you heard this conversation?''

Her gaze flickered away. "I was working. I had to close the café that night.''

She must have been the waitress Clancy saw cleaning the grill.

"You couldn't have heard their conversation from inside the café,'' Jake said quietly.

She flushed to the dark roots of her blond head. "I wasn't. I was…in the trees. I had to run an errand.''

Right beside the deck. "Did you see anyone else while you were there?''

She shook her head. "I was only there a few minutes.''

"Just long enough to overhear their entire conversation,'' Jake said.

"I gotta get back to work,'' she said, turning to walk away.

"What was so interesting about that conversation that you hid in the pines to listen?''

Her steps faltered, but she didn't stop or turn around. Nor did she deny it. "I was just curious,'' she said flatly. "There's no law against that.''

No, if there was a law against curiosity, Jake would be doing time right now, he thought as he watched Clancy hurry down the dock to her boat. What had she learned from the cabin girl that had put a spring into her step? More important, how could he convince Clancy she wasn't going to be doing any more investigating on her own?

CLANCY STRETCHED OUT in the back of the boat, pretending to be asleep. It was hard to do since she couldn't help but steal a peek at Jake from under her large straw fishing hat. Jake strode down the dock, his cap pulled low over his eyes, his jaw set in concrete. She didn't have to see his eyes to know he was furious. Or to know who he was furious with. Obviously he knew that she'd left the boat.

"I thought you agreed to stay here where I could see you," he said the moment he reached her.

She leisurely pushed back her hat and looked up at him. "I *did* stay in the boat. For a while." She grinned, too pleased at what she'd discovered to hold it in any longer. "Don't you want to know what I found out?"

"Dammit, Clancy, I won't have you messing up my investigation with your amateur sleuthing." He glowered at her.

"I found out some pretty good stuff," she said. "For an amateur, of course. Dex was romantically involved with one of the waitresses."

"Liz Knowles."

She stared at him. "How did you know that?"

"She's one of the witnesses who overheard your conversation with Dex."

Clancy sat up. "Really?" How interesting. "Wait a minute, why didn't I see her that night?"

"She was hiding in the pines right beside the deck."

Excitement coursed through her. "Then, she wasn't the person Dex saw in the darkness. It *was* someone else, just as I suspected." She hurriedly told Jake about the note the cabin girl had left under a bait can and how Dex had been on the island an extra day and night before he contacted her. Also how he'd left the island Thursday to meet someone, maybe a date, and returned in a good mood. "That's when he left the note."

She waited for Jake's reaction, expecting him to be as excited about this as she was. He bent to untie the boat, and, if anything, he seemed more angry.

"Don't you realize what this means?" she demanded. "Dex knew someone else on the island, someone he left a note for. He also left the island to meet someone. It's a lead."

Jake looked up, leveling his gray-eyed gaze at her. "Clancy, I realize telling you what to do is a waste of my breath," he said. "But it would help if you'd let me do the job I've been hired to do. And if you'd just stay put like you're told. This is my case, and whether you believe it or not, I know what I'm doing."

"No wonder I keep firing you," she said in exasperation. "This may be your case, Jake, but it's my life. Even if I trusted you to do the job my aunt hired you to do, which you have already admitted isn't why you're here, I couldn't stay put. Someone tried to kill me. The sheriff isn't even looking into other leads because he believes he already has his killer, and you don't believe I'm innocent any more than he does. If I stay put, I might end up dead. At the very least, in prison for life."

Jake jerked off his cap and raked his fingers through his hair. "Dammit, Clancy, sometimes I'd like to—" He slapped his cap back on his head and leveled his gaze at her. "You were always like this. Too independent, stubborn and fearless for your own good. Remember that time you went swimming off Angel Point in the storm?"

She'd almost drowned. Probably would have if it hadn't been for Jake. She'd only done it because he'd told her not to. What he was saying was true. Often in the past, she'd let her stubborn pride get her into trouble. "You're wrong, Jake. I'm not fearless. I'm scared to death."

In one swift motion, he pushed off the boat and stepped in. "You should be scared. There's already been one murder. If you didn't kill Dex, or whoever he was, then the killer is still out there. It's too dangerous for a—"

"Woman?" She raised a brow at him.

"Amateur," he said with that soft southern drawl.

She pushed back her sunglasses to glare up at him.

"We'll discuss this back at the lodge." He tossed her the boat key. "You can drive."

She caught the key easily enough but bristled at his tone. It sounded as if he thought he was going to have the last word on this. He was even going to let her drive her own boat. And then take the key again when they got to the lodge. She tossed the key back to him. "Some things aren't debatable," she said, pulling down her sunglasses as she stretched out on the seat in the sun again.

She heard him mumbling as he started the boat and pulled away from the resort. She had the feeling that Jake Hawkins was used to women he could mold like soft clay. Well, not this woman. And he had a fight on his hands if he thought he could.

It was more than her stubborn pride, Clancy told herself. She was tired of feeling like a criminal. And while she appreciated Jake's help, she had no intention of letting him investigate her case alone. She had to prove her innocence. And she couldn't depend on anyone to do it for her. Not even Jake Hawkins. Especially not Jake Hawkins.

Jake slowed as they rounded the island. Clancy pretended to sleep until she felt the boat bump the dock. She sat up, studying Jake out of the corner of her eye to see if his mood had changed.

He still looked irritated with her, but as he passed on his way to tie up the boat, he handed her the boat key. That simple sign of trust touched her more deeply than she wanted to admit.

"Jake?" She started to tell him that she was glad he was here. That she liked being around him, even when he was ill-tempered. That his being here made her feel like she had a chance to prove her innocence. He gave her strength. And hope. Even if he was here for all the wrong reasons— "Thanks."

He grunted in response and offered her a hand out of the boat. "I still don't want you interfering in my investigation."

She smiled. "But you're smart enough to know that I will whether you like it or not."

"You are the most disagreeable woman I've ever—" Before she knew what was happening, he grabbed her and hauled her out of the boat—and into his arms, into his kiss. It was a kiss that brooked no arguments. He took her lips, the same way he took her body to his. Her lips responded to his demands, parting of their own volition to allow him access to her. Against her counsel, her body answered his, molding its softness to his hardness.

"Excuse me?"

Clancy's eyes popped open as she recognized the voice and realized it was directly behind her. Abruptly Jake broke off the kiss and swung Clancy around, shielding her before he realized just who had joined them in the small bay.

"Sorry to interrupt," her attorney said from his boat, which now bumped the edge of the dock. Funny, but Tadd didn't sound sorry. Nor could Clancy remember hearing his motor when he pulled into the bay. She had a feeling he'd cut his engine and drifted in when he'd seen the two of them kissing.

But then she'd heard nothing but the throb of her heart against Jake's chest, felt nothing but his lips on hers. Now she felt her face flush, wondering how long Tadd had been watching them.

"I'd ask you how the investigation was going but I can pretty well see the course it's taking," Tadd commented.

Jake swore and released Clancy. She stumbled and fought to regain her composure.

"Did you bring the flier?" Jake said a little hoarsely.

Clancy tried to still her pounding heart, not even kidding herself that it was Tadd's sudden appearance that had caused it to pound, not Jake's unexpected kiss.

"Why don't we go up to the lodge," Tadd said, his look growing serious. "I've got some news you might want to sit down for."

Chapter Eleven

Clancy led them into the living room. Tadd took a seat on the western-style couch her family had bought when she was a child. It had horses embossed in the thick leather and wide wooden arms. She stood, too nervous to sit, remembering the night of the resort fire when she'd come down the stairs to find her parents sitting on that same couch, arguing about Warren Hawkins and the missing money.

Clancy had that same sick feeling now as she looked at Tadd. He sat on the edge of the couch, at odds with the warm, inviting character of the room with its large rock fireplace that Jake now leaned against, the rich golden pine floors, the bright-colored rugs.

Tadd pulled a sheet of paper from his shirt pocket. "The sheriff needs to know if this is the man you knew as Dex Westfall," Tadd said, unfolding the flier.

Clancy found herself unable to move. Instead, Jake crossed the room, took the paper from Tadd's hand and brought it over to her.

She could feel his gaze on her as well as Tadd's. She took the flier in her hands, a zillion thoughts whipping through her mind. The last thing she wanted to do was look at the photograph she knew she'd find reprinted on the sheet of paper. What if it wasn't the man she'd dated? What if it was?

She braced herself, her gaze flicking to Jake, his look

sympathetic, supportive. She looked at the face in the photo. Her heart leaped into her throat.

"Is that the man you knew as Dex Westfall?" Tadd asked again.

She nodded, looking away from the dead man's face to stare into the darkness of the empty firebox.

Jake took the flier from her. "Are you all right?"

She nodded, avoiding his gaze. She wasn't all right and wondered if she'd ever be all right again. The man she'd known as Dex Westfall was dead. So who had been snooping around her lodge last night? Who had she seen who looked like Dex? Who'd run out of the lodge? Who had pulled her into the lake and tried to drown her?

"Have you got an ID on the body yet?" Jake asked Tadd as he handed back the flier.

Out of the corner of her eye, Clancy watched Tadd carefully fold the sheet of paper and put it into his shirt pocket. He's stalling, she thought, and faced him, realizing he'd brought news. Bad news.

"The sheriff got a positive ID from the family this morning," Tadd said. "What Dex told you, Clancy, about being raised in eastern Montana on a farm turned out to be true."

The air in the living room crackled. "Who was he?" she asked, her voice no more than a whisper.

Tadd's gaze shifted to Jake. "His real name was Dexter Strickland."

"Strickland?" Jake asked.

"Strickland?" Clancy repeated, the name not registering.

It was Tadd who answered. "Dex Strickland was Lola's son."

Lola. A chill stole across her skin. "Lola Strickland, the resort secretary?" The woman Jake's father had gone to prison for murdering.

Clancy looked over at Jake. He stood, his muscles tensed, all his attention on Tadd.

"Dex was her son?" Jake asked, sounding not all that surprised.

"I never knew she had a son." Was Clancy the only one shocked here? "I didn't even know she'd ever been married."

"No one did," Tadd said. "Dex lived with his father on a farm near Richey. The father had custody. I guess Lola just up and disappeared one day, leaving her husband to raise his infant son alone. Allan Strickland never heard from her again."

"What about during the trial?" Clancy asked. "It was in all the papers. Surely he would have heard about his wife's death."

"From what I can gather, Allan Strickland's farm is pretty isolated," Tadd said. "But you're right. He knew about her death. He says he was trying to shield his son."

Clancy's legs wobbled beneath her. "If Dex was Lola's son..."

"The murders have to be connected," Jake said.

"We don't know that," Tadd said. "But it could explain why Dex had the newspaper clippings of the trial in his closet and why he might have wanted to meet Clancy."

"Why Clancy?" Jake asked.

Clancy saw the pain etched in his face and wished with all her heart that she wasn't responsible for him being here, for him having to relive all this. They were talking about the woman his father had been convicted of murdering.

Clancy wanted to reach out to Jake but knew she was the last person he'd take sympathy from. Especially right now.

"Why wouldn't Dex come after *me?*" Jake demanded. "If he wanted retribution, it was my father who...he believed killed his mother."

"Who knows what Dex had in mind?" Tadd said. "Maybe he was just looking for some connection to his mother."

"Or to his mother's murder," Jake interjected.

That seemed more a possibility now that Clancy thought

about it. "He did say something that night about his mother's legacy and how it linked the two of us."

"But what was that legacy?" Jake asked.

"Well, it seems to be death," Tadd said quietly, making the hair stiffen on Clancy's neck.

Dex had stalked her. With a shudder, she realized Dex was still stalking her. "Did Dex have any brothers?"

Jake's gaze swung around to meet hers.

"I already thought of that," Tadd said. "I asked Allan Strickland if there were any more like Dex at home."

"And?" Jake asked impatiently.

"Dex didn't have any siblings."

Clancy felt the air rush out of her. The floor wavered and threatened to come up to meet her.

"You should sit down," Jake said, suddenly appearing at her side.

She gave him the best smile she could manage. "I'm okay. I'm more worried about you."

He seemed surprised that she would be worried about him right now. He returned her smile. "Thanks, but I'm tough."

She knew that. And tender. Her heart ached to take some of the pain from those gray eyes. She wished she *had* lied on the stand about his father. At least now she could rectify things. "I think I'll get a drink of water."

"I'll get it for you," Jake said, already heading for the kitchen.

She stopped him. "Please, I need a little fresh air. A few moments alone."

He studied her for a long moment, then nodded.

Was he worried about her? Or just worried she'd jump bail? She felt a stab of annoyance. Just when she let down her defenses, he'd remind her again exactly what his stake in her case was. Revenge. Nothing more. She was on her own, now more than ever.

She left the two of them in the living room and went straight to the porch, where she gulped the summer afternoon air and tried to quit shaking. Dex was Lola Strickland's son. She couldn't even comprehend all the ramifications of that. What had Tadd said? Maybe he was just looking for a connection to his mother. Or to his mother's murder, Jake had added. Is that why he went to so much trouble to get close to her?

A connection. Like the string of beads. Dex said the beads were a legacy from his mother. But Lola was dead, and all of her belongings had burned in the fire. So where had he gotten the necklace? From someone who was still on the island who'd known Lola? Or someone on the mainland?

That silly necklace, why was it so familiar? The memory came in a flash. The string of tiny blue beads. Light glinting off the small dark blue ceramic heart. Clancy knew she'd seen them before. Now she knew where.

The memory brought her little pleasure. She'd seen them the night Jake Hawkins had promised her *his* heart. That's why the tiny navy heart had stuck in her memory. She reminded herself that not only had Jake broken that promise—he was now on the island to, as he put it, get the goods on her.

Grabbing her mountain bike from where she'd left it against the porch railing, Clancy took off up one of the trails without thinking of anything but reaching her destination and getting back before Jake missed her. If she was right, she might have some answers to keep her out of prison when she returned.

THE LODGE SEEMED EMPTY after Clancy left. Almost eerie. Jake found himself pacing, too keyed up to sit.

"I'm worried about Clancy," Tadd said, leaning forward as he watched Jake wear out the rug in front of him.

"You should be," Jake said, stopping his pacing for a moment. He fought the urge to check on Clancy again. Not long after she'd gone outside, he'd looked out to find her standing on the back porch. He wanted to give her the space she'd asked for, but not too much. She couldn't get into too much trouble for a few minutes on her own back porch in broad daylight, right?

"She thinks someone is trying to kill her," Jake said, resuming his pacing. He told Tadd about the near drowning incident and filled in more detail about last night's supposed intruder. "She thinks someone who looks like Dex Westfall is still stalking her."

Tadd gave him one of those calculated lawyer looks. "Is that what you think?"

Jake didn't know what to believe. "There's a scrape on her ankle, and if you'd seen Clancy's face last night— She saw something," Jake said in Clancy's defense. "Someone. Someone she thinks looks enough like Dex to make her believe he's still alive."

"You don't believe Strickland's come back from the dead?" Tadd inquired.

"Of course not." Jake pulled off his cap and rumpled his hair with his hand.

"At some point, Clancy's going to have to see a sleep specialist and have some extensive tests run on her," Tadd said. "If we can prove she has a sleeping disorder. That Dex's death was the result of noninsane automatism, an act committed by a sane person but without—"

"Intent, awareness or malice," Jake interrupted. "I know, I've read about it." He shook his head at Tadd. "If Clancy killed Dex, it wasn't in her sleep. Dex Strickland stalked her, lied about who he was, cheated on her. All the more reason for Clancy to want him dead. Add to that the mountain of evidence against her—"

"I *have* to sell the jury on the sleepwalking defense or she's going to prison," Tadd interrupted.

Jake groaned, realizing how true that probably was. "Unless I can find some evidence that proves she didn't kill him." And if he couldn't? Then he'd have no bargaining chip. Funny how that didn't matter as much as it had just a few days ago. "She thinks Dex has come back from the grave for her."

"Ever read any Edgar Allan Poe?" Tadd asked.

"There's no heart thumping under the floorboards here. Unless it's Lola Strickland's."

Tadd gave him a long look. "You think Dex came back to either avenge his mother's death or solve her murder?"

"You have to admit, both are possibilities," Jake said. "But if he believed my father was guilty, why wouldn't he come after me instead of Clancy? Unless he believes Clancy's father, Clarence Jones, is somehow involved."

"That's what you think, isn't it?" Tadd said as he got to his feet. "Maybe you should solve one murder at a time, preferably the one you're being paid to solve."

"The murders are connected."

"Maybe. Maybe not. My only concern is for my client. What's yours?"

"Clancy," Jake said, realizing that was true. "But these murders are connected."

His entire theory rode on the premise that the two murders were connected, and Dex turning out to be Lola's son only supported that. The hunch discoing at the back of his brain was that whoever killed Dex had killed Dex's mother. Clarence Jones could have embezzled the money, either used Lola to do it or killed her because she found the discrepancy, and started the fire to cover his own misdeeds. Warren Hawkins had come along after the fact, just as he said, and tried to save Lola and the books to prove his innocence.

But Clarence and Lola were dead. And Warren was in prison. So where did that leave Jake? All the prime suspects were now out of the picture. Too many things were blowing holes in his hunch.

Not only that, ten years ago he had found it easier to believe that Clancy had perjured herself than he did now— perhaps being around her had altered his perspective.

"I don't see how the murders could be connected," Tadd said.

"Clancy's the connection," Jake insisted. "Maybe she saw something that night that someone doesn't want her to remember."

Tadd lifted a brow. "They waited ten years to shut her up?"

Jake admitted it didn't make a lot of sense. But what did about this case?

Tadd let out a long sigh. "I'm worried about Clancy's mental state. I'm concerned she might be on the verge of a major breakdown. The sooner we get to trial, the better."

"I beg your pardon?"

They both swung around at the sound of a sharp, female voice from the doorway.

"Kiki!" Jake said. Her name came out like an oath.

"I can assure you my niece is not on the verge of a major breakdown, as you so delicately put it," she said firmly. She stormed into the room, giving them both withering glares. "Nor is she a murderer."

Jake wondered how long she'd been standing in the doorway listening. He didn't have to wonder long.

"If my niece says someone is trying to kill her, I expect you to believe her," Kiki said, biting off each word.

Tadd was on his feet, trying to explain himself, but Kiki cut him off.

"How can you fools *not* believe her?" Kiki snapped, some of her highly bred composure slipping. "Clancy's no murderer. She didn't care enough about the man to kill him. Asleep. Or awake." She narrowed her eyes at Jake. "Why aren't you out looking for the real killer instead of sitting around speculating on Clancy's mental health?" She shook her head in disgust. "Where is my niece, anyway? I came by to see how she was doing."

Jake stared at Kiki. "Didn't you pass her on your way in? She was out on the porch just a—" He was already racing toward the back of the lodge. He pushed through the door and out onto the porch. "Clancy?" She was nowhere in sight. A breeze rippled the water. The tops of the tall pines swayed overhead. Her boat was still at the dock. The beach was empty. He glanced around, thinking she might have just gone for a walk.

Then he noticed her mountain bike was gone. He swore, knowing he'd never be able to catch her on foot. Nor did he have any idea which trail she might have taken. The island was a labyrinth of trails.

"It's a small island," he heard Tadd trying to reassure Kiki. "How could she get into trouble on such a small island in broad daylight?"

"Find her. Hurry." The emotion in Kiki's command clutched at Jake's heart. He felt the tentative strum of a hunch at the base of his spine. He knew the name of this tune. Trouble. And Clancy, as usual, was right at the center of it.

Chapter Twelve

Clancy rode up the narrow mountain trail through the cool pines. The sun sliced down, making patterns of gold on the dry pine needles covering the path. The trail climbed the steep terrain through a series of switchbacks to the top of the ridge. The exertion felt good; she pushed herself harder, stopping at the top to catch her breath.

The lake stretched for miles, a mosaic of blues and greens. The Mission Mountains rose up from the valley floor to the east. Pines, dense and dark as the ones around her, edged the other side of the lake as far as the eye could see. To the north, boats churned the water in a bay near the resort. Laughter and the roar of engines drifted up the mountainside, making Clancy ache for happier summer days.

She headed down the main trail that ran along the ridge-line. Occasionally she'd catch a view of the lake from the dense pines. The island was a web of narrow trails; most she'd ridden at one time or another during her childhood. Ridden with Jake, she thought. Back when their lives had held nothing but promise.

As she rode, she tried to understand everything she'd learned over the last few hours and where she fit into it. Some things started to make an odd kind of sense to her. Why Dex had stalked her. Why he'd followed her to the island. This is where his mother had died, and Clancy Jones had been the only witness.

That is what tied her to Dex Strickland. The same thing that distanced her from Jake.

JAKE AND TADD SPLIT UP and, lacking a bicycle, Jake began his search for Clancy on foot. Tadd opted to go by boat. Her bike tires had left no tracks on the needle-covered path, so Jake had no way of knowing which way she'd gone or where she was headed. He took the trail directly behind the house.

He stormed up the trail, that hunch of his dancing to that same old little ditty. Clancy was the key. Had always been the key. Now that he knew Dex was Lola's son, there was no doubt in his mind that their deaths were connected. Nor did he have any choice but to dig into the old murder and his father's case.

What bothered him like a bad headache just getting started was his father. Why had Warren Hawkins asked him not to get involved? Well, Jake was involved now. And he was going to learn the truth. About his father. About Clancy.

But first he had to find her. She couldn't have gone far, he told himself. Jake couldn't believe she'd taken off again. He knew the shock had thrown her—just as it had him. But if she really believed someone was trying to kill her, how could she have taken such a chance?

Because she was too impetuous, independent and stubborn for her own good. But Jake knew he was partly to blame. He'd made it clear to her that she couldn't trust him. She was alone and scared. Now he had to find her before she got into more trouble.

CLANCY CRUISED DOWN the mountain on a narrow trail that came out directly behind Johnny and Helen Branson's place at the edge of the cliffs.

Helen spotted her as she came out of the pines and waved from the kitchen window for her to come on in.

Helen was petite with short blond hair that showed no gray, blue eyes and fair skin. Unlike Johnny, Helen didn't look as though she'd aged at all the last ten years. In fact, Clancy noticed with surprise, Helen looked as if she might be closer to thirty than she was fifty.

"I hope I didn't catch you right at dinner," Clancy apologized as she was met with the smell of pot roast.

"Don't be silly," Helen said from her wheelchair in front of the stove. Johnny had built the house to accommodate Helen's disability; everything was wheelchair level. "Stay for dinner. Johnny should be here any moment. We'd love to have you."

Clancy's stomach growled, and she remembered she hadn't eaten anything since breakfast, but she declined the offer. She had to get back before Jake called out the National Guard.

"Maybe some other time," she told Helen. "I just stopped by to ask you something."

"I heard about all that nasty business. I've been so concerned for you."

"That's why I wanted to talk to you. You remember Lola Strickland, the secretary at the resort?"

Helen frowned. "Why, yes."

"That man, the one who was killed upstairs at my lodge. His real name was Dex Strickland. He was Lola's son."

Helen's eyes widened. "My word. The woman had children?"

"One," Clancy said. "A son."

"But how can that be?" Helen asked. "I never saw her with a child, and she certainly never talked of children."

Clancy felt a surge of hope. "Then you did know her fairly well?"

Helen chuckled. "It's a small island, dear. Everyone knew her. But it sounds like you know more about Lola than I do. I didn't even know she had a son."

"Oh, I thought you might have befriended her," Clancy said.

"What would make you think that?" Helen asked as she turned to take a peek into the oven at her roast.

The smell was enough to make Clancy drool. "I remembered that you were both involved in the Flathead Community Theater Company in Bigfork that summer."

Helen laughed. "I just did some of the makeup and helped with costumes."

"Didn't Lola star in one of the plays right before her death?" Clancy asked.

Helen frowned as she reached into the refrigerator and pulled out a bowl of salad. "It's been so long, but now that you mention it, I think she did. Why do you ask?"

"I remember the play," Clancy said, suddenly hesitant. Earlier her theory had made sense. Right now it seemed silly. "I wondered if you knew what happened to the necklace she was wearing opening night?"

"A necklace?" Helen asked in surprise. She wheeled over to the dining-room table by the window with the salad. Clancy noticed the table settings for the first time. Fresh flowers, cloth napkins, candles and fancy china?

"Is it your anniversary?" Clancy asked, even more ashamed for interrupting Helen's cooking.

"Oh, dear, no." Helen smiled. "I just wanted to spoil my husband tonight. He's been a little under the weather lately."

Clancy felt tears pool in her eyes. They threatened to overflow and spill down her cheeks.

"I'm so fortunate to have a man like Johnny," Helen said, straightening the napkins she'd folded by each plate. "We've been married for almost thirty years. We were childhood sweethearts, you know." She turned and seemed surprised to find Clancy near tears. "Are you all right, dear?"

Clancy hadn't thought much about true love, marriage or love-ever-after. Not since Jake had left the island ten years ago. Dex certainly hadn't made her realize what she'd been missing. But standing here, smelling pot roast, seeing this romantic dinner scene, having earlier kissed her own childhood sweetheart—

"What's wrong?" Helen asked again.

Clancy made a swipe at her tears. She was exhausted. Overstressed. Overemotional. But then, why wouldn't she be? She was a suspected murderer who wasn't even sure she was innocent, and a dead man was after her. That would make anyone a little teary at unexpected moments. "I'm fine." She wondered how many more times she could say those two words before she started to scream.

"You're not fine," Helen said, taking her hand. "Tell me what's wrong."

Clancy found herself pouring out her heart. From Dex's death, to the hand coming out of the water and scraping her ankle with the silver watchband, to Jake.

Helen smiled kindly when she finished. "It sounds like Jake being back might be putting even more stress on you. You have feelings for him, haven't you?"

Clancy tried to deny it and couldn't. She brushed away her tears, feeling relieved to be able to talk to someone who believed her. "Thanks for listening to me."

"Anytime, dear. I'll always have a strong shoulder for you to cry on. Now, what can I do to help you?"

"Was there anyone else involved in the theater company that summer who might still be around?" Clancy asked.

Helen seemed to think for a moment. "Frank Ames. I believe he helped with some of the scenery." She straightened one of the place settings. "Why are you looking for a necklace of Lola's, dear?"

Clancy knew it sounded ridiculous. What could a string of tiny blue beads have to do with finding Dex's murderer? "I just thought she might have given it to a friend. Or left it with someone for safekeeping."

"You thought I was that friend." Helen smiled kindly.

"I was probably as close as anyone to Lola, but I wouldn't say we became friends. I'm sorry, dear."

Johnny came in then. "Clancy, what a nice surprise. Something sure smells good. I hope you're staying for dinner."

"Pot roast," Helen said, sounding pleased. "Wash up. I tried to get Clancy to join us, but she can't. I want her and Jake to come to dinner soon."

"Real soon," Johnny called as he headed down the hall.

"What did this necklace look like?" Helen asked.

"Tiny blue beads. Like hippies used to wear. There was a small handmade dark blue ceramic heart at its center."

Helen seemed surprised. "I thought maybe it was diamonds. You made it sound so important."

Clancy knew she must seem irrational, worrying about a string of beads at a time like this. "Dex had it the day he was killed. I just wondered where he might have gotten it." And where it was now.

"I wish I could have helped," Helen said.

Clancy thanked her and made a hasty goodbye, promising she'd come back soon. Once on her bike, she headed for home.

The air felt cool against Clancy's flushed cheeks. It had been hot in the kitchen, she assured herself. She wasn't flushed and embarrassed about her silly behavior. Crying over nothing. As she rode through the shadowy trees, she made excuses for her tears back in Helen's kitchen. They had nothing to do with Jake Hawkins. Nothing at all, she told herself.

JAKE REACHED THE TOP of the ridge and stood for a moment, scanning what little of the island he could see through the dense pines, disappointed Clancy was nowhere to be seen. Down the mountain at the resort, an American flag snapped above the treetops in the wind; whitecaps dotted the water beyond the bay. Jake wondered if Clancy had gone back to the resort. Or if she was just out riding and thinking. Or maybe making a run for it?

He'd tried not to think on his hike up the mountain. It made his head hurt, trying to put together pieces of a puzzle he'd spent ten years trying to solve. Worse yet was worrying about Clancy. And that latest stupid kiss.

Not that he regretted either kiss. Unprofessional, yes. Totally out of line, unquestionably uncalled for. And yet he couldn't get either one out of his head, let alone out of his blood. He'd planned to do more than kiss her when the opportunity arose. But the kiss on the dock had been as unexpected for him as it was for her. The real problem, however, was the effect it had on him.

Now he was out wandering in the woods looking for the most frustrating woman in the world. Stubborn. Hell-bent determined. Too brave for her own good. Grudgingly, he admitted he admired her.

Under normal circumstances. But now he worried that Clancy might not have just gone for a bike ride. He worried she might have taken off. Tricked him again.

There was one way to find out. If she'd run, she'd need a boat to get her off the island. As he hurried down the trail, he realized he'd spent most of his time on this case chasing that woman.

At the resort office, the clerk assured him that no one matching Clancy's description had rented a boat.

Jake used the phone to call the lodge, hoping Clancy had returned by now. He hadn't seen Tadd since they'd split up to search for her. Aunt Kiki quickly informed him that neither Clancy nor Tadd had returned.

He hung up, more worried. Unless he missed his guess, Clancy was still on the island. The question was where?

As he started to leave the phone booth, he remembered the Bransons and dialed their number.

"Clancy was here, Jake, but she left just a little while ago," Helen told him. He could hear the clatter of dishes in the background and apologized for interrupting her dinner. She assured him they were just finishing. "I invited Clancy to join us, but she said she had to get home."

He hung up, wondering why she'd gone to the Bransons', and started back up the trail. So she was headed home. That was a good sign. He told himself he'd known she hadn't taken off again, at least not far. But he still felt a sense of relief that lifted his spirits. All right, maybe he'd started to trust her a little and he was glad she hadn't broken that trust by skipping the island to parts unknown.

Come on, Hawkins. When are you going to be honest with yourself? You desperately want to believe in Clancy's innocence. You're such a chump, you even want to believe she didn't perjure herself at your father's trial, that maybe there's another explanation.

Jake cursed his own foolishness. As he topped the mountain and started down the other side, he spotted Liz Knowles. Two things struck him as odd. One was the way she was dressed. The other was her hurried pace. He went after her on the side trail she'd taken, wishing he had enough time to tail her secretly and find out where she was headed in such a hurry.

"Hello," Jake said, catching up to her.

She jumped, startled. Scared, too, he noticed. Like a turkey on Thanksgiving morning. He couldn't help but wonder if he was the cause of her fear. Or someone else. After all, if the cabin girl was right, Liz had spent some quality time with Dex right before his death.

"You haven't seen Clancy, have you?"

"Clancy?" She wore a freshly ironed shirt with matching shorts and sandals. Her hair was pulled up, her lips painted pink, her cheeks flushed with blusher, and she smelled of perfume. He figured she had a date and must be meeting him on the trail somewhere since there was nothing but rocks and trees the way she was headed. She seemed a little overdressed for a roll in the pine needles.

"Clancy Jones, the woman you said you overheard

threaten Dex Westfall on the day he died,'' Jake said through gritted teeth.

''Why would you ask if I'd seen her?'' The drone of a dirt bike broke the stillness. Liz glanced up the mountain, her look agitated. He was keeping her from something. ''I don't even know the woman. Of course I haven't seen her.'' When she looked again at Jake, she seemed all the more anxious to be on her way.

He decided to let her go. She started down the trail, turned once to see if he was following her, then took a side trail that headed off to the west. He had a feeling that wasn't the way she'd intended to go, that she'd changed her plans because of him.

Jake headed down a trail that would eventually lead him back to Clancy's lodge. As he walked, Clancy crowded his thoughts. Flashes of her making pancakes. Lounging in the boat with that silly fishing hat hiding her eyes. Standing in his arms. Looking up at him, her eyes filled with— He stumbled and swore. Love.

CLANCY HEARD THE BUZZ of a dirt bike coming up the mountain. The engine whined, the bike bucking as it climbed the steep terrain. The sound grew louder. She felt a chill and realized how dark the sky had gotten. Shadows hunkered in the pines. A wind blew up from the lake, swaying the tops of the trees. She pedaled faster through the growing darkness of the approaching storm, anxious to get back to the lodge. And Jake. Her sense of security ebbed with the light.

She was almost at a trail that dropped down to her lodge when she heard the dirt bike behind her, saw its headlight flicker in the trees in front of her as the bike gained on her. The bike was coming up behind her fast. Too fast. Didn't he see her? She took a side trail, stopping partway down the narrow path, waiting for the motorbike to go by.

She didn't realize she'd been holding her breath until she heard the biker stop. Clancy looked up to see a figure wearing a shielded dark helmet standing astride an old motor-bike. She couldn't see his face behind the helmet, but she could feel him staring at her. Her heart thundered at the thought of whose face was hidden behind the shield.

She jumped on her bike and took off down the tree-lined trail, wanting only to get home. Above her on the mountainside she heard the bike motor rev. In horror, she realized he was chasing her. Panic tore through her. She pedaled as if the devil himself were at her heels. But when she stole a glance back, the trail behind her was empty, and she could hear the whine of the dirt bike dying off into the distance.

Clancy's heart thumped wildly in her chest. Paranoia. Maybe Jake was right. She *was* imagining things. Her legs felt weak and shaky from her scare. What had made her think that biker was chasing her? Was it the same thing that had made her think someone had tried to drown her? The same thing that made her think she saw a light in the lodge last night? Made her think she saw Dex?

The sky darkened to charcoal overhead. In the distance, she heard the rumble of thunder. The wind picked up, whipping the tops of the pines. Ahead, the trail forked, the trees opened a little. The path to the left circled up the mountainside to the east end of the island, the one on the right dropped rapidly in a series of switchbacks to the beach and her lodge. Clancy relaxed. She'd be home soon. An image of a furious Jake filled her mind. Even he would be a welcome sight.

A bolt of lightning splintered the sky above the treetops, making her jump. Thunder boomed, drowning out the sound of the dirt bike.

The biker appeared in a flash of movement. Leaping from the pines. All she saw was a blur. All she felt was the bike hit hers. A scream caught in her throat. The ground came up to meet her. She hit it hard, knocking the air from her lungs. Then she fell, tumbling down the steep mountainside.

Chapter Thirteen

As Jake wound his way through the dense pines, he heard the unmistakable whine of the dirt bike again. It cut through the softer evening sounds, irritating his already fried nerves. He cursed himself with each step. He was handling things poorly. He should have stashed Clancy with her aunt Kiki. Or had her bail revoked. At least if she was in jail, he wouldn't have to worry about her. And right now, he was worried.

One of his faithful hunches pounded at the back of his brain to a little ditty that had started the moment Kiki Talbott Conners had set one high-heeled foot on the dock beside his boat in Galveston. It reverberated like the thunder overhead and promised a darkness far beyond the storm bearing down on the island.

THUNDER RUMBLED and the sky darkened like night. Clancy's skin was cut, scraped and gouged as she fell, plunging down through brush and branches, dirt and rocks. She fought to find purchase, grabbing at anything, everything, to keep from tumbling all the way down the steep mountain to the beach below. Finally, when she thought she'd never stop, she plunged over a large, old fallen log, decayed from the years, dropped into a hole rimmed by a thicket of fresh new pines and slammed to a halt.

That's when she felt the pain. It shot through her, making

it hard to tell if she was seriously hurt or not. She tried to get to her feet, but her body screamed with pain for her to lie still a little longer.

Overhead, thunder clapped with a startling closeness. She glanced around to see that she'd fallen into a hole below the rotted log. Squirming away from the prickly pines, she leaned back against the warm earth, stared up at the blackened sky above her, and assessed her injuries. None fatal, few that required more than a bandage. She'd been very lucky. Again.

She replayed the accident over in her head. Then slowly she sat up, her heartbeat accelerating to breakneck speed. It had been no accident. The biker had waited in the pines and deliberately hit her. But why? And where was he now?

She glanced up the mountainside but couldn't see past the fallen log blocking her view. Suddenly the day seemed too quiet. In that deafening silence before the storm, she heard a sound above her that congealed her blood. The soft scuffle of footfalls, half stumbling, half sliding, coming down the mountain.

A flash of lightning electrified the sky and illuminated the darkness. The light died in an instant, leaving thunder to rattle across the treetops. Dirt showered down on her, cascading over the log, as someone drew closer. The biker. Her mouth went dry, her pulse pounded so loudly she feared he could hear it.

She didn't move, just waited, knowing that any moment he would peer over the log and see her lying there.

A voice in her mind, which sounded a lot like Jake's, yelled for her to move under the log. And yet she waited, with a sickening sureness that he'd find her before she could move. Then the lightning splintered the sky; thunder boomed. Clancy scrambled under the log, wedging herself into the small, narrow space between rotting log and earth. She held her breath and waited.

A boulder cartwheeled over the top of the rotted log with a resounding thump, then crashed through the new pines below her and on down the mountainside to the rocky beach below. It was followed by the thud of boots on top of the hollow-sounding log. She could almost feel him standing up there, looking down the mountainside, looking for her. To finish the job?

Rain splattered on the ground next to her, large, hard drops that pummeled the earth. Clancy closed her eyes, praying he wouldn't come any farther down the mountainside. If he did, he'd surely see her and— She squeezed her eyes tighter, concentrating on Jake's handsome face, the sound of that soft southern drawl, the feel of his arms wrapped around her. She prayed for Jake, clinging to the log and hope as she waited.

THE FIRST DROPS OF RAIN pelted down, angry and wet, as Jake would soon be. He told himself that when he found Clancy, he'd wring her neck. He'd bodily carry her to her aunt's for safekeeping. He'd take her over his knee and—

The dirt bike. It took Jake a moment to realize why the sound had pulled him from his frenzied thoughts. Its engine. Revved to the max. He looked up to see the headlight coming out of the blackness of the storm. The light flickered wildly as the bike roared down the pine-lined trail. Jake had only a moment to realize its rider didn't see him, couldn't see him in the rain and the darkness. He leaped from the path as the bike sped past.

Jake watched it go, not surprised to see Liz Knowles on the back of the bike, her russet hair blowing in the wind.

He cursed the biker and his close call. Then he turned and headed down the trail, following the path he knew would take him directly to Clancy's lodge. He hadn't gone far when something glinted in the trail ahead.

Dread clamped down on his heart as he thought he recognized the object at the edge of the trail. His breath caught as he drew closer. A bicycle, broken and twisted. His legs forced him forward, his mind arguing it wasn't Clancy's.

Couldn't be hers. Clancy's ruined bike lay mangled at the edge of the steep drop-off in the rain.

"Clancy!" Jake screamed her name, a cry of fear and anguish, hope and despair. He stumbled past the bike to stare down the mountainside. The wind howled in the pines; rain bit into his skin, hard as stones. He bent down, saw the tracks where she'd slid down the mountainside and practically threw himself down the slope after her.

CLANCY THOUGHT SHE HEARD the high-pitched whine of the bike fade. But she stayed wedged beneath the log, afraid to move. Had he really left? How could she be sure?

In the end, it was thoughts of Jake that made her slowly edge out of her hiding place. The wind whipped the pines, making them groan. The rain splattered down, wet and cold, promising a torrent shortly. She looked up, half expecting to see the biker standing on the log above her, his body in silhouette, his face as black as the shield he'd hidden behind earlier.

But no one waited on the log.

Had he really gone? And more important, who was he? Why did he want to harm her?

Clancy pulled herself to her feet. Her body throbbed with so many pains she couldn't isolate one from another. Her right hip ached with a dull throb where she vaguely remembered hitting it on something as she tumbled down the mountainside. The rain stung her skin, but she hardly noticed. She thought she heard her name on the wind. She thought she heard Jake's voice because she'd wished it so.

JAKE'S HEART THREATENED to burst from his chest as he slipped and fell his way down the mountainside. He didn't even realize he'd screamed her name until he heard her call out to him and look up. He saw her just below him.

Her face was covered with a mixture of dirt and blood, her clothes were torn and stained, her hair a nest of weeds and decomposed wood. He thought she'd never looked more beautiful.

"Clancy?" His voice came out a whisper and was quickly carried away by the wind. "Clancy."

He stumbled down to her, grabbed her and pulled her into his arms. "Oh, baby. Are you all right?"

He felt her nod against his chest as she tightened her hold on him. Relief washed over him, making him weak. The rain began to fall in sheets, drenching him and everything it touched.

"He tried to kill me again," she said, her words muffled against his chest. "The man on the dirt bike. This time you believe me, don't you?"

He pulled back to look into her face. Words stuck in his throat. "Yes," he whispered. "I believe you." He swept her up into his arms and took her to the closest shelter—his lodge.

CLANCY COULDN'T STOP shivering as Jake kicked open the door and carried her up the stairs, straight to his room and the shower. She leaned against him as he got the water going, refusing to give up the warmth of his body or breach the bond between them even for a moment.

He turned and, without breaking contact, pulled her into the shower with him. The warm water felt wonderful, but not as wonderful as Jake as he drew her to him. He cupped her face in his hands. His mouth dropped to hers, taking her as his own, possessing her in that single kiss in the same way he'd possessed her heart for more than a decade.

His lips lingered on hers, savoring her, seducing her with his lips, his tongue, his breath. He drew back. She looked up at him, breathless from the kiss, from the look in his eyes. "Jake," she whispered, a plea.

Slowly, his gaze on hers, he unbuttoned her shirt, opening her bare skin to the warm water and the fire of his touch. She leaned into the spray and him, letting the water wash away the dirt and blood, letting Jake wash away the years of hurt.

He caught his breath as her shirt dropped from her shoulders to the shower floor. His gaze alone hardened her nipples, making them ache with longing. He reached to unhook her bra, freeing her breasts to his gaze, to his touch, to his mouth and the rough, wet feel of his tongue.

Warmth sprinted from her hardened nipple through her body, making her weak. She ached for the feel of his skin on hers as she hurriedly unbuttoned his shirt, pushing aside the wet cloth to brush her palms across the solid wet heat of his flesh.

With a groan, he stripped off her jeans and panties and dragged her to him. Her pulse matched the thunder outside as he backed her up against the shower wall, trapping her there, her body now at his mercy. She surrendered as he devoured her swollen breasts, sucking her nipples red and hard. Then his mouth trailed down her belly to her open thighs, where he consumed her with the same kind of desperate need. She buried her fingers in his hair, arching against his mouth, as a hot current raced through her. There was no need for words; for once, they completely understood each other. There were no walls. No fences. Nothing to keep their hearts from running free.

"Jake," she whispered as she unbuttoned his jeans. A plea. A promise.

Jake stepped out of his wet jeans and lifted her, hip to hip. He breathed her name, husky with desire. "Clancy." Not a question. An affirmation. He thrust her against the shower wall, his gaze locking with hers. She gasped as he filled her so completely, and with each drive, he took her spiraling up, the water pounding them as the rain beat down on the skylight overhead. As the thunder rumbled and lightning lit the sky, he took her higher and higher, further and further, until they both soared like hawks over the island.

Jake said nothing as he pulled her into his arms. She buried her face in his shoulder, hugging him tightly, grazing his skin with a kiss. He placed a hand on the back of her blond head and gazed down at her. So small. So strong. So beautiful. He should have been surprised by his feelings for her. But instead he was more surprised by her feelings for him. After everything he'd done to her, she still loved him.

She leaned back to look up into his eyes. Then she picked up the bar of soap and gently glided it over his skin, lathering his shoulders, his chest, his belly.

He watched her eyes, still dark with pleasure, and he knew he had to have her again. One time would never still the need inside him. He doubted a hundred thousand would.

He took the soap from her and slowly slid it over her, from the pounding pulse at the hollow of her neck, over her luscious, full, rounded breasts, down to the hollow of her stomach, to the silken V of her thighs.

She groaned softly, her eyes darkening as her hands trailed over his skin.

He pulled her to him, their bodies slick and slippery. He buried himself in her again, losing himself in her body, in her eyes, in her.

CLANCY CAME OUT of the bathroom, her wet hair curled at her neck, her skin pink and bare except for the towel wrapped around her. Jake tossed another log on the fire and closed the screen.

"Do you want to go home and get something on your scrapes and scratches?" he asked as he closed the distance between them. "You must hurt all over from your fall."

She shook her head. Thunder boomed overhead, rattling the windows. Rain streaked the glass and pounded the deck. "I've never felt this wonderful."

He laughed as he swept her up and carried her to his bed. Before he joined her, he picked up the cell phone and dialed Clancy's number. Kiki answered on the first ring.

"Clancy's fine," Jake said. "She'll be back in the morning. Go home." He hung up and pulled Clancy into his arms. They lay together watching the storm rage outside, the fire crackle and glow inside until they fell asleep, spooned together in the middle of the bed.

THE NEXT MORNING, Clancy woke to find Jake propped up on one elbow, looking down at her. He smiled as he brushed hair back from her forehead and planted a kiss between her eyes, then dropped to place one on her lips.

She lay on her back, watching his face. When she'd first opened her eyes she'd caught him frowning down at her. She'd gone to sleep happier than she could ever remember being. Now she felt as if an elephant had just sat on her chest. "What is it?"

He seemed surprised by her question, then his smile faded. "You really don't miss anything, do you?" He trailed a finger across her shoulder.

She could almost hear the wheels turning in his head as she sat up, pulling the sheet over her bare breasts and leaned against the headboard, bracing herself. Outside, the storm had let up. The lake lay slate gray and flat. Water dripped from the eaves. In the distance, Clancy could see a slit of blue sky on the horizon.

Jake pulled himself up and leaned back against the wall next to the bed so he could face her. "Clancy, I've never been closer to anyone than I am to you."

She feared what was coming. She promised herself she wouldn't cry. "Why don't you just say it. This was a mistake."

She started to get up but he grabbed her arm and kept her on the bed.

"No, dammit, I'm trying to tell you that making love to you has made me realize that now more than ever, I want—I *need* to know—"

She knew the words before he said them.

"The truth. I have to know, Clancy. For my sanity's sake. For...our sake."

She stared at him. For a few hours she'd forgotten why he'd come back to Montana. Didn't he say he'd get the truth out of her at any cost? "Is that why you made love to me?" she asked. She shoved him away and got out of bed, anger soothing the dagger of hurt that was stuck in her heart. "Is that what this was all about? You thought if you got me naked and in a weakened enamored state, maybe I'd break down and confess everything?" She remembered her clothes were still on the shower floor, soaking wet.

"No! Dammit. You're not listening to me."

"Oh, I hear you just fine, Jake." She jerked a pair of jeans from Jake's closet. From the few items of clothing he'd brought, he obviously hadn't planned to stay long. Just get the truth out of her—whatever it took, even seducing her. Then he'd be gone back to Galveston. Oh, what a fool she'd been. Did she really think making love meant anything to him? Just a means to an end.

The jeans were way too big, but that didn't stop her. She tugged them on, grimacing at her aches and pains. Just hours ago, she'd felt nothing but pleasure in Jake's arms. But this morning, her sore body reminded her painfully that some things hadn't changed. Making love with Jake had solved nothing.

"Dammit, you're wrong," Jake said, flying out of the bed to tower over her. "You think last night was just part of my plan?"

She looked up at him. "Don't tell me it didn't cross your mind."

His gaze slithered off. "I'll admit it did cross my mind but—"

"That's what I thought." She shoved her way past him to the closet and jerked one of his shirts from the hanger.

"Listen to me, woman. I used to imagine making love with you." He took her bare shoulders and drew her around to face him. "Nothing in my imagination would ever come close to actually being with you."

"Now, if I'd just quit lying to you, everything would be perfect, right?" She shucked his hands from her shoulders and tried to get the shirt on without him seeing how hard she was shaking. She didn't want him to see how much he'd hurt her. She didn't even want to admit it to herself.

"Where do you think you're going?" Jake demanded, stomping around to face her in all his nakedness.

She pushed past him. "Leave me alone, Hawkins."

"I can't stand this between us. Can't you understand that, Clancy?"

She angrily thrust one arm into a sleeve, then the other, making him have to step back to keep from getting slugged. "Nothing I can say or do will ever convince you."

"You can't just stomp off. Not now." She stepped back when he reached for her. He raked a hand through his hair and let out a frustrated curse. "Are you forgetting that someone tried to kill you?"

She fumbled with the buttons, not caring which holes they went in. "No, Jake, something like that doesn't exactly slip your mind, especially when I'd been telling you someone was after me all along and you didn't believe me." She stuffed her feet into her wet sandals and headed for the door.

"Just a minute, you aren't leaving like this. Let me get dressed. You took off by yourself yesterday and look where it got you."

She turned to see him hopping on one foot as he tried to pull on a pair of jeans. He looked so flustered, so much like the boy she'd fallen in love with. She cursed the emotions that drew her to him, the heart that threatened to break at just the sight of him. "Damn you, Hawkins. There are worse things than having a crazed killer after you. Like having a crazed ex-boyfriend who pretends to want to help you. Especially one you've been in love with your entire life." She turned and left, slamming the door on the way out.

"WHERE HAVE YOU BEEN?" Aunt Kiki demanded the moment Clancy slammed into the lodge. "Are you all righ—" She glanced from Clancy's flushed, scraped and scratched face to Jake's shirt, improperly buttoned with one tail hanging lower than the other. Clancy had to hold up the much too-large jeans with one hand.

"I'm fine," Clancy snapped, sweeping past her, feeling like a teenager caught necking. "Someone on a dirt bike tried to kill me. Other than that—" She turned and walked to her aunt, whose eyes widened in obvious disapproval at this inappropriate display of emotion. "And *someone* brought Jake Hawkins back into my life. If the guy on the bike doesn't get me, Jake will convince the state to hang me instead of just send me to prison. Other than that, I'm just fine. Didn't Jake tell you to go home?"

Kiki looked highly offended, but then she often did. "I don't take orders from Mr. Hawkins. And believe me, *this*—" she waved a hand at Clancy's postcoital condition "—isn't what I had in mind when I hired him."

It gave Clancy some satisfaction to see how displeased her aunt was over Clancy's liaison with Jake Hawkins. "Sometime you'll have to tell me just what it was you *did* have in mind when you hired him. In the meantime, I will just continue to assume that you've lost your mind."

Clancy turned and, with all the dignity she could muster, limped toward the stairs, her body hurting with each step.

"By the way," Kiki said behind her, "your lawyer called. It seems he fell while looking for you and broke his leg. He's at the hospital but said he plans to be home later. You might want to call him. That's if you are still interested in not going to prison."

"Actually, prison is looking better all the time," Clancy said without turning around.

She heard her aunt sniff in disapproval, then leave quietly. Always the Talbott, she thought, thankful that she had enough Jones in her to rant and rave and show some good, honest emotion.

Clancy started up the stairs, changed her mind and went back to lock all the doors. The last person she wanted to see again was Jake Hawkins. She'd much prefer Dex West-fall's ghost.

As Clancy climbed the stairs, she concentrated on the pain from her fall instead of the warmth inside her where Jake had been. Her skin still simmered from where his skin had touched hers. She used anger as a salve. What had she thought? That once they made love, Jake would realize she couldn't have possibly lied? That she was a woman who would never betray her man? That he'd been wrong? Oh, sure. A man as stubborn, intractable and incorrigible as Jake Hawkins? Fat chance.

JAKE TOOK A FEW frustrating minutes to try to find a shirt, then gave up and went after Clancy, realizing that all he'd done in the three days since he'd hit Montana was chase this woman and he was getting damned tired of it.

He threw open his front door to find Kiki poised under the dripping eave ready to knock. It didn't take a genius to see that she was madder than an old wet hen. She glanced at his bare chest with distaste. She was lucky he hadn't come to the door stark naked. He almost wished he had just for the shock value, although he doubted much could shake up Kiki.

"What?" he demanded. Before she could speak, he added, "Whatever it is, I don't have time for it."

"Perhaps we misunderstood each other, Mr. Hawkins," she said, her look darker than the storm that had passed through. "I hired you to help my niece, not seduce her."

He bit back a nasty retort and tried not to bite off her head. "It's none of your business who Clancy…sleeps with or doesn't." In his case, it would be "doesn't" in the future, he was sure, but he wasn't about to tell her that.

Kiki narrowed her gaze at him. "Please don't be offended, but you're not right for my niece. She deserves better than some…private investigator. Her mother married poorly. I won't let that happen to Clancy. I hope that's clear enough for you."

"Marrying your niece isn't even an option," Jake snapped.

Kiki's look would have frozen boiling water. "How nice to hear. Do you know who killed Dex Westfall yet, Mr. Hawkins?"

"No, as a matter of fact, I don't. If I could keep your niece from disappearing every time I turn around, I might be able to find out."

"See if you can do that." With a haughty flip of her head, she turned and headed for her boat.

Furious, he slammed out of his lodge and stalked the distance to Clancy's. *Some private investigator.* The nerve of that woman. He'd marry anyone he damned well pleased. As he stormed up Clancy's steps, he wasn't sure who he was the most angry with. Kiki. Clancy. Or himself.

He'd blown it, plain and simple. The case. But mostly Clancy. And, he realized with a start, he didn't give a damn about anything else. But she was right; what the hell was he doing making love to her when he still thought she was a liar and possibly a murderer?

Because I'm in love with her! He felt like he'd been struck by lightning. *You're in love with a liar and a possible murderer?* He stood for a moment, trying to get his bearings. He'd prove she was neither, dammit. He'd prove it to himself and then... And then what would he do? Throw himself at her mercy? Good luck.

But first he had to get back into her good graces somehow. It wasn't going to be easy. But for once, he thought he knew what to do.

CLANCY WAS CURLED UP on the couch in her robe, a heating pad on her back, a bag of crushed ice on one ankle, her scrapes, scratches and cuts disinfected and bandaged, when Jake burst in.

"I thought I locked that door," she demanded.

"Like everyone else in the world, I know where you keep your key."

She gave him a sour look. "Did you come to make love to me again to see if I'd crack this time?"

He cocked a brow at her. "I want to make love to you again, yes. But not for the reason you think."

Her look, as she got up to escape to another room, said his chances of that weren't good.

"But I'm not going to make love to you," he said.

She stopped and raised a brow at him. "No kidding."

"You were right. There's enough going on in your life right now without me complicating things by making mad, passionate love to you. We have a killer to find." He moved toward her, wanting desperately to take her in his arms and do exactly what he was about to promise he wouldn't. "We have to concentrate. For now. So, I promise I won't even kiss you." He reached out to run his thumb along her lips. "Or make love to you. Not until you ask me to."

"Well, there's no chance of that." Clancy took a ragged breath. Just when she thought things couldn't get any worse, he'd promised not to even kiss her until she asked him to. Right. How could she be around him and not beg him to kiss her, beg him to make love to her? Prison was starting to look like a picnic.

"So, we'd better get back to business. We have to go to the resort and talk to Liz," Jake said. "She knows who was driving that bike."

Clancy told herself at least now he believed someone really was trying to kill her. She supposed that was something. Although, she did wonder about this sudden turnaround of Jake's. What was he up to with this promise of his? Something.

Out of the corner of her eye, she looked into his wonderfully handsome face and felt her dark mood lighten like the blue sky through the window. Even as a kid she could never stay mad at him.

"All right," she said, hoisting herself up from the couch. The parts of her body that weren't bruised, scraped, scratched or gouged, ached. All of her still ached for one man. She gave Jake a resigned look. "Let me get some clothes on."

He gave her a wide berth as she passed. Fool that she was, she already missed his touch.

IT LOOKED LIKE OFF-SEASON at Hawk Island Resort. The storm that had hammered the island most of the night still had everyone curled up inside their cabins. Only a handful of hard-core fishermen bailed their boats at the docks for a morning fishing trip. Everything dripped, wet and cold. June in Montana.

"I'd tell you to stay here—" Jake started, then smiled "—but what would be the point? You might as well tag along. One look at that scraped-up face of yours and Liz is bound to talk."

"Thanks a lot," Clancy said, climbing out of the boat and sweeping past him.

But when they reached the café, the only person banging around at the back of the small kitchen was Frank Ames.

"What do you want?" Frank said, glancing up from the dirty grill.

"We're looking for Liz Knowles," Jake said.

Frank cursed and continued scraping the grill with a large metal spatula. "Isn't everybody."

"What does that mean?" Jake demanded, amazed at how quickly he could lose his patience with Frank.

Frank gave him a smirk. "She didn't show up for work this morning."

A bad feeling settled in the pit of Jake's stomach. "When was the last time anyone saw her?"

"I wouldn't know," Frank said, throwing down the spatula in disgust. "What's the big deal with you, anyway? I'm the one who has no waitress."

Jake leaned over the counter toward Frank, hoping he wouldn't have to cross it to get what he wanted out of him. "Did you check her cabin?"

Frank had the good sense to look a little nervous. "Of course. She hadn't slept in her bed. One of the cabin girls said she had plans last night with one of the dock boys. He says she never showed up for their date. She probably left the island with some guy she met. Happens every summer." He turned back to his dirty grill.

"Who has a dirt bike on the island?" Jake asked.

Frank stopped scraping and turned around slowly. "Why?"

Well, that answered that question. "Who besides you?"

Frank looked suspicious. And worried. He laid down the spatula again. At this rate, he'd never get that grill cleaned. "No one. Why?"

"Someone on a dirt bike tried to kill Clancy," Jake said.

"What?" His gaze shot to Clancy, surprise registering in his expression when he saw her injuries. "Just a damned minute here," he said to Jake. "You're not pinning me with that. I haven't ridden that bike since last summer."

"Where is your bike?" Jake asked. "I want to see it."

Frank ripped off his apron and threw it down on the counter. With a mean look, he led them to the back of his place and a dilapidated shed. Frank swung the door open and stood for a moment staring into the semidarkness inside.

Frank's shoulders sagged. He swore but didn't turn around.

Jake stepped past him to look inside the shed. Junk had been piled waist-deep in a U-shaped heap that left only a small, narrow space at the center. Just small and narrow enough for a dirt bike. But there was no bike.

"Someone stole my bike," Frank said. "Not that I'd expect you to believe me."

Jake didn't. "How could someone take it? Where was the key for it?"

Frank avoided his gaze. "I always left the key in it and the helmet on the seat."

"That's handy," Jake said.

"It was handy," Frank snapped.

Jake couldn't believe this. "And I suppose everyone knew the key was in it?"

Frank kicked at the shed door in answer. "No one's ever stolen it before, so why would they now?"

"Is there any reason anyone would want to incriminate you in a murder?" Clancy asked from behind him.

Frank's head flew up. "You mean someone took my bike to make it look like I tried to kill you?"

"Bingo." Jake watched Frank's eyes widen in surprise, then narrow in meanness.

"No. No one." The lie seemed to catch in Frank's throat. "That's the craziest thing I've ever heard."

"If Liz turns up, have her call me," Jake ordered.

Frank nodded distractedly.

Jake would have given a penny for his thoughts.

ON THE BOAT TRIP BACK to the lodge, the sun burst through the clouds, making the morning golden if not exactly warm. A few thin clouds scudded across the blue. A light breeze rippled the top of the water, bringing with it the smell of wet pines.

Jake's obvious disappointment in not finding Liz or the bike hung like a dark cloud over him. Clancy knew he was worried about Liz. Had Liz seen the biker run Clancy off the trail? Is that why she'd disappeared? Then, what had she been doing on the back of the bike just after that? She must have known Clancy's assailant. Did that mean Liz was part of whatever was going on? She *had* spent time with Dex.

Clancy felt a shiver as she and Jake walked up the beach toward the lodge. As hard as she tried not to, she kept seeing Dex's face beneath that bike helmet.

As Clancy opened the door, she could hear the phone ringing. She raced to it. "Hello?"

Silence.

Her heart began to pound. Another one of those crank

calls. She motioned for Jake to pick up the extension in the living room. "Hello? Is anyone there?"

For a moment all she could hear was the labored breathing. Then came the distinct sound of a match being struck as the person on the other end of the line lit a cigarette and took a long drag. "Please say something," Clancy urged.

"Clancy Jones?" The hoarse voice was a woman's. At least Clancy thought it was. "I need to talk to Clancy Jones."

"This is Clancy."

"I need your help." The woman sounded scared. And maybe a little drunk. Clancy wondered if that wasn't why she'd finally decided to speak rather than hang up like she had the other times.

"My help?" Clancy asked in surprise.

"My name is Glenda Grimes," the woman said. Clancy could hear her tapping nervously on something as she spoke. "You don't know me. I'm Lola Strickland's sister. Half sister."

Clancy looked across the room at Jake. His eyes widened in surprise. He nodded for her to keep talking.

"What can I do for you?" Clancy asked.

"Could you come up to Somers? I've got to talk to you. It's about Dex. I know who killed him."

Chapter Fourteen

Jake turned off Highway 93 and drove the Mustang through downtown Somers, a community with little more than a bar, post office, café and hardware store. He drove up one of the dirt streets to the top of a rise and parked in front of a small dilapidated cottage overlooking the highway.

"Are you feeling all right?" Jake asked. "You've been awfully quiet."

"Just thinking." Clancy brushed her hair back from her face and gave him what she hoped was a reassuring smile. After what Jake had told her, she was worried about Liz Knowles. She agreed with Jake; there was a killer out there and she felt if they didn't stop him, he'd kill again. As she opened her car door, she hoped Glenda Grimes really did know something that could help them.

A woman in her sixties answered the door with a cigarette and a beer. She held little resemblance to her half sister, Lola. A bright-colored scarf tied around her head hid most of her frizzy dyed red hair; a faded chenille robe the color of dirt hid most of her body, except for a pair of bony bare feet poking out the bottom of the robe, the toenails painted bright red. The same color as the lipstick smear on her beer can.

"Yes?" the woman asked, suspicion as much a part of her face as the wrinkles.

"Glenda Grimes?" Jake asked.

Eyes narrowed, she looked from Clancy to Jake and back. Clancy could smell her perfume. A mixture of cigarette smoke, beer and perm solution. At one time, she might have been pretty, Clancy thought. But not as pretty as Lola.

"What do you want?" She had the voice of a woman who'd spent a good deal of her life on a bar stool. She took a drag off the cigarette and blew the smoke out the corner of her mouth as she eyed them.

"I'm Clancy Jones." It didn't seem to register at first, and Clancy felt her initial rush of hope dissolve. Either the woman was a crackpot or Glenda Grimes hadn't called her at all.

Glenda looked around warily before she settled her gaze on Jake. "Who's he?"

"He's a private investigator," Clancy said, then added, "and a good friend of mine."

Glenda studied Jake for a moment, then glanced past him as if she thought someone might be watching them. Hurriedly she pushed open the screen and ushered them inside, closing and locking the door.

And Clancy thought *she* was paranoid.

Clancy stepped into a small, cramped living room. The place was filled with...stuff. Every flat surface had something on it from chipped figurines and old perfume bottles to ashtrays with the names of Montana bars.

"All I have is beer," Glenda said, shuffling into the cluttered kitchen to swing open the door of an old fridge with so many magnets on it Clancy couldn't tell the color.

Both Clancy and Jake declined, and Glenda finished the beer in her hand and pulled out a fresh one. It was obvious she'd already had a few as she came into the living room.

"Sit down." She motioned to a broken-down couch in a dark corner and dropped into a faded chair across from them. Clancy watched her put her beer next to an overflowing ashtray beside her chair. Her fingers trembled.

"There's something I don't understand," Clancy said.

"If you have information about Dex's murder, why did you call me instead of going to the police?"

The woman took a drag off her cigarette, then fumbled it back into the ashtray. She popped the top on the beer and took a long drink as if she thought it would steady her nerves. Clancy wondered what Glenda Grimes had to be nervous about.

"You're the one they arrested for Dex's murder, right?" Glenda asked.

Clancy nodded, wondering where this was going.

"I figured you'd care more than the police about who really killed Dex."

That made an odd kind of sense to Clancy. "On the phone you said you knew who killed him."

Glenda reached for another cigarette, fingers shaking violently. "I did."

"You?" Clancy asked incredulously.

"I wasn't the one who bashed his head in, mind you, but I killed him just as sure as you're sitting here." Glenda reached for her beer and a tissue.

Clancy shot a look at Jake. Glenda Grimes was a crackpot, just as they'd feared. A morose woman who cried in her beer and blamed herself for her nephew's death. Another dead end.

"Why should you feel responsible?" Jake asked.

"I was the one who got him all stirred up about the past." She started to cry. "Got him digging into things that should have been left buried."

"What kind of things?" Jake asked.

Glenda just shook her head and cried. "I've never been to Vegas. I'm an old woman. I want to go before I die. That isn't too much to ask, is it?"

What did that have to do with Dex's death?

"So you really don't know who killed your nephew," Jake said, getting to his feet. "Why did you call Clancy and waste her time?"

Glenda wiped her tears and narrowed her eyes at him.

"I don't know who actually killed him. But I know why," she said, anger making her cheeks pink.

"Why?" Jake demanded. When she didn't answer, he swore softly under his breath. "Two people have already died. If you really do know something—"

"Somebody doesn't want all that old stuff about Lola coming out again. You've got to find the murderer before he finds me." Glenda finished her beer as if it were an antidote.

"Why would someone want to kill you?" Jake asked. "What is it you know?"

"It isn't what I know," she cried. "It's what he might think I know. Don't you see, I talked to Dex and he figured it out. If the killer finds out I talked to Dex, he might think I know more than I do and come after me."

"Wait a minute," Clancy interrupted. "How do you know Dex figured it out?"

Glenda studied the end of her cigarette. "He came by here the night before he died. He told me he knew who killed his mother."

Jake shot Clancy a look she recognized instantly. Total disbelief. "He didn't tell you who that person was?"

"He didn't want to get me involved," Glenda said. "Just believe me, Dex was positive he'd figured it out."

"Based on what?" Jake demanded.

Glenda shook her head. "He'd collected everything he could find on his mother's murder."

The newspaper clippings, Clancy thought.

"He'd even hatched some lamebrain scheme that involved getting to know Clancy, thinking, I guess, that she might know something. I told him the rest, about the trial, his mother..." Glenda said with a look of disgust.

Clancy thought of the beautiful, dark-haired woman who had worked at the resort office. "I don't remember very much about Lola. Can you tell us what you told Dex?"

Glenda let out a long sigh, making Clancy think it was going to be a long story. "Lola looked like her daddy. All that dark hair, those dark secretive eyes, a face that stopped traffic.''

"You didn't have the same father?" Clancy asked.

"No, my daddy died when I was young. Mama remarried and had Lola." Glenda wagged her head. "Lola was spoiled, wild and foolhardy from the get-go. She ran off at sixteen and got herself into trouble. Then she goes and runs off again after Dex is born." Glenda leaned back, as if that pretty much covered Lola's entire life history.

"Did you see much of her when she lived on the island?" Jake asked.

"She'd stop by just to lord it over me. Tell me about the parties she'd been to, important people she'd met."

"Do you know where she was going the night of the fire?" Clancy asked.

Glenda raised a brow. "She *thought* she was taking off with her lover."

"Her lover?" Jake and Clancy asked in unison.

Glenda seemed surprised by their surprise. "Lola always had a lover, but this time she thought she'd met her Prince Charming." She rolled her eyes. "But he turned out to be just another loser."

"You knew who this man was?" Jake asked.

"Lola never told me, just that I'd find out soon enough and I should expect fireworks," Glenda said. "Lola loved drama in her life."

"You think he was married," Jake said.

Was Jake thinking of his father, Clancy wondered.

"Could be why Lola kept him a secret." Glenda made a production of lighting another cigarette. "Who knows? But I can tell you this, he was no Prince Charming."

"What makes you say that?" Clancy asked.

"Where were his suitcases if he planned to run off with her?" Glenda asked. "All her talk about how sweet he was, loving, caring, considerate. I knew he sounded too good to be true."

"You think he's the one who killed her?" Jake asked.

"He could have been," Glenda said as she got up and headed for the fridge. "Probably over the money."

Clancy and Jake exchanged a glance. "What money?" Clancy asked first.

"The money Lola stole." Glenda gave them a look as if to say they weren't as bright as she'd hoped.

"Are you talking about the money that was missing from Clancy's and my father's businesses?" Jake asked. The money Warren Hawkins had gone to prison for embezzling. "Lola stole it?"

"If there is one thing Lola loved even more than men, it was money." Glenda dug around in the fridge. "I wonder if she ever really planned to run off with this guy."

"What do you mean?" Clancy asked.

"She could have led the guy on, planning to double-cross him all along," she said as she slammed the fridge door and popped another top. "Maybe he found out and killed her."

"If you thought Lola embezzled the money, why didn't you come forward during the trial?" Jake demanded.

Clancy could have cut the tension in the room with a dull knife.

Glenda came back into the room, sat and dug another cigarette out of a half-empty pack. "Why? I don't know she did it. Why get involved in something I didn't know squat about?"

"You were her sister," Jake shot back.

"Half sister. Maybe I didn't want anyone knowing I was related to her. It wasn't like she told anyone about me. Anyway, she'd made someone mad enough to kill her. I didn't want to get involved."

"But you did get involved," Clancy pointed out. "When you told Dex. Why did you decide to tell what you knew now?"

Glenda looked toward the front door as if she expected someone to come bursting in at any moment. "I want to go to Vegas before I die."

It took Clancy a moment. "You told Dex because you thought he would uncover the missing money."

Jake swore.

Tears filled Glenda's eyes. "How did I know it was going to get Dex killed?" she demanded. "I just thought he might be able to solve the mystery of what happened to that money."

"What made you think the money was even still around?" Jake asked, sounding surprised. "It had been embezzled over a period of time. What makes you think the embezzler didn't spend it as fast as he stole it?"

She shrugged. "I figure if Lola stole the money, she would have been real careful. She'd know better than to spend it. So she'd hide it somewhere. She was probably going to pick it up that night but she got killed. Her lover might or might not have known where she'd hidden the money. Either way, he probably didn't have time to rehide it before he was arrested for her murder."

That was quite the theory, Clancy thought. *If* Lola took the money.

"But now Warren Hawkins is coming up for parole," Jake said, an edge to his voice. "You wanted to get to the money before he could. Just in case he was that man."

Glenda took a swig of her beer.

"Wait a minute," Clancy said, frowning at the woman. "You're saying now that you don't believe it was Warren Hawkins?"

"Someone murdered Dex because he was getting too close to the truth," Glenda said with certainty.

Jake shook his head. "You had to have told Dex more than this for him to figure out who killed Lola."

"I told you everything I told him," Glenda said stubbornly. "When he came by, he wasn't here long. We talked, he looked through a box of junk Lola left here, but he didn't take anything except for some silly necklace, and he left."

Clancy's head jerked up. "Necklace?"

"What box of junk?" Jake demanded with a pained look.

"What did this necklace look like?" Clancy questioned.

"Just a string of beads," Glenda said.

Clancy felt her heart rate accelerate. "Pale blue with a navy ceramic heart in the center?"

Glenda nodded, eyeing her suspiciously. "How did you know that?"

"Dex showed me the necklace. He said his mother left it to him."

The woman snorted. "Lola didn't leave him nothing. She could have cared less about the boy. It was just some stuff she dumped here and a few personal things the police turned over to me after the fire."

So Glenda had come forward after the trial to collect her sister's valuables. Only they hadn't turned out to be valuable.

"You should have seen the way that boy rifled through that box," Glenda was saying. "Like he thought she'd left him buried treasure or something." Glenda wagged her head. "It was pathetic to see—"

"You still have the box?" Jake interrupted.

"It doesn't have a thing in it that's worth anything," she said. "That's probably why Lola left it with me."

"I'd like to see the box," Jake insisted.

With effort, Glenda pushed herself out of the chair and went into one of the rooms off the living room. She returned a few minutes later with a shoe box and handed it to Jake. He set it on the coffee table and carefully removed the contents. Clancy slid closer.

Glenda was right. It contained little of monetary value. Several pressed dried roses. Ticket stubs from the local theater. A faded fishing lure. A plastic bubble with fake snow falling over a fat, red-cheeked Santa. A cheap dime-store mood ring. A pair of tarnished silver half-moon earrings. An envelope of photographs from the resort, mostly scenic, Clancy noticed as she flipped through them. A stack of play programs, ones Lola had had roles in. A handful of greeting cards. It reminded Clancy of the kind of things a young girl keeps from her first love affair.

It seemed odd that Dex would take nothing but the bead necklace. Had he just taken it because it belonged to his mother? Then, why didn't he take some of the other things? "Was the necklace in the box when Lola gave it to you?"

Glenda shook her head. "She must have been wearing it. The cops gave it to me with that ring and those earrings." She pointed to the mood ring and the half-moon earrings Jake had pulled out of the box. "That's the lot of her belongings," Glenda said with disgust. "And all that talk about her ritzy friends."

Jake handed Clancy the photographs he'd found. She leafed through them, stopping in surprise at a photo of Lola with a man she recognized. The man stood next to Lola on the dock in front of the resort, his arm around her shoulders, a smile on his face as he looked down at her. There was what Clancy would describe as a longing in his eyes. The man was Tadd Farnsworth.

"Could this have been Lola's Prince Charming?" Clancy asked.

Glenda squinted at the photograph, then shook her head. "Why the fuss over keeping it a secret if she was going to pose right in front of the resort with him?"

Clancy had to agree. She suspected Lola's great love had been a forbidden one. She just wondered why.

Jake glanced through the greeting cards, then handed them to Clancy. They were all in the same hand, all the kind of cards a man in love might buy a woman, all with the same inscription: "With love, your Teddy Bear."

Glenda nodded with a smirk. "Teddy Bear. Can you believe that?"

It didn't sound to Clancy like anything a grown man would call himself, but what did she know about men? She put the cards back into the box.

"Do you think Teddy Bear was this man she planned to run off with?" Jake asked.

Glenda shrugged. "If a guy who calls himself Teddy Bear doesn't have something to hide, who does?"

"This stuff meant something to her," Clancy said, glancing at the odd items from the box. "That's why she brought it here." But why? Was she worried that something might happen to her? Was there a clue in this box as to who killed her and had Dex recognized it? Then, why had he taken only the necklace, which hadn't even been in the box?

Out of the corner of her eye, Clancy saw Jake slip one of the cards into his pocket when Glenda wasn't looking. Clancy hoped he hadn't taken it because he'd recognized the handwriting as his father's, and that Teddy Bear was Warren Hawkins. If Glenda's theory was right, Lola's lover was still on the loose—and a killer. And if that were true, then Warren Hawkins had gone to prison for a murder he hadn't committed.

"Do you mind if we take this photograph?" Jake asked, holding up the one of Lola and Tadd.

"Take the whole box," Glenda said. "I want it out of here."

Chapter Fifteen

Clancy was too quiet as they left Somers. Jake drove along the lakeshore, his own thoughts tangled. The storm had left the day cooler than usual, but Jake cracked his window, anyway, to let in some of the fresh air. He found himself going over what Glenda had told them, trying to fit the odd-shaped chunks of truths and lies together. It made his head ache.

"Glenda Grimes knows more that she's telling us," Jake said with a silent curse. He looked over at Clancy when she didn't respond. "Want to tell me what's bothering you?"

They'd gone a few miles along the Flathead Lake shoreline, everything lush and green after the storm. He suspected Clancy had seen him pocket the card. She didn't miss much. Or was he losing his touch?

"You've never believed your father was guilty," she said quietly. "So who did you think was?"

Jake knew this discussion had been coming for years. Actually, he was surprised they hadn't gotten into it sooner. He pulled the Mustang over at the first wide spot and turned off the engine. Sunlight flickered on the water. A canopy of clouds still hung over the mountains. It had seemed clear to him. "Your father," he answered.

"That's what I thought." She didn't sound angry, just sad.

"It was the only thing that made sense," Jake admitted. "I knew you wouldn't perjure yourself except to protect your father."

"That's what you think I did, knowing what it would do to you?" she asked. "Jake, I adored my father. But I didn't love him as much as I loved you. I would never have lied for him. He wouldn't have let me."

Jake felt a pain at heart level stronger than any he'd ever known. "At the time, all I saw was that either you'd lied to save your father or that my father was not just a thief, but a murderer and an arsonist."

"And now?" Clancy asked.

He shook his head. "Now everything seems different than it did then." Because of the large amount of money that was missing, it seemed that one of the two partners, Warren Hawkins or Clarence Jones, had to be guilty. "Maybe Lola did embezzle the money. All I know is that now I can see that there might be another explanation, even though Lola's dead and the money's never turned up."

"Maybe she spent it or gave it to someone. Maybe it's still hidden somewhere like Glenda thinks it is."

He looked over at her. "You don't want my father to be guilty any more than I do, do you."

She smiled. "I never did, Jake."

"The problem is, if Lola had been skimming that much money from the businesses, my father would have caught it." Warren Hawkins had been in charge of the financial end of the businesses.

"Your father may have been…distracted," Clancy said.

He glanced over at her. Had everyone known about the problems his parents had been having or just Clancy? He'd always believed his parents would have worked things out if his father hadn't gone to prison. Now he wasn't so sure of that. He knew they'd been having financial problems partly because of the way his mother had liked to live, throwing large, extravagant parties. She loved to entertain, and there was nothing wrong with that. They could afford it. Couldn't they?

"I thought we'd stop by Tadd's and ask him about that photograph," he said as he started the Mustang.

"You think he's Teddy Bear?" Her tone made it clear she didn't.

"His name is Theodore."

THEY FOUND TADD AT HOME, his leg up and a ballgame on the television.

"How's the leg?" Jake asked, taking the chair Tadd offered. He noticed Clancy didn't sit. She'd gone to the mantel, where she seemed to be inspecting a series of framed photographs.

"Hurts like hell," Tadd said, grimacing. "Doctor says I'm lucky I didn't break my neck." His gaze followed Clancy. "How are you, Clancy?"

She turned. "Sore, but otherwise just glad to be alive."

He nodded, and continued to watch her inspect the photos. "The sheriff called. They found the dirt bike."

"Where?" Clancy asked.

"Paradise Cove." Tadd seemed to hesitate. "They also found Liz Knowles's body."

"Oh, no," Clancy said, slumping down into a chair by the fireplace. "She wasn't..."

"She'd drowned," Tadd said. "She was wearing the bike helmet."

Jake slammed a fist down on the arm of the chair. "No way. Someone else was driving that bike when I saw her. Whoever it was killed her as sure as I'm sitting here. Don't tell me the sheriff thinks it was an accident?"

"He's waiting for the results of the autopsy," Tadd said. "But it looks like Liz might have ridden the bike off the cliffs and drowned."

Jake swore. "What about the bike?"

"Belonged to Frank Ames, all right. He's sticking to his original story that someone stole it."

"With Liz gone, we don't know who was driving that bike and we can't prove Frank's lying," Jake said.

Tadd nodded. "I think Frank Ames is up to his neck in this. I asked for a copy of the police report." He reached beside his chair, picked up a manila envelope and handed it to Jake. "These are the photocopies of the evidence you asked for along with Dex Westfall's autopsy report and copies of the clippings from Dex's closet wall."

Jake took the envelope but he didn't open it. He studied Tadd, a dozen suspicions buzzing around in his head like angry wasps. "Where were you when Liz went off that cliff, Tadd?" Jake asked, trying to keep the accusation out of his tone.

Tadd's eyes widened. "What?"

Jake saw Clancy tense. "You used to own a dirt bike. I remember when you raced in local competitions. You were pretty good."

Tadd let out a laugh. "You can't be serious. I haven't ridden in years. I'd kill myself."

"Or break your leg," Jake added.

"Wait a minute," Tadd said, holding up his hands. "Why would I want to kill Liz Knowles and my own client?"

"Because of Lola," Jake said quietly.

"Lola?" Tadd asked, looking uncomfortable.

"We had an interesting talk with Lola Strickland's sister this morning in Somers," Jake said.

Tadd looked surprised. "Lola had a sister?"

"Half sister. Glenda Grimes. She told us she thinks the person who killed Lola also killed Dex."

"You're not accusing me?" Tadd laughed. I told you what happened. I got out of the boat to look around and fell. Fortunately I wasn't far from the boat and could get to the hospital. I had the doctor call as soon as I could."

"Lola's sister told us something else interesting," Jake said. "The night Lola died she thought she was running off with some man she'd fallen in love with."

"No kidding," Tadd said.

"Were you that man?" Jake asked.

"You aren't serious. I was engaged to marry a senator's daughter. Why would I run off with Lola?"

"Because you were in love with her," Clancy said as she reached into her pocket and pulled out the photograph Glenda had given them. She handed it to Tadd.

He took it with obvious reluctance and stared down at it for a long moment. "Where did you get this?"

"From a box of special mementos that Lola left at Glenda Grimes's house. This was in the box along with numerous cards from her Teddy Bear."

He looked up and seemed surprised at their expressions. "You think I'm Teddy Bear?" Tadd asked, sounding amazed.

"Isn't your real name Theodore?" Jake asked.

Tadd groaned. "I've never been called Teddy in my life. I certainly wouldn't call myself Teddy Bear."

"We think the man who wrote the cards is the same one Lola planned to run off with," Clancy told him.

Tadd laughed. "You've got the wrong man."

"But you did have an affair with her," Jake said.

Tadd let out a groan. He met Jake's gaze. "Okay, I had an affair with her. But it was just that, a brief affair. When she threatened to go to my fiancée, I bailed out."

"But you never married the senator's daughter," Clancy pointed out.

Tadd nodded. "When I broke it off with Lola, she went to the senator. Not only did Suzanne drop me like a hot rock, it set my political career back a good ten years."

"What did you do about it?" Jake asked.

Tadd laughed. "It was too late to do anything. I'd lost Suzanne and the senator. By then, Lola had already moved on to her next victim. Lola didn't go long without a man," he said bitterly. "I got over it." He looked up and must have seen their skepticism. "Come on, you don't really believe I was Teddy Bear. I'm a lawyer. I'd never put anything in writing."

Jake didn't want to, but he believed him. He'd also compared the handwriting on the back of the business card Tadd had given him with the note on the Teddy Bear card. The handwriting wasn't even close.

"Any guesses who this Teddy Bear might have been?" Jake asked.

Tadd shook his head. "I'll tell you who used to have it bad for Lola. Frank Ames. He was always hanging around her like a lost puppy." He turned his gaze on Clancy. "Well, are you going to fire me?"

"You have more reason than any other attorney to keep me out of prison. The upcoming election and Aunt Kiki's money. That's good enough motivation for me."

"I've been doing some research on sleep disorders," Tadd said. "Did you know that severe stress or some type of trauma often triggers sleepwalking?"

"You mean like being arrested for murder?" Clancy asked sarcastically.

"I was thinking more like Dex Westfall showing up on the island," Tadd said.

"Or showing up at the lodge after he's dead?" Jake asked.

CLANCY WAITED UNTIL they reached the car and Jake started to pull away from the curb before she asked, "I've walked in my sleep again, haven't I?"

"Yes."

"Oh, my God." She buried her face in her hands for a moment. "What did I do? Where did I go?" When he didn't answer, she looked at him. "Why didn't you tell me?"

He shrugged.

"You thought I was faking it." She turned to look out the passenger-side window, a volatile mix of emotions making her want to strike out at him.

"I'm not sure where you went—somewhere on the beach," Jake said. "You had sand on your feet. And—"

She looked over at him, her pulse rate accelerating. "And what?"

"You had something in your fist. A tiny blue bead."

Clancy let out a groan. "You weren't going to tell me?"

"I haven't really had a chance."

"You could have said something when I told you about the necklace and my other sleepwalking episode when I came back with a bead."

Jake said nothing. But then, what could he have said in his defense?

"Don't you realize your lack of trust in me is hampering this investigation? Can't you, the professional P.I., see that?"

"I should have told you."

No kidding. "Just like you should have told me about the card you took from the box."

He reached into his pocket. "Here." He handed her the greeting card. "I was going to tell you."

"Sure you were." She opened the card, wondering if that were true. The card was like the others in Lola's junk box. Only this one had a sailboat on the cover with a man and a woman watching a sunset. They presumably were in love. Inside it read: Each day with you is a dream come true. It was signed: Your Teddy Bear. "Do you recognize the handwriting?" Clancy asked.

"It's not my father's, if that's what you're asking." His voice had an edge to it. He knew that was exactly what she was asking. "You want to talk about trust here?"

He was right. But it was that lack of trust between them that was breaking her heart.

Jake took the card from her and turned it over and returned it to her. Written on the back in an entirely different hand were the words: I have to talk to you. Meet me at the usual place. Frank.

Clancy looked up at Jake. "Frank and Lola?"

"Lola seems to have been a busy woman. Makes you wonder, doesn't it? I'd like to pay Frank a visit. What do you think?"

"Why not?"

CLANCY COULD FEEL the weight of the few days' events on her sore and aching body as they parked the car at the marina and went by boat to the island resort. She wanted this case over with as quickly as possible so Jake could go home to Texas. Being around him wore down her heart. She told herself it would be easier not to see him. Not to be near him. Not to hear his voice. Not to know he was just down the hall.

Frank wasn't in his cabin. He didn't come to the door when Jake knocked and the door was locked.

"He's not home" came a male voice from the darkness.

Clancy recognized the youth as the dock boy she'd seen working the day before. "Do you know where he is?" she asked.

The boy shrugged. "He left earlier by foot." He pointed to the mountain.

Frank didn't seem like the hiking kind.

"You didn't happen to be around the night Dex Westfall was murdered?" Jake asked.

The boy looked up, surprise in his expression.

"I was wondering if Dex might have taken a boat out that night."

He shook his head. "The only time Mr. Westfall left the island was that first day. He rented a boat."

Jake looked disappointed. He thanked the boy and they started back down the trail.

"Mr. Westfall did have a visitor who came by boat the night he died, though," the boy added from behind them. "A woman."

Clancy stopped and turned slowly. "Can you describe this woman?"

The boy smiled. "Oh, yes." He proceeded to describe her in detail.

Clancy shot a shocked look at Jake.

Jake swore. "Kiki." He turned to the boy. "About what time was this?"

He shook his head. "It was late, well after dark. She went up to Mr. Westfall's cabin. I didn't see her leave."

"Did you tell the sheriff this?" Clancy asked.

The boy shook his head. "No one ever asked me. I figured it wasn't important."

Jake thanked him again. They walked back to their boat. "Kiki?" Jake exclaimed the moment they were out of earshot. "Had your aunt ever met Dex?"

"Not that I was aware of." She bit her lower lip, feeling sick. "You don't think she—"

"Is somehow involved in his death?" Jake asked. "No, but I've thought from the very beginning that Kiki knew a lot more about this than she told either of us."

JAKE DOCKED THE BOAT in front of Kiki's rented condo in Bigfork. The condo hung over the water, a huge monument to commercial development. Clancy didn't wait for him to tie up the boat. She jumped out, charged up to her aunt's door and pressed the doorbell.

Kiki opened the door in a caftan with a champagne-colored poodle under her arm and what smelled like a banana daiquiri in her hand. "What a nice surprise," she said.

"You might not feel that way when you find out why we're here," Clancy said.

Kiki raised a finely sculpted brow as Clancy stepped past her. "Can I offer you something to drink, dear?"

"I'd love something to drink," Jake said from behind her, although Clancy noted Kiki hadn't offered him one.

Jake closed the door, then he and Kiki followed Clancy into the living room.

Clancy spun around to face her aunt. "What were you doing on the island the night of Dex's murder?"

"I'll fix that drink myself," Jake said to Kiki, and headed for the wet bar.

Kiki set the poodle down. It was the only color in the room. Everything else was white. Even the marble fireplace was white.

"Visiting Dex Westfall," Kiki said, and took a sip of her drink.

"Where's the ice?" Jake called from the bar.

"In the bucket," Kiki called back, her voice sounding a little strained.

"I didn't even know you knew Dex!" Clancy cried.

"I made his acquaintance shortly after the two of you met," Kiki said, walking over to sit in one of the large white chairs in front of the fireplace. "I offered to pay him not to see you anymore. Are you sure you wouldn't like something to drink?"

Clancy gasped. "You tried to buy him off?" Her aunt had always interfered in her life, offering unwanted advice, but this was way beyond that.

"What was I to do?" Kiki asked, nonplussed. "He wasn't the right man for you."

"Did he take the money?" Jake asked from the bar.

"No," Kiki said in disgust. "He said he deserved much more and he intended to get it."

"Aunt Kiki, I can't believe you'd do such a thing," Clancy said. "What else did you do?"

"If you're asking if I killed him, of course not," Kiki said. "But I can't say I'm sorry he's dead. He was a deplorable man."

"If he refused your money the first time, why did you go to the island to see him?" Jake asked as he joined them. He handed Clancy a glass of brandy she hadn't asked for and went to sit across from Kiki.

"To offer him more money," Kiki stated flatly. "I knew he had a price, I just had to find it."

Clancy rolled her eyes. Life was so simple for her aunt as long as she could solve her problems with money. While she almost appreciated Kiki's efforts, she resented her aunt's continued attempts to control her life. Had always resented it.

"Dex didn't take it?" Clancy knew no large quantity of money had been found in Dex's cabin or on his body. Although, she was surprised that Dex hadn't taken her aunt up on the offer.

"The opportunity didn't present itself," Kiki said with a sigh. "I caught him with some woman and did the next best thing."

"Let me guess," Jake said. "Blackmail."

Clancy glanced over at him, keyed to the way he'd said "blackmail." Was that how Kiki had gotten Jake to Montana? She felt sick.

"While blackmail is always a possibility," Kiki said, smiling at him, "it really wasn't necessary. He was planning to leave the island that night, anyway."

"But he didn't," Jake pointed out.

Kiki shot him a dour look. "Something must have kept him from it. Someone. He told me his business on the island was finished. He seemed quite pleased about leaving."

"Who was the woman?" Jake asked.

Kiki shrugged. "I never saw her, but I smelled her perfume. It was expensive."

"Did he look like you'd interrupted something?" Jake asked.

"He was clothed, if that's what you're asking," Kiki replied primly. "But yes, now that I think about it, I did see him kick something under the bed. A pair of white Jockey shorts, I believe."

Kiki didn't miss a thing, Clancy thought, and took a sip of the brandy. It burned all the way down. She took another.

"I was astounded to hear the next morning that he'd been murdered," Kiki continued. "Even more appalled to learn the sheriff thought Clancy had killed him."

Clancy drained her glass and stared dumbfounded at her

aunt. "What do you do when you can't buy what you want or blackmail someone to get your way?"

Kiki studied her niece for a moment. "The problem's never come up." She glanced pointedly at Jake. "But I could see how it might."

He finished his drink and got up to take Clancy's empty glass from her fingers. "You ready to go?" he asked her.

"Yes." She marched to the door, opened it and stopped to look back at her aunt. "One of these days you're going to go too far. Maybe you already have."

Jake tipped his baseball cap at Kiki on the way out. He didn't say anything until he and Clancy reached the boat. "She's something, isn't she?" he said, and laughed.

"It's not funny, Jake."

"Oh, come on. It's her way of trying to protect you. As strange and twisted as it is. And you have to admit, her instincts about Dex were right."

Clancy spun on him. "How can you defend her?" She narrowed her gaze at him. "How did she get you up here, anyway? Money? Or blackmail?"

"Money?" He sounded insulted.

She studied him for a moment, remembering that she'd heard his father was coming up for parole soon. "If not money, then it had to be blackmail. Initially."

He tried to look insulted, but she knew her instincts had been right. "What makes you think I didn't come up here because I wanted to?" Jake demanded.

Clancy glared at him. "I remember how mad you were that first night when you had to save me from drowning. Then, when you realized you could get revenge—"

"Hey." He grabbed her and spun her into his chest. "You're wrong. Maybe at first. But surely you realize it isn't like that anymore."

"Isn't it?" she asked, looking into those gray eyes. The lights from the marina came on, making them gleam a slick silver. She felt the strength of his grip on her arm as he pulled her to him. For a moment, she thought he'd kiss her.

Hoped he would forget his promise. Hoped he'd take her in his arms and tell her he believed her.

With an oath, he let go of her and climbed into the boat without another word.

Clancy said little on the boat ride back to the island.

"I need to do some work," she said the moment they walked into the lodge. Jake watched her disappear up the stairs to her studio, kicking himself.

He couldn't stand the wall between them. But at the same time, he seemed incapable of tearing it down. He cursed himself and went to his room just down the hall from Clancy's studio. He dumped the envelope of evidence in the middle of his bed. He had to find out who killed Dex and keep Clancy from going to prison. Maybe, if he got lucky, he'd also find Lola's killer. For his father. For his own sanity. But he wondered if by then it would be too late for him and Clancy.

He picked up the cellular phone and called Tadd.

"I need to know if Frank Ames inherited a bunch of money. Or maybe won the lottery. I need to know how he bought Hawk Island Resort. Now."

"Tonight?" Tadd croaked.

"Tomorrow would be fine," Jake said.

"I'll put my secretary on it at daybreak."

After Jake hung up, he felt restless. The lodge seemed uncommonly quiet, the summer night almost too still. He didn't want Clancy to think he was checking up on her. But he couldn't help himself. He couldn't get her off his mind any more than he could forget the feel of her in his arms. Or her steadfast conviction that she hadn't perjured herself, hadn't lied about his father.

Quietly, he sneaked down the hall. Clancy's studio was a second-floor addition that overlooked the bay. It had been a surprise birthday present from her father for her fifteenth birthday. Johnny Branson, who'd been a carpenter back then, had built it. That was before he ran for sheriff.

Jake heard music filtering through the open doorway. He

stopped. Classical? He and Clancy had grown up on country music. The long-haired stuff coming off her stereo only reminded him of how much had changed between them. He was wondering if she ever listened to country anymore when the song ended and another came on. A Don Williams tune. One he used to know all the words to. He smiled to himself. Maybe things hadn't changed that much.

The actual studio was a large room with a bank of windows on three sides to catch the light. As Jake peeked in, he remembered the times he'd come here, moving quietly, hoping not to disturb her. He remembered how seriously she'd taken her sculpture. That's one reason he'd loved to watch her work.

Now he stood at the edge of the doorway, just looking at her. Watching the way her fingers molded the mound of clay on the table in front of her. She pinched, prodded, slicked and smoothed. Her fingers strong, her movements precise. He studied her face, not surprised by the intensity of her expression. Clancy had been fourteen the summer she confessed to Jake she wanted to be an artist. She'd felt it was a frivolous desire. How many artists actually made a living with their work?

But Jake and her parents had encouraged her. And surprisingly, so had her aunt Kiki. Kiki saw to it that Clancy got her first sculpting lessons. Jake could still remember Clancy's first work. It was crude but showed potential, her art teachers had said. Hell, one of her first pieces was a part of the breakwater at his beach house in Galveston, he thought with a curse.

Clancy frowned now as she stepped back to inspect her latest creation. She wore her glasses instead of her contacts. He liked them on her. They made her look even more sexy, if that was possible. The frown deepened as if she wasn't quite satisfied with it. That would be the perfectionist in her. She stepped forward again and began to reshape and resculpt, working quickly, meticulously, totally immersed in the clay and the vision inside her head, totally oblivious to everything else. Including him.

So intent on studying her, Jake hadn't even noticed the sculpture she'd been so engrossed in until she suddenly pushed it back to inspect it again. The back of it faced him. A bust of a man's head.

She gave the sculpture a turn. It slowly revolved around on the lazy susan. Jake caught his breath as he saw the face she'd molded into the clay. The likeness was so striking it shocked him.

It was *his* face in the clay. Younger. His nose straighter than he remembered it. His face far more handsome than he'd ever been. But he could see the resemblance to the boy who'd grown up on this lake with Clancy.

It unnerved him, reminding him too much of the past and the way things had been between them.

He stepped back into the hallway, pressing against the wall. Emotions surged through him, waves that threatened to wash away everything he'd believed, everything he'd held on to for ten years, everything he'd let go of ten years ago. What if he'd been wrong?

He thought about the sculpture, the man she'd somehow captured in the clay. He felt moved and, at the same time, torn.

He sneaked back to his room. Clancy's phone rang. He heard her pick it up. He listened to her tell Helen about Lola's half sister. From the conversation, it seemed Helen didn't know about Glenda Grimes, either.

He turned his attention back to the evidence on the Westfall case. The answer was here, somewhere, and damned if he wasn't going to find it.

JAKE SIFTED THROUGH the pile of papers again, his head aching from lack of sleep and the craziness of this case. At some point, he could always feel the pieces start to fall into place. There'd be that rush as he started to see glimpses of a pattern. But not in this one.

He pushed back the papers and stretched, surprised, when he glanced at his watch, at how much time had gone by. Surely by now Clancy had gone to bed. But he hadn't heard her.

He walked down the hallway. Her door stood open. He peeked in. The covers were thrown back on her bed. Her shoes were by it on the floor. But her room was empty.

This time, he made noise as he went down to her studio. But when he rounded the corner, she wasn't sitting at her worktable. The sculpture of him wasn't on the table anymore, but a large mound of battered-looking clay sat in its place. His face was long gone. And so was Clancy.

Panic rocketed through him. "Clancy?" He raced down the stairs, calling her name as he went. "Clancy?"

The kitchen door stood open. He charged outside, wondering how much of a head start she had on him.

That's when he saw her. She looked ghostlike walking down the beach, her long white nightgown billowing around her bare ankles. He went after her, telling himself she was fine. But he couldn't throw off the bad feeling.

He'd almost reached her when she suddenly stopped and, in slow motion, bent to pick up a small piece of driftwood in her path. An icy chill shot up his spine as she started walking again, the driftwood dangling from the fingers of her left hand, forgotten.

He felt a stab of shock as he caught up with her and looked into her blank face, the face of a sleepwalker.

"Clancy?" She moved along on some agenda, programmed like a robot. The only problem was that the program was often flawed, senseless. Or was it? Was Clancy headed somewhere she really wanted to go? But she was headed for the end of the island and the cliffs.

"It's time to go to bed." He touched her arm. Hadn't he read that you shouldn't wake a person who's walking in her sleep?

But she didn't wake. Nor did she fight him. He turned her toward the lodge, then trailed along beside her. Almost home, something must have clicked, some kind of wake-up call. She blinked. "Where—"

"I'm here," Jake said quickly.

She turned in surprise to see him there. Tears flooded her eyes. "I did it again," she whispered. "Where did I go?"

"Just down to the beach. I saw you and brought you back."

She looked down, startled to find the piece of driftwood in her hand, and dropped it quickly as if it were a poisonous snake. She began to shake.

Jake swept her into his arms and carried her inside the lodge and up to her bed. He sat beside her, holding her hand until she fell asleep again.

He took the chair, positioned it in front of the door, and made himself as comfortable as possible. It was going to be a long night.

Chapter Sixteen

Thursday morning, Jake woke to the ringing of a phone. He hurried down the hall to his room and picked up the cell phone. "Yeah?" He could hear a television in the background.

"No inheritance. No lottery," Tadd said, sounding as sleepy as Jake felt. "No bank loans. Frank Ames couldn't have bought a candy bar with his earning power before he purchased the resort."

"Then, how did he?" Jake asked, starting to wake up.

"Good question," Tadd said. "As long as he put the money down as income on his tax returns, he's legal and there's no way we can track it. Hold on." Jake heard Tadd turn up the volume on the TV. "Lola's sister lives in Somers right? Glenda Grimes?"

"Why?" Jake asked, afraid he wasn't going to like the answer.

"Her house is on fire and her neighbors think she's inside."

Jake hung up and raced down the stairs to turn on the television in the living room. Glenda Grimes's home was nothing but a ball of flames.

"What is it?" Clancy asked from the stairs. She still had on her nightgown, her expression worried and afraid. Not as worried and afraid as Jake was for her at this moment.

"Glenda Grimes," Jake said, turning off the TV. "She didn't make it to Vegas."

CLANCY STOOD IN the hot shower, letting the water pound her skin. Desperately she tried not to think about Glenda. Had Jake been right? Had Glenda known more than she'd told them? Well, her secret had died with her.

Clancy shifted her thoughts to something more pleasant. Jake. Knowing he was just outside the door gave her a sense of security and well-being. She'd seen her own fears mirrored in his face. Was she next?

When she reached for the soap, Clancy had a quick flash of her shower with Jake. Her skin tingled, and that ache low in her belly almost brought her to her knees. Having him right outside the door made her more aware of her naked body. Having once had it, she now ached for Jake's touch. She remembered his fingertips on her skin. His mouth. His tongue. The weight of his body on hers. She groaned.

"Clancy?" Jake asked on the other side of the door, his voice full of concern. "Are you all right?"

"Fine!" she called back quickly, and turned up the cold water. Well, he wasn't going to make love to her until she asked, and she couldn't ask until he believed that she wasn't a liar and a murderer. The way things were going she would never know the feel of him again.

When she came out of the shower wrapped in her modest robe, she heard Jake on the phone. He hung up when he saw her. "What is it?" she asked.

"I just talked to the sheriff's department."

"Arson?"

Jake nodded. "And deliberate homicide. Glenda was inside. She'd been bludgeoned to death before the fire was started."

Just like Lola. Clancy clutched the front of her robe, the look in Jake's eyes making her more afraid.

"We've got to find this guy, Clancy. And soon."

Clancy couldn't agree more. "How would you suggest we do that?"

He hesitated. "Helen was close to Lola. Didn't you say they were involved in summer theater together?"

Clancy nodded. "You think Lola might have confided in Helen about this mystery lover of hers?"

"Maybe." He rubbed a hand over his stubbled jaw. His hair hung over his forehead. He looked as though he hadn't gotten a lot of sleep last night.

Clancy felt a twinge of guilt for that, but had to admit Jake Hawkins had never looked more handsome to her.

"Even if Lola never told her, Helen still might recognize something in Lola's keepsakes that at least would give us a lead," he said, and stopped. "What are you smiling about?"

Clancy quickly looked away. "I was just thinking that I could make us some breakfast while you—"

"Do I look that bad?" Jake asked.

She shook her head. "You look—" Sexy. Seductive. Wonderful. "Fine."

He grinned. "I won't take but a minute. Promise me you'll be here when I get back."

Clancy had to laugh. "I promise." There was no place she wanted to be more than with Jake, she thought with a curse.

Jake was as good as his word. He was back by the time she had the eggs and toast ready. He'd showered, shaved and changed into a shirt and chinos. He looked good enough to eat.

"Not bad," she said, sliding a plate of food in front of him. As she sat across from him and picked up her fork, she realized her sudden hunger had nothing at all to do with food.

"WE'RE GOING ON the assumption that Teddy Bear killed Lola, right?" Clancy asked as they took her boat to the Bransons'. "And he's still killing to keep his secret?"

The lake's surface mirrored the clear, sunny sky overhead. The air smelled fresh and clean. In the distance, she
could hear a boat's motor running.

"Because he's never come forward, I think that's a pretty
good assumption," Jake said. "Or he knows who did. I'm
not sure how Frank Ames fits into all of this. I talked to
Tadd this morning. No one knows where Frank got the
money to buy the resort."

"You think it's the missing money?" Clancy asked.

"Maybe," Jake said. "If it is, then Frank had to have
someone on the inside embezzling it for him."

"Lola." Clancy looked up at the cliffs as they rounded
the end of the island. The Bransons' place sat on the highest
bluff, with the elevator Johnny had put in for Helen running
from the dock up to the house. There were also wooden
stairs that switchbacked up the face of the cliff.

"Clancy, could you see Frank Ames as Teddy Bear?"
Jake asked.

Clancy laughed. "Not hardly. But maybe Lola did. Frank
would have been a lot younger. From what Tadd said,
Frank had a huge crush on her."

"Yeah, it sounds like she enjoyed attention," Jake
agreed.

"Maybe she encouraged that attention," Clancy said.

"That's what I was thinking," Jake said as he pulled
alongside the Bransons' dock. "Especially if Frank could
be useful to her."

"Like helping her hide the embezzled money?"

Jake looked over at Clancy. "Yeah. Then maybe he got
greedy. More than likely he found out she was seeing other
men. I mean, Frank's note to Lola is on the back of one of
the cards. Frank could have decided to get rid of Lola and
keep the money for himself."

Clancy tried to imagine Frank's face behind the motorbike helmet, in the water off the end of the dock as he
dragged her under, beneath the sweatshirt hood as he ran

out of her lodge. But all she could see was Dex Strickland's.

Jake closed the door on the cagelike elevator and pushed the button. It lurched with a noisy groan and began to climb. He'd been disappointed to note that Johnny's boat wasn't tied at the dock. Jake had hoped Johnny would be here.

The elevator grumbled to a jerky stop. Jake opened the door and Clancy stepped out.

"I've always wondered why Johnny would build up here, especially with Helen's handicap," Clancy said quietly.

"You have to admit, it's an amazing view," Jake said, joining her at the railing. "And it's isolated. I get the impression that since the accident they pretty much keep to themselves."

Jake stood on the top deck. He couldn't help but admire the Bransons' house. Johnny had always been a master carpenter, but he'd outdone himself on this place.

It was built on three levels, all connected by ramps in such a way that they didn't call attention to Helen's handicap. Along the side of the house were three decks set at the same levels as the house, also with ramps. It gave the place a spacious feel. Each deck had a view, but the top deck, where he and Clancy stood now, was the most panoramic.

They found Helen in the pool on the second deck, swimming laps.

"Sorry, I didn't hear you come up," she said from the side of the pool. "I force myself to get exercise every day, and today was so beautiful—"

"Don't let us keep you from it," Clancy said.

"No, actually, I was just finishing," she said, hoisting herself up onto a step.

"Here, let me help you," Clancy said.

"No." Helen smiled to soften her words. "I have to do it myself. I refuse to be an invalid."

"You look great," Clancy said as Helen lifted herself into the wheelchair, making it look effortless.

"So what are you up to this morning?" Helen asked, pulling a white robe around her shoulders.

"We brought something we'd like you to look at," Jake said, indicating the small shoe box under his arm.

"Come on in," Helen said. "I think Johnny put some coffee on before he left."

They followed her into the living room, which opened up into the kitchen to the left and what looked like bedrooms off to the right. It had that same open, airy feeling inside as it had out. A two-way radio near a large window squawked as they went past.

"Where's Johnny?" Jake asked. "Fishing?"

"No, he had a doctor's appointment," Helen said on her way to the kitchen. "He hasn't been feeling well lately."

Jake saw that Clancy had stopped in front of a glass cabinet filled with trophies. He joined her, noticing a photograph of a smiling Helen beside a balance beam.

"Gymnastics. It was my first love," Helen said from the kitchen. "Then I got into theater and met Johnny and found my true love."

Clancy followed Helen into the kitchen. "You and Johnny both were actors?"

Helen laughed and shook her head. "Johnny on stage? No, he built sets. That's how we met. I'd seen him around at school, but he was so shy. So I joined the drama club, hoping he might notice me. I liked acting, but found helping with the costumes and makeup put me closer to Johnny. The rest is history, as they say."

Helen poured them both a cup of coffee. "Sit down," she said, motioning to the table set against the big bay windows.

"I've been so worried about you," Helen said to Clancy. "Have they got any closer to finding out who killed Dex Strickland?"

Clancy shook her head. "That's why we're hoping you

might recognize something in the box. It contains Lola's things.''

Helen looked surprised. ''Lola's? I thought all of her belongings burned in the fire.''

''Not everything burned,'' Jake said. ''Some things were saved from the fire, the rest were in this box of…keepsakes that Lola left with her sister before her death.''

''This half sister you told me about who lives in Somers?'' Helen poured herself a cup of coffee before joining them at the table. ''A son and a half sister we knew nothing about. I sometimes wonder if I knew Lola at all.''

''Her sister died in a fire early this morning,'' Clancy said.

''I saw something on the news, but I had no idea that it was Lola's sister,'' Helen said. ''Oh, how awful. What was her name, Linda Grimes?''

''Glenda,'' Clancy corrected her. ''She told us yesterday that Dex had figured out who killed his mother. We think that person murdered Dex because of that.''

''And probably Glenda,'' Jake added.

Helen looked shocked. ''You mean, you don't think the fire was an accident?''

''No,'' Jake said.

''Well, I'll try to help in any way I can,'' Helen said.

Jake pushed the box over to her and watched as Helen riffled through the items.

She frowned. ''Why would Lola's sister have hung on to this for all these years? It doesn't seem to contain anything…important.'' She picked up one of the cards. ''Teddy Bear?''

''Do you have any idea who that might have been?'' Clancy asked. ''Glenda seemed to think that he was the man Lola planned to run off with the night she was killed.''

''I knew she was leaving the island, but she planned to run off with some man?'' Helen asked, sounding surprised. ''That is certainly news to me. Lola seemed to date a lot of men, but none for very long.''

"Glenda thought Lola had embezzled the money from the resort. This man might have been someone who helped her."

"Lola?" Helen shook her head, her look full of sympathy as she shifted her gaze to Jake. "I know how badly you want to clear your father's name, but that just doesn't sound like the Lola I knew. Did this Glenda person have proof of any of this?"

Jake stared into his coffee cup, his mood as dark as Helen's coffee. "No. That's why I was hoping you might recognize something in the box. If we could figure out who the man was—"

"I'm sorry, Jake," Helen said. "Lola never mentioned him to me, and you'd think she would have."

"For some reason she kept him a secret," Clancy said.

"You're sure she didn't...dream him up?" Helen asked. "I mean, Lola loved acting, playing different roles. It suited her. She didn't seem happy with real life. Never satisfied with what she had, whether it was a man or a job. That's why she told me she was leaving the island. She said she needed a change." Helen took a sip of coffee. "No, if her 'Teddy Bear' existed, he wouldn't have stayed with her long. It's a shame. She was a very beautiful woman, but so...needy and dependent. That puts a lot of men off."

THE SUN HUNG HIGH in Montana's big sky as Clancy and Jake headed back to the lodge. Clancy couldn't help thinking about Helen's last remark and how lucky Helen was to have a man like Johnny. Clancy doubted Johnny could have loved her more. Just seeing that kind of love made Clancy ache inside for what she and Jake had had.

Jake said little on the boat ride back, and Clancy knew he'd hoped Helen would provide one of the missing clues. Finding the elusive Teddy Bear was proving much more difficult than Clancy had hoped. She wondered if maybe Helen was right; maybe Lola had made the man up. Hadn't even Glenda said he sounded too good to be true?

Jake brought the boat into the dock and Clancy jumped out to tie it up. She could feel Jake's frustration. It matched her own. They were no closer to finding out who had killed Dex Westfall, and her trial was coming up quickly. Without some sort of new evidence—

As Clancy bent down to secure the stern of the boat, she noticed something shiny in the water beyond the dock.

"Jake?" she said.

He joined her and squatted to look into the clear green water. "I'll take a look." He stripped off his shirt, then slipped out of his Top-Siders and reached for the zipper on his chinos.

"I'm going in with you," Clancy said, pulling her shirt over her head.

Jake stopped undressing. "You sure that's a good idea?" he asked, raising a brow. "You wouldn't purposely try to get me to break my promise?"

She mugged a face at him, slipped out of her skirt and sandals, down to her bra and panties, and dove into the water. It felt cold after the hot sun and the heat of Jake's gaze. Was that exactly what she was doing? Trying to get him to break his promise?

Jake did a shallow dive and came up next to her. They dog-paddled for a few moments just looking at each other, neither touching. His bare shoulders glistened, slick with water. They were so close she could feel his legs churning the water in front of her. It brushed her thighs, sparking a need to feel his skin against hers again. Desire flashed in his eyes as bright as the summer sun overhead. In that instant, the water no longer felt cold. Her skin ached, hot and sensitive to his gaze.

He groaned and dove into the water. She followed. Jake reached the bottom first, scooping the object into his hand. He looked over at Clancy and gave her a thumbs-up.

They burst to the surface almost in unison. Clancy watched as Jake inspected the object in his hand, then passed it to her. She stared at the silver watch for a moment, then up at Jake.

"Just as you described it," he said. "A flash of silver."

Proof that someone had tried to drown her that night. She smiled in relief and swam to the dock, hoisting herself up. Sitting on the edge of the dock, she turned the watch over in her hand. She heard Jake dive under the water and saw that he'd disappeared from sight. She looked down at the watch; something on the back caught her eye. Lettering. An inscription. She read the words in shock. Then realized Jake hadn't surfaced yet.

Getting to her feet, she stared into the clear water but couldn't see him. Where had he gone? She clutched the watch and waited for him to reappear, suddenly worried. How long could he stay under?

Just when she was about to dive in to search for him, he reappeared beside the dock.

"You scared me," she admonished.

He grinned up at her, his eyelashes jeweled with water droplets. "Sorry. I think I know where your attacker disappeared to that night." He pointed to the dock beneath her. "There're large air pockets under here between the flotations where he could have waited until we were gone."

Jake lifted himself onto the dock beside her, making her uncomfortably aware of how little they had on and just how wet and body-conforming their clothing was. She could feel Jake's gaze caress her, traveling across bare, wet skin to what was no longer hidden beneath her underwear. The air stilled around them. Time stopped.

"Dammit, Clancy, you can't do this to me."

"Do what?" she asked innocently.

He threw himself back into the water. She reached down and grabbed his hair, gently pulling him to the surface. She handed him the watch. "It's inscribed."

It seemed to take him a moment to drag his gaze from her to the watch. He flipped it over. "To Frank, love Lola," he read. His gaze flew up to Clancy's. "You have to be kidding."

JAKE CALLED TADD with the news about the watch.

"Even with the watch and the motorbike, I'm not sure the sheriff has enough to hold Frank," Tadd said. "It would help if we had something more tangible."

Jake agreed. "Clancy and I will go over the evidence. Maybe there's something we've missed."

After he hung up, Jake dumped everything he'd collected on the Dex Strickland murder case in the middle of the kitchen table. But his attention was on Clancy. He felt a pull toward her stronger than the gravity on Jupiter.

"Where do we begin?" She leaned toward him.

He could smell her scent. It brought a rush of memory—the feel of her skin, the sound of her voice as she pressed her body to his, the look in her eyes as they made love. Damned if he couldn't still see her on the dock, wet and in that skimpy underwear. Why had he made such a foolish promise?

"Here's Dex's autopsy report," he said, trying to concentrate on the report. "This is interesting. Dex was struck from the right. That would indicate he was hit by a right-handed person."

"I'm left-handed, and the sculpture was in my left hand when I woke up. But that really doesn't prove anything, does it?"

"It helps," Jake said, flipping through the report. "If we have to go to trial, everything that puts doubt into the jurors' minds will help."

Clancy picked up a stack of photocopies of all the newspaper clippings, photos and other materials Dex had tacked to his closet wall. He saw her shudder as she sorted through them, quickly passing over an old play program from the summer Lola died. Jake recognized it. It was the play he'd taken her to the night he told her how much he loved her and that he wanted to marry her.

"You don't have to do this if you don't want to," he said. But she didn't seem to be listening.

"Look at this," she said, stepping over so he could see. It was a newspaper article. The headline read Local Woman Injured in Wreck Near Angel Point. Jake saw that it was an article about Helen Branson. The subhead read Sheriff's Wife Critical After High-Speed Rollover.

Jake read over Clancy's shoulder. Johnny Branson was driving at a high rate of speed when he lost control and rolled down an embankment. Helen was thrown from the car. She was listed in critical condition at the local hospital. Johnny was uninjured.

"It's dated the night of the resort fire," Clancy said in surprise.

The night Lola was murdered. Jake scanned the story again for the time of the accident. "It would have been just hours after the fire and Lola's murder."

Clancy looked up at him. "Dex had this tacked on his closet wall, too?"

"Johnny was the sheriff, and it was the same night as Dex's mother's death."

Clancy moved away from the table to look out into the night. "Johnny was driving the car," she said. "I didn't know that. How awful for him to know that he was responsible for Helen being in a wheelchair for the rest of her life. Why was he going so fast on that road, I wonder?"

"And what were they doing on Angel Point that time of the morning?" Jake said.

Clancy shook her head. "He was probably upset after what had happened at the resort, having to arrest one of his best friends. I guess I never realized how many lives were affected by what happened that night."

"Neither did I." Jake got up to take his empty cup to the sink. He'd been so filled with anger for so many years. He hadn't even thought about the other people who'd lost something that night. He leaned over the sink for a moment. Like Clancy. She'd lost her family first to Alaska, then to a plane crash. Her pain had been amplified by him walking out on her. And he'd spent the last ten years in his own kind of sleepwalking. Pretending he could forget about her.

He glanced over at her, remembering the way she'd looked last night on the beach. Her eyes open. Her expression glazed. Picking up that piece of driftwood in her path and not even realizing what it was.

He felt goose bumps on his arms as a chilling thought whipped past. Had she picked up that driftwood the same way she'd picked up the murder weapon the night Dex was killed? He remembered what he'd read about the total amnesia sleepwalkers experienced from the time of falling asleep until waking. The confusion on waking.

"Clancy," he said, excited by how right this felt. "Last night on the beach when you were sleepwalking, you picked up a piece of driftwood in your path. What if that's exactly what you did the night Dex died? If that's how you ended up with the murder weapon in your hand?"

Clancy stared at him.

"Don't you see? You must have heard someone upstairs. Still asleep, you walked up there. The murder weapon was in the middle of the floor. You picked it up and went to the balcony." Jake shuddered. "The killer must still have been in the room. Clancy, that's it. You must have seen him. That's why he's after you now."

"But I can never remember anything about my sleep-walking episodes."

"The killer wouldn't know that," he pointed out. "He may be afraid that you'll remember." The thought came out of left field, fast and hard. "Oh, my God. Clancy, if I'm right and the same person killed Lola and Dex, you might have seen him *both* times." Jake slapped a hand to his forehead. "You could have seen him the night of Lola's murder when you were sleepwalking. God, Clancy, that could be what woke you up."

"And he waited ten years to come after me?" Clancy asked in disbelief.

"No, he felt safe. Then Dex turns up, asking questions, maybe even actually knowing who the killer is. Dex could have tried to extort money from him. Or maybe just threatened to go to the cops. Remember what Kiki said about Dex being in a good mood and saying his business on the island was completed and he was leaving?" Jake stood, pacing the floor, excited by the way the pieces seemed to fit. "He thought he was getting money. And somehow the killer got him to go to your garret, then killed him and set you up."

Jake pulled off his cap and raked his fingers through his hair. "And you played right into the killer's hands, picking up the murder weapon."

"Oh, Jake, is it possible?" Clancy cried. She got up to get them more coffee, excitement in her movements.

More than possible, he thought as he watched her, his heart so full of love for her that it felt as if it would explode. And she loved him. He believed that with all his heart. Then, how could he not believe everything else she'd told him?

"I know you didn't kill Dex Strickland," Jake said, feeling a rush of emotion as he knew something else in the only place it mattered. In his heart. "And I know you didn't perjure yourself at my father's trial."

She didn't turn. Her hand clamped down on the handle of the coffeepot as if she needed support.

"I believe you, Clancy," he said.

"But?" she asked, her back still to him.

"But I believe my father, too. There's an explanation for what you saw that night, because I know in my heart that you didn't lie."

She turned slowly, her eyes welling with tears as she looked at him.

In two strides, he came around the table and pulled her into his arms. "Oh, Clancy," he breathed against her hair. "I love you," he said, thumbing the tears from her cheeks. "God, I would give anything to have never hurt you." He drew her closer. "I'm so sorry I didn't believe you. Can you ever forgive me?"

She drew back to look up into his face. "I love you, Jake. I've always loved you."

"I know." He held her to him tightly, promising himself he'd never let her go again.

"Kiss me, Jake. Please. Then make love to me."

He laughed softly. "I thought you'd never ask."

THEY MADE LOVE in front of the fireplace. Slowly. Gently. Touching each other as if for the first time. Lovers at long last.

Later Jake cooked steaks on the barbecue and they sat on the front deck watching the sunset. Jake felt a contentment he hadn't known in years. Not since he'd left Flathead and Clancy.

He sat holding her hand, watching the last of daylight disappear behind the mountains, when he heard a sound behind them.

"Did you hear that?" Clancy asked, turning to look back into the lodge. Jake's gaze leaped to the window behind them as Clancy let out a startled cry. A figure moved through the shadows of the unlit living room, headed for the back door.

"Stay here," Jake commanded without thinking. Had he had time to think, he would have asked her, pleaded with her, begged. Because commanding Clancy had always proved a mistake. But there wasn't time to beg. Jake wasn't about to let the intruder get away. Not again.

He circled around the side of the lodge just as the figure broke into a run down the beach. Jake tore after him, stretching his legs and lungs with everything he had in him, closing the distance.

The figure headed for a rental boat pulled up on the beach on the other side of Jake's lodge. Jake knew he had to reach him first.

The moon had just started up the backside of the Mission

Mountains. Dusk lay deep in the pines. Jake concentrated on only two things: the dark figure running up the beach and the shoe box tucked under the man's arm. The man raced for his life. It was a race Jake wasn't about to let him win.

Just before the thief reached the boat, Jake made a flying tackle. He caught the man by the lower legs and brought him down hard. Not hard enough, Jake thought, scrambling to his feet.

The man tried to get up. Jake put a boot toe into the man's ribs and flipped him over onto his back, noticing that he wore a dark hooded sweatshirt, the hood up, hiding his face. Next to him was a crushed shoe box. Some of Lola's keepsakes had tumbled out when he'd fallen.

Grabbing the scruff of the man's coat collar, Jake jerked him to his feet and, pulling down the hood of the sweatshirt, finally got a good look at his face. The man held no resemblance to Dex Strickland.

"Frank Ames." Jake swore and tightened his grip on the man's throat. "I ought to kill you right now with my bare hands."

Chapter Seventeen

Fear shone in Frank's eyes. "You wouldn't do that." He didn't look in the least bit convinced.

"Wanna bet?" Jake demanded. "You're the one who's been trying to kill Clancy."

Frank shook his head violently. "That's not true."

Jake shoved Frank down into the sand again. "Don't lie to me, Ames. I swear—"

"I'm telling you the truth," Frank cried, gasping for breath. "It wasn't me. Why would I want to kill Clancy?"

"That's what I want to know. We found your watch near the dock where you tried to drown her," Jake said, getting angrier by the minute.

"What watch?" Frank asked, almost sounding surprised.

"The one Lola gave you."

"Lola never gave me a watch."

Jake towered over him. "It was engraved. 'To Frank, love Lola.' Ring any bells?"

"I don't know what you're talking about."

"Are you also going to deny you were in the lodge tonight?" Jake demanded.

Frank swallowed and took a shaky breath. "Helen told me you had some of Lola's things in an old shoe box."

Jake wondered why Helen had told him that.

"I wanted to get my letters back."

"Your letters?" Jake asked. Frank couldn't be Teddy Bear.

"Personal letters."

"Love letters?" Jake demanded. "You sent Lola love letters? How did you sign them?"

Frank looked confused. It wasn't a new look for him. "I signed my name."

Not Teddy Bear.

"I want them back. They're mine."

Frank thought Lola had saved his letters? What would make him think that? Unless— "You're not trying to tell me that Lola responded to your sick fantasies."

That mean look Jake had seen many times before showed up on Frank's ugly face. He flushed with anger. "It wasn't like that. She cared about me. She talked to me when other people wouldn't. We were friends."

"Were you friends with Liz Knowles, too?" Jake demanded.

Frank frowned. "She was my waitress, that's all."

"How did she end up on your motorbike, then, Frank?"

"Maybe Liz was the one who stole it and chased your girlfriend. Did you ever think of that?"

"No." Jake figured Frank would finger anyone to save his own neck. "What possible motive would Liz have had?"

Frank shook his head. "I'm supposed to know that?"

"Look, Frank, I saw Liz on the back of your motorbike not long before her body was found in Paradise Cove," Jake told him. "Someone was driving that bike. I think it was you."

"Well, you're wrong."

Jake tried another tack. "I found a note you wrote Lola to meet you at the 'usual place.' Where was that?"

"It was just this little stand of pines," Frank mumbled. "She liked it there. Not that it's any of your business."

Jake had had about all he could stand. He moved toward Frank, determined to get the truth out of him. "Not that it's any of my business, but where did you get the money for the resort?''

Fear crossed Frank's face as he groped in the sand behind him. ''I don't have to tell you nothing,'' he said, coming up with a hefty chunk of driftwood. He scrambled to his feet, brandishing the weapon, then turned and made a run for it.

Jake would have gone after him but Clancy grabbed his arm.

''The sheriff's on his way,'' she said. ''Let him handle it.''

Chapter Eighteen

Jake hung up the phone and pulled Clancy into his arms. "Tadd just called to say the sheriff picked up Frank Ames at the airport this morning. He was trying to make a run for it."

Clancy buried her face in his shoulder. "Then it *was* Frank?"

"He hasn't confessed, but the deputies found a mask at his cabin, and last night he was wearing a dark hooded sweatshirt."

"Mask?" Clancy asked.

"It's the kind of thing they use in the movies," he told her. "It's eerie how much it looks like Dex Strickland," Tadd said.

She stared up at him. "Frank went to the trouble of having a mask made that looked like Dex Strickland just to scare me?"

Jake tightened his grip on her. "I don't think he did it to scare you. More than likely it was to trigger your sleepwalking. Tadd agrees with me that Frank had to have been in the garret that night and saw you sleepwalking. He couldn't chance that you'd remember seeing him, not again. Nor did he need another murder on his hands. So, by triggering your sleepwalking, he could make your death look like an accident."

"They're sure it was Frank?"

Jake had been a little surprised himself. Frank didn't seem smart—or patient enough—to use Clancy's sleepwalking to his benefit. "With the mask, the hooded sweatshirt and his watch that we found off the dock, Tadd thinks the county can make a pretty good case against him for attempted murder," Jake said. "Tadd's convinced they'll be able to tie him to Lola's murder and the others." He brushed a kiss into her hair. "Do you realize what this means? You're finally safe."

She hugged him tightly. "I was thinking more about what it will mean for your father, Jake."

"Yeah." Jake pulled back to look at her. "I'd like to tell him about this in person."

She nodded. "I really need to get back to work. I might still be able to make my art show in August."

Jake knew Clancy wanted to give him time alone with his father and he loved her for that. But it was hard to leave her, even with Frank locked up in jail. He thumbed her hair back from her forehead and planted a kiss between her eyes. "I'll be back before you know it." Jake didn't tell her he had one stop to make on his way to the prison.

AFTER JAKE LEFT, Clancy poured herself a cup of coffee and went out on the deck. The sun felt warm as she leaned against the railing to stare out across the lake. The water shimmered, gold. No breeze stirred the surface. Only an occasional boat made waves that lapped softly at the shoreline. Why did she feel so antsy? The killer was behind bars. Jake loved her.

She went back into the kitchen to pour herself another cup of coffee and wandered the lodge, trying to put a finger on what was bothering her. According to Jake's theory, Lola had embezzled the money with Frank's help, Frank had found out about Teddy Bear, taken the money, killed her and burned down the resort.

But how did Clancy explain what she'd seen that night, ten years ago, when she woke up on the docks? She saw

Warren Hawkins and Lola fighting and Warren push her. Jake had tried to blame it on the confusion she normally felt when she suddenly awakened in a strange place. That she hadn't really understood what she'd seen. Or had she?

She took a sip of the hot coffee and stared at the lilac bushes framing the window. Something didn't feel right. The other time Frank had come to the house, he wore a mask to make him resemble Dex Strickland. Why hadn't he last night?

Don't buy trouble, she told herself. All the evidence pointed at Frank Ames. Just as all the evidence in Dex's death had pointed to her, she reminded herself.

Not even the coffee could take away the sudden chill in the room. Clancy put down her cup. What was it that tugged at the back of her brain? The necklace. Why hadn't the rest of those tiny blue beads turned up? *Did it really matter,* she asked herself. Yes.

FRANK AMES LOOKED like a man who belonged behind bars, Jake thought as he watched the deputy bring the prisoner into the room.

"What the hell do you want?" Frank demanded when he was ushered into the small interrogation room. "You aren't going to leave me alone with this guy?" Frank asked the jailer who brought him in.

"You can always call a cop if you need one," Jake told Frank as the jailer went to stand just outside the door. "Okay, Frank, we're alone. Whatever you tell me will just be my word against yours. But I need to hear the whole story. Start with Lola and why you killed her."

Frank eyed Jake warily. "I've already told you. I loved Lola. I wouldn't have touched a hair on her head."

Jake took a seat at the far end of the table.

Frank seemed to relax a little. But he sat as far away from Jake as he could get.

"Come on, Frank," Jake cajoled. "Lola hurt you. She fell for someone else—and planned to leave the island and you to run off with him. I'll bet you wanted to kill him, too.''

"There wasn't any man," Frank said adamantly. "She flirted with guys sometimes. But it didn't mean anything. I was the only one who really cared about her and she knew that.''

It was all Jake could do to keep from going for Frank's throat. "We're not going to get anywhere if you keep lying to me, Frank.''

"You're lying to yourself," Frank said nastily. "You want to wrap up this case, get your old man out of prison, clear your girlfriend. You want it to be me so badly that you're blind to what's right in front of your face." Frank shook his head at Jake in disgust. "What kind of killer would use his own motorbike, leave his engraved watch at the scene of the crime, hide the mask he used in his top dresser drawer? How stupid do you think I am?''

Jake decided he'd better not answer that one. Nor would he listen to that little voice at the back of his head arguing that Frank was making sense. No one was that dumb, not even Frank Ames. Maybe especially Frank Ames.

No, Jake thought, Frank was smart. He'd played it this way on purpose. Making it look too obvious.

"Who would want to frame you, Frank?''

He stared down the table at Jake. "I can think of only one person. Your father.''

"My father?" What kind of bull was this?

"But since he's still in prison, someone on the outside would have to be setting me up for him," Frank said. "Maybe that explains why you've been dogging me. You're working with your old man.''

Jake slammed a fist on the table, making it rattle and Frank jump. "That's a crock, Frank, and you know it. Why would my father want to frame you?''

"Where have you been, Hawkins?" Frank said, coming back like a mean, cornered snake. "You're supposed to be this amazing private eye.''

He leaned toward the man, reminding himself that Tadd had gone out on a limb for him, pulling a lot of strings so he could be alone with Frank.

"Why don't you spell it out for me?" Jake said, also reminding himself he'd promised not to lay a hand on Frank, let alone give in to the urge to kick Frank's scrawny behind.

"Where do you think I got the money to buy the resort?" Frank asked in that cocky, "about to get his butt kicked" tone. "Why don't you ask your father."

"What?"

Frank shook his head, sympathetically. "I got the money from your father."

"My father didn't have any money after the fire. Especially to loan you. He fired your sorry butt."

"A loan?" Frank's laugh almost changed Jake's mind about thumping him, cops or no cops, promise or no promise.

"He didn't fire me," Frank said. "I quit after I found out what was going on. Your old man paid me to keep my mouth shut."

Jake felt like he'd been kicked in the gut. He gripped the edges of the table and bit off each word. "What did you have to keep your mouth shut about?"

Frank got up and shuffled around the table to put the most distance between them, all the time eyeing the door. "I caught him skimming the money from the businesses. He paid me to keep quiet. I invested every dime of it and waited. I told you your old man was an embezzler."

"You're lying," Jake growled.

"I've got the proof. I stole the doctored books." A smile curved Frank's thin lips. "You were right, Hawkins, Lola did play me for a fool. I thought she was in love with me and I made the mistake of telling her about your father and how he'd been skimming money from the businesses. Then I found out that she was leaving the island with some man and had told Clancy's old man about your father, his partner and friend, so Clarence Jones wouldn't think she'd been taking the money." Frank let out a bitter laugh. "So I went to the resort that night and I took the books before your father could destroy them."

Jake leaned into the table, sick at heart. His internal arguments that Frank was lying fell on deaf ears.

"So you see, Warren didn't destroy the doctored books in the fire because he couldn't find them. That's probably what he was fighting with Lola about when Clancy saw him. He must have thought she'd taken them. That's probably why he killed her. In the end, they both got what they deserved. And I got the resort. So who's the fool now, Hawkins?"

CLANCY HADN'T BEEN into the storage room in years. She waded through musty old weathered orange life jackets, past rods and reels and water skis, to the dusty boxes at the back. The one she wanted, of course, was on the top shelf.

She pulled out another box to stand on and reached up for her mother's old hatbox, remembering Lola's box of mementos. Clancy's was much the same. A box that most people would think was nothing more than junk. Little things that would remind her of summers spent on the island. With Jake.

As she stepped down she noticed that the large box she'd used for a stool held her father's yearbooks. Clancy pulled his senior yearbook from the box and carried it and the hatbox upstairs to the kitchen where there was more light.

Not ready to delve into the box and all those memories just yet, she opened her father's yearbook.

When she found her father's senior picture, her eyes filled with tears. He looked so young, she thought as she ran her fingers over his face. Oh, how she missed him. He hadn't been handsome by most standards, but he had been to her. He'd been voted class clown, she noted with a smile.

She found another photograph of her father with his two best friends, Warren Hawkins and Johnny Branson.

She looked up their senior photographs. Johnny appeared uncomfortable in an outdated brown suit and garish tie. She studied his face, remembering what her father had told her about Johnny. He'd had to go to work at a young age to help support his family and was always ready to help anyone in need. He'd been voted nicest guy in the class.

She turned a page and found Warren Hawkins. His smiling photograph was in stark contrast to Johnny's. Captain of the football team. Star quarterback. Senior class president. Voted by his classmates as most likely to succeed.

As she thumbed through the yearbook, she looked for Helen. What had her maiden name been? Clancy thought she was a couple of years younger than Johnny. She found Helen in the sophomore section. Helen Collins. Her hair, a pale blond, was long and straight. A pretty girl. No wonder Johnny had fallen for her. Talk about contrast. Johnny had come from one of the poorer families around Kalispell; Helen from one of the richest.

Clancy started to close the book when she noticed a group photograph. The drama club. Johnny Branson would have stood out in the back row for his size alone, but no one could miss the smile on his face.

Helen Collins stood in front of Johnny in a simple shift, her hair hanging past her shoulders. She smiled into the camera. It tugged at Clancy's heart just looking at the two of them. Childhood sweethearts. They had married right out of high school.

Clancy pushed aside the yearbook and opened her treasured hatbox. Like Lola's box of keepsakes, it was filled with memories from summers of love. An odd-shaped smooth rock that Jake had picked up off the beach and handed to her. The lure she'd caught her largest fish on; Jake had netted it for her. The photo he'd taken of her holding it. Ticket stubs from movies, concerts and plays.

Clancy spotted a play program, the same one she'd seen in Dex's stuff on the back wall of his closet, she realized. Clancy remembered that play. For two reasons. It had been a special date. Jake had surprised her with dinner on the mainland and then a play at the community theater in Bigfork. It was over dinner that he'd told her he loved her and wanted to marry her.

But the play was also where she'd remembered seeing Lola wearing the bead necklace. As she'd sat next to Jake, with him holding her hand, everything about the play had been magnified. Not that she could remember the name of the play or even what it was about. But she remembered the necklace. Probably because of the tiny handmade ceramic heart. It had caught the light at the end when the cast and crew took their bows. It had stuck in her memory because she and Jake had promised their hearts to each other that night.

She opened the play program. The photographer had taken a large wide-angle shot of the cast and crew. Clancy found Lola in the front row. Her heart sank. Lola's neck was bare. Why had Clancy been so sure that's where she'd seen the necklace before?

Clancy's gaze fell on another woman in the photo. Around her neck was the tiny string of beads, the stage lights catching on the ceramic heart. Helen Branson had been wearing the necklace the night of the play. Not Lola.

JAKE DROVE INTO the state prison yard under the heat of a summer sun. His head ached. He kept telling himself he couldn't believe anything Frank said. Frank would do anything to cover his own behind. The problem was, he believed him. Hadn't Jake always prided himself on being able to tell when someone was lying? Well, he'd been wrong about Clancy. Could he be wrong about Frank, as well?

"Jake," Warren said, sounding surprised and nervous as he was ushered into the visiting room. He started toward his son but stopped as if suddenly scared. "What's wrong? Nothing's happened to Clancy—"

Jake shook his head. "The sheriff just arrested the man he believes killed Lola and Dex Strickland."

Warren slumped into the nearest chair. "Thank God they finally found the killer. Who is he?"

"Frank Ames."

Warren looked surprised. "Frank Ames?"

Maybe it was his father's look. Maybe it was realizing earlier that Clancy would never lie to him. Or maybe it was that bad feeling, thumping at the back of his brain. But he knew. "You lied to me."

Warren sat perfectly still, his gaze locked with his son's.

"It was you all along. You stole the money. And you let a slimeball like Frank Ames blackmail you."

Warren's eyes swam behind tears. "I tried to warn you. I asked you to stay out of this."

Jake felt his stomach turn to stone. "Frank thinks you're orchestrating all the evidence against him from here. He actually thought I might be a part of it."

"That's ridiculous," Warren said.

"Why, Dad? Why did you do it?"

He suddenly looked years older. "I was losing your mother, Jake. I knew she was unhappy and I thought more money would keep her. I planned to pay it all back. But then Frank found out and I found myself getting in deeper and deeper. I didn't know how to stop."

Jake swore.

"It just got so crazy after Lola was murdered. I wanted to tell the truth, but I was afraid it would make me look more guilty. Then it was too late."

"Mother knew." Her attitude toward his father suddenly made sense.

"I told her. She couldn't forgive me. It didn't matter that I did it for her. What about you, son? Can you forgive me?"

The pain was too raw right now. Jake just kept thinking about Clancy. "Clancy saw you arguing with Lola that night, just like she swore she had."

Warren nodded. "But I didn't kill Lola. I swear to you. When the fire started, I got out. I thought she was behind me. I realize now, whoever was in that adjoining room started the fire and killed Lola."

Jake stared at his father, unable to believe anything he said. A mystery person in the adjoining room. For years he'd wanted to believe that. But he hadn't believed Clancy, who'd told the truth. Now he wanted desperately to blame his father, to blame someone other than himself, something other than himself for all those years of lack of trust in the woman he loved.

"The killer is after Clancy," Jake said. He moved to the door, needing desperately to get back to Clancy. What had started as a notion, jitterbugging at the back of his mind, was now a death march. The killer was still out there.

Jake stopped at the door, all his fears pounding him like hail the size of walnuts. He thought of Clancy alone at the lodge. If Frank hadn't killed Lola— If Warren hadn't—

"Who was Lola in love with?"

Warren slumped into a chair. "He wouldn't hurt Clancy."

"Are you willing to gamble Clancy's life on that? Because if you are—" Jake opened the door to leave.

"Wait."

Jake looked back at his father. He could feel time slipping away. He had to get to Clancy.

"He loved Lola," Warren said more to himself than Jake. And Jake realized his father had sat in his cell for ten years having this same argument with himself. "He couldn't have killed her."

"Who?" Jake demanded, losing his patience with this tangled web of misplaced loyalties.

"Johnny Branson."

"Johnny?" Jake cried.

"He fell head over heels for Lola. He'd never loved anyone like he loved her, but in the end he made the right decision. He was going to tell Lola that night that he couldn't leave Helen.''

"Johnny was meeting Lola at the resort office?"

"He'd already been there when I found Lola," Warren said. "She was very upset, so I figured Johnny had told her. But I swear to you, she was alive when I left that room."

"How do you know Johnny wasn't still there?" Jake asked.

Warren blinked. "Johnny loved her. He's the kind of guy who wouldn't hurt a fly."

THE PHONE RANG, making Clancy jump. She glanced at the clock on the wall, surprised how long she'd been working. The rest of the morning had passed in a blur of creative expression.

Clancy stretched, content with the work she'd accomplished. It hadn't taken her long to get back into it. She'd always worked best when something was bothering her. While her fingers shaped the clay, her subconscious worked on any problem on her mind. Like the string of beads. Clancy could see where Helen might not remember a cheap bead necklace after ten years. But how had Helen's necklace ended up in Lola's keepsake box? Not that it probably mattered, she told herself as she wiped her hands and went to answer the phone. The killer had been caught. With any luck, Frank would confess and this nightmare would be behind her.

"Clancy?" Tadd asked. "Is Jake there?"

"No, he's gone to Deer Lodge to see his father. Why? Is there a problem?"

"No, I just wanted to talk to him. When do you expect him back?"

Clancy glanced at the clock on the wall. "Any time, actually. What's going on, Tadd?"

"It's Frank Ames. The sheriff had to release him for lack of evidence."

She sat down hard on the stool at her worktable. "Lack of evidence? What about the watch, the hooded sweatshirt, the mask?"

"Frank had an alibi for the night you said someone tried to drown you, Clancy. He also had an alibi during the time Lola was murdered. Everything against him is circumstantial. The sheriff couldn't hold him. Also, that watch you found off the end of the dock. It might have been ten years old, but the engraving on it wasn't, the lab says."

Someone had planted the watch off the end of the dock? Who had even known about the scrape on her ankle? Jake. Tadd. Helen. Helen had probably told Johnny. Clancy glanced through the window at the lake shimmering under the summer sun. "When was Frank released?"

"Not long after Jake's visit this morning. I just heard about it and wanted to let you know."

Jake had gone to the jail to see Frank? "I thought you were so sure Frank was the one."

Silence. "There's been some new evidence. An eyewitness got the license plate number from a car that was seen near Glenda Grimes's just before the fire. We're waiting to get a name from the Department of Motor Vehicles. Their computer's down. I'll call you as soon as it comes in. Do you want me to send someone out there to stay with you until Jake gets back?"

Another call beeped on Clancy's line.

"No, I'm fine," Clancy said. "My aunt's coming over. That's probably her calling now."

Absently she pulled the play program out from under her sculpting tools and opened it again to the photograph, thinking about the necklace.

She clicked to the other call. "Hello?" As she answered, she pulled the photograph closer, noticing that Helen wasn't looking at the camera but off to her right. She looked upset and seemed to be glaring at—

"Clancy?" It wasn't Kiki's voice. "It's Helen, dear."

"I was just thinking about you," Clancy said, wondering

if it had been ESP or just a coincidence. She looked more closely at the photograph. Helen was definitely looking at someone else. Clancy followed her gaze over to...Lola? Or— Clancy blinked. Or was Helen glaring at the man standing next to Lola? A big teddy bear of a man, Clancy thought with a jolt. That man was Johnny Branson.

"I hate to bother you." Helen sounded upset.

"Is something wrong?" Clancy asked, her heart pounding as she stared at the photograph. Johnny Branson. Teddy Bear?

"I was digging around and I found something I think you should see. Can you come over?"

What had she found? Something to do with Lola's death? Or had Helen found a receipt for the engraving of a silver watch?

"Helen, does this have something to do with Johnny?" she asked, voicing her worst fear.

"Yes." Helen sounded close to tears.

Clancy looked down at the play program photo. "I'll be right over."

"Please hurry." Helen hung up.

JAKE LEFT THE PRISON and headed for the airport, his chest aching with worry. As he drove, he dialed Clancy's number on the cell phone. No answer. Then he tried Helen Branson. The phone rang and rang. Jake hung up and dialed Tadd Farnsworth's office.

"Can you get the sheriff to send a deputy to Clancy's right away?" Jake asked.

"Clancy's?" Tadd said. "I just tried to call you to tell you about Johnny."

"What about Johnny?" Jake asked, dread settling in his chest.

"There's an eyewitness who saw a car parked near Glenda Grimes's house right before the fire. When the Motor Vehicle Department ran the plates—"

"The car's registered to Johnny Branson," Jake said.

"How did you know that?"

"Johnny is Teddy Bear."

"No kidding?" Tadd sounded genuinely surprised.

And Warren had been so sure that Johnny couldn't hurt a fly. Right. "You said you tried to call me earlier."

"I talked to Clancy and warned her that Frank's been released. He had alibis for the nights in question. The sheriff couldn't hold him any longer."

Jake swore. As hard as he tried, he couldn't convince himself that Frank Ames wasn't a danger to Clancy. "Did you tell her about Johnny?"

"I hadn't received the information yet from DMV the first time I talked to her. I tried a few minutes ago, but there was no answer."

"Tadd, I'm worried about her. Something's wrong. She said she was going to spend the day in her studio."

"When I talked to her she told me her aunt was coming over," Tadd said reasonably. "In fact, she got a call from Kiki while I was on the line. Maybe the two of them are outside and can't hear the phone."

Jake wanted to believe it was that simple.

"If you're worried about Johnny Branson, the sheriff sent a deputy out to bring him in for questioning. The deputy should be there by now."

Jake tried to relax but knew he wouldn't be able to until he had Clancy safe in his arms. "I'm in Deer Lodge. I'm flying out on the first plane I can charter." Or steal. "Call me when Johnny's in custody."

Chapter Nineteen

"Helen?" Clancy called after her knock at the kitchen door went unanswered. A warm wind blew off the lake, whispering through the tops of the pines at the edge of the deck. Large white cumulus clouds scudded across a backdrop of clear blue. Clancy knocked again and tried the door. Locked. She headed up the ramp to the second level, wondering if Helen was in the pool, swimming laps. That seemed odd, considering how urgent the woman had sounded on the phone.

"Helen?" Clancy called again. The pool glistened a pretty turquoise blue, but Helen was nowhere around. A knot of worry settled in Clancy's stomach. She'd told herself all the way over that she was just jumping to conclusions. Just because it had looked like Helen was glaring at Johnny and Lola in an old photo. Just because Johnny had changed so much since Lola's death. Just because he was indeed a big teddy bear of a man. That didn't mean that he was Lola's lover. Helen could have found out something else about Johnny—

Clancy had started toward the ramp to the top deck, but stumbled to a stop as something in the crack between the boards caught her eye. She knelt. More than a dozen tiny blue beads were wedged between the wood of the deck. Using her thumbnail, she dug one out. Her hand shook as she held it up to the light. This was a bead from the necklace. Helen's necklace. The one Dex had had the night he died.

She held the single bead in her palm, all the ramifications of finding it here battering her brain. This is where the string of beads had been broken. Dex Strickland had been here.

To see Johnny? To talk to him about Lola's murder because he was the former sheriff? Or because Dex thought that Johnny Branson had been in love with his mother and had killed her?

Clancy straightened, suddenly even more worried about Helen. What had she found out about Johnny? That he really was Teddy Bear? That he was the one who'd killed Lola? That he'd killed three more people to keep his secret?

Her steps quickened. Where *was* Johnny now? Had he returned from fishing? Clancy had ridden her mountain bike instead of coming by boat to avoid the climb up the cliffs by either the elevator or stairs. She hurried up the ramp, anxious to get to the top deck so she could see if Johnny's boat was tied at the dock.

Helen sat at the far edge of the deck, her back to Clancy, her wheelchair facing the lake. She wore her white terrycloth robe, the hood up. The wind whipped at one corner of the robe tucked around her legs.

Something about the way the woman sat made Clancy hesitate. Her shoulders were slumped forward, her head bent as if she were crying. If Clancy was right about Johnny and Lola— She tried to imagine what Helen must be feeling. Betrayed. Johnny had been her life. She must be devastated. How could a woman accept that the man she'd been married to all these years was a murderer?

"I came as quickly as I could," Clancy said as she approached Helen from behind. The woman had probably been sitting here, waiting, expecting her to arrive by boat. "Are you all right?"

When Helen didn't respond, Clancy laid a hand on her shoulder.

"Helen? It's Clancy."

Helen suddenly slumped forward in the wheelchair. Clancy rushed around to help her. "Helen," she cried as she knelt in front of her and gently pushed her back into the chair.

"Oh, my God!" Clancy threw herself backward, slamming into the deck railing. Her feet slipped out from under her and she sat hard on the deck floor at the foot of the wheelchair as a high-pitched scream shrieked from her lips.

JAKE DIALED CLANCY'S number again as he turned into the mainland marina. It was answered on the first ring.

"Kiki?" he asked. "Where's Clancy?"

"I was going to ask you the same thing," she said. "I just got here— Just a moment. Clancy left you a note. It says, 'Sorry. Helen called upset. I'm going over there. I think I know who Teddy Bear is and that Helen's figured it out, too.'"

Jake swore and hung up as he swung into a parking space beside the deputy's car. But it was the boat tied at the dock that stopped him dead.

He climbed out of the Mustang and walked down to the dock. Johnny Branson looked up from his boat and smiled.

"You must be that special fare I'm supposed to pick up," Johnny said.

Jake shook his head.

Johnny looked around and frowned. The marina parking lot was empty except for Jake's and the deputy's cars. Johnny seemed to study the cop car for a moment, then turned his attention to Jake. "That's funny," he said, still frowning. "I was supposed to meet a client here more than half an hour ago."

"Have you seen Clancy?" Jake demanded.

The older man looked surprised. "No, why? What's wrong?"

"I just got back from Deer Lodge."

Johnny's gaze dropped to his feet. "How is Warren?"

"How do you think he is?"

When Johnny raised his head, worry etched the man's thin face. Worry and a deep sadness that Jake knew only too well at this moment.

"He's the one who embezzled the money, but you knew that, didn't you?" Jake said, trying hard to hold down his anger. What had happened between two best friends that one would let the other go to prison for a murder he didn't commit?

Johnny slumped back against the side of the boat.

"You were Lola's lover. You were Teddy Bear." Jake had spent the last few hours trying to put it all together, but it still didn't fit. He told himself he was just too close to it. "You went to the resort that night to meet Lola. The two of you were taking off."

Johnny shook his head. "I went to tell her I couldn't go with her. I couldn't hurt Helen."

Jake stared at the former sheriff. At one time he'd been a big bear of a man. Now he looked frail and broken, a man worn down by secrets and sorrows. With a shock, Jake realized that Johnny Branson looked like a man who was dying. Jake knew that look; he'd just recently watched his mother die. "Cancer?"

Johnny raised his head slowly and nodded.

"How long?" Jake asked.

"I won't see fall."

Jake looked out over the lake, then back at Johnny. Jake's father was right; Johnny didn't seem like much of a killer. Nor could Jake understand why a man with only three months to live would keep trying to cover up a ten-year-old murder.

"The cops have an eyewitness who saw your car at Lola's sister's house just before Glenda Grimes was murdered and her house set on fire,'' Jake said. ''A deputy is at your house now with a warrant for your arrest.''

Johnny's gaze flicked up. He glanced toward the island, worry in his eyes. Jake followed his gaze, a thought hitting him between the eyes like a brick. A dying man *wouldn't* keep killing to protect himself. Jake felt his heart lunge in his chest. He swore and looked again at Johnny's gentle face.

''You didn't kill Lola,'' Jake said, the first thing he'd been truly sure of. ''My God. Who told you to pick up a fishing client here?''

''I probably just got it wrong.''

''Who, dammit?'' Jake demanded.

''Helen said Frank Ames set it up—''

''Call her.'' Jake vaulted into the boat and handed Johnny the two-way radio. ''Dammit, call Helen now. Clancy's on her way there. Helen phoned her and asked her to come over.''

Johnny stumbled to the radio. Just as Jake had feared, Helen didn't answer.

Jake shoved Johnny aside to start up the dual engines on the large, powerful fishing boat. It would be faster than his rental boat. He only prayed they could reach the island in time.

''You don't understand,'' Johnny said as they sped across the water. ''Helen loves me. She's always loved me. She was so pretty and popular. I was poor and a...nobody. She made me somebody, don't you see? She gave me everything. And look what I did to her.''

Jake's fears multiplied with each beat of his heart. He could see. That's what frightened him so. ''You fell in love with someone else. That's not the same as murder.''

Johnny's eyes clouded over. ''Helen didn't know I'd changed my mind about leaving her. She didn't know.''

The island grew closer, but Jake's fear grew with it.

"I was going to tell the truth," Johnny said. "Then after the accident— We were arguing. I was driving too fast. It was all my fault."

Jake could see only too clearly why Johnny had covered for Helen all these years. "She's killed three more people, Johnny. How long were you going to sit back and let her keep killing?"

He frowned. "She couldn't have killed them. How could she? A woman in a wheelchair?"

Jake had asked himself that same question. He picked up Johnny's binoculars. The home Johnny had built Helen high on the cliffs shone in the afternoon sunlight as Jake glassed it with the binoculars. The deputy's boat was at the dock. So was a bright red jet boat. "Whose jet boat is that?" Jake asked.

Johnny took the binoculars. "Frank Ames's."

Jake's heart dropped. "Maybe Helen had help." Someone like Frank Ames. Had Helen been Frank's alibi? That would explain how he'd gotten out of jail and why he was at Helen's now. To collect whatever amount she'd agreed to pay him. With a fresh rush of fear, Jake reminded himself that Helen had called Clancy to come to the house.

"Try the radio again," Jake commanded, praying that Johnny would be able to stop Helen. But who would be able to stop Frank Ames? Jake assured himself that a deputy was there—everything was fine. Except the hunch stomping at the back of his neck said everything was not fine. Not fine at all.

IN HORROR, CLANCY STARED at the face beneath the hooded robe in the wheelchair. Not Helen's face. But a man's. A man Clancy didn't recognize. Couldn't have recognized. The face purple, tongue protruding, eyes bulging. Around his neck was a white cord. The same white cord Clancy had seen Helen tie around her slim waist the day before. The cord was now taut around the strangled man's throat.

Unable to pull her gaze from his face, Clancy stumbled
to her feet. The wind caught the edge of the robe and
whipped it open. Clancy's heart thudded against her rib
cage as she backed her way along the railing toward the
house. The man wore a uniform from the local sheriff's
department. Clancy's heart rate rocketed upward. His holster was empty.

"Helen!" she screamed, frantic to put distance between
her and the death in the wheelchair, her brain tangled and
confused. Where was Johnny? She looked over the side of
the railing, down the cliff to the dock floating in the dark
green of the lake below her. Two boats. Neither was Johnny's fishing boat. Two boats? Her thoughts came like bul-
lets. A Sheriff's Department boat. But who did the other
one belong to?

Clancy inched her way along the railing toward the
house without consciously realizing what she was doing.
Who had killed the deputy and put him in Helen's wheelchair? Where was Helen? "Helen!"

Clancy's shoulder slammed into the glass door to the
living room. *Run!* The deputy was dead. Helen wasn't answering; she'd answer if she were still alive. The killer was
still here. His boat was still at the dock. *Just get out of
here. Get help. Don't go in the house.* She glanced toward
her bike, leaning against the deck railing, but her feet
seemed incapable of moving another step. She slumped
against the glass door. Panic made thinking almost impossible. Where was Helen? Who else was up here?

The door began to open. Clancy felt her breath catch in
her throat as she found the strength to push away from the
glass. She turned, in slow motion, hoping to see Helen in
her wheelchair, praying to see Helen. The sun ricocheted
off the glass. Behind it nothing but darkness. The door slid
open slowly. Clancy felt a scream rise in her throat.

Frank Ames stood in the doorway, smiling, his shirt
soaked with blood. Clancy screamed.

Frank stumbled toward her, his face contorted in not a smile but a grimace. He tried to speak but the words came out slurred. All Clancy caught was one word, "Helen," before Frank lurched forward and fell at her feet.

Clancy would have turned and run, but she heard a faint cry for help from within the house. Helen. She slipped past Frank's lifeless body into the living room. Empty. "Helen?"

"In here," Helen called from the front part of the house.

Heart hammering, Clancy rushed into the master bedroom.

Helen lay on the floor near the bed.

"Where's Frank?" she cried as she pulled herself up to a sitting position to lean back against the foot of the unmade bed. A bloody baseball bat lay on the floor beside her.

"I think he's dead," Clancy said, rushing to her. "Are you all right?"

"He tried to strangle me," Helen said, her hands going to her throat. She jerked off the scarf that had been wrapped around her neck and cast it away from her in disgust as she reached for a smaller wheelchair near the bed.

Clancy didn't mention the deputy, strangled outside in her other wheelchair. "Here, let me help you."

"Don't worry about me," Helen snapped, shooing her away. "Call Johnny. I need Johnny."

Clancy rushed back into the living room but went to the phone instead of the radio. She punched out 911 before she realized the line was dead. As she hung up, she noticed the drawer in the desk, partially closed on a stack of papers. Unconsciously, she opened the drawer to push the papers in. Her gaze fell on the word *Sleepwalking*.

She pulled the drawer open a little farther. There were dozens of photocopies of articles about sleepwalking. One sentence, underlined in red, leaped out at her. "Sleepwalking episodes are often triggered by severe stress or trauma.''

Clancy's heart thundered in her ears as something else in the drawer caught her eye. A tiny ceramic heart. The heart from the necklace.

Clancy staggered and grabbed the desk to keep from falling. Helen's necklace. It had been the clue all along. Dex had had the necklace. And the old play program. He *knew* it was Helen's. That's why he'd come here.

The two-way radio squawked. Clancy jumped.

''Helen?'' Johnny's voice came over the radio. ''Helen?'' Desperation laced his voice. She could hear the boat's motors in the background and the sound of his boat's hull slapping the water as it crossed the lake.

''Clancy?''

A chill streaked across her skin at the sound of Jake's voice. She lunged for the radio. ''Jake? Where are you?''

''We're almost there. Clancy, thank God, you're all right. Where's Helen?''

''In the bedroom. But there's a deputy here— He's dead, Jake. And Frank—'' The elevator. It groaned and clanked as it climbed the cliffs. Clancy could feel the hysteria rising like lava in her throat. ''Someone's coming up the elevator.''

''Clancy, listen to me—'' The radio crackled.

The elevator clanged to a stop. Clancy turned slowly, afraid of who she'd see in the contraption. The sun caught on the dull metal, then passed through the bars. The elevator stood empty.

''Clancy, do you hear me?'' Jake yelled over the radio. ''Get out of there! Helen killed Lola. Get out of there! Now!''

Clancy turned to look toward the bedroom as she set down the radio receiver. ''Helen?'' She moved cautiously toward the open bedroom doorway. ''Helen?'' A deathly quiet fell over the house. Her pulse thrummed in her ears.

She fought for each breath. At the edge of the doorway, she peered around the corner into the bedroom.

Helen was gone. So was the wheelchair and the baseball bat.

Chapter Twenty

Clancy stumbled to the door and stepped gingerly over Frank. The top deck was empty except for the deputy. He sat slumped over in the wheelchair, the wind snapping the tail end of the robe. Helen was nowhere in sight, but Clancy knew she couldn't have gone far.

Cautiously, she walked to the back edge of the deck to look down past the pool and the lower deck. Her bike still leaned against the railing. If she could reach it—

She could hear Jake's words in her head saying he was on his way. He would be at the dock soon. Take the elevator down to the dock and wait for him. She turned and looked back at it still sitting empty at the edge of the deck. Then she hurried over to it and pulled open the door. She stared at the empty elevator for a moment. Why had Helen brought it up? Just to slow down Johnny and Jake? Or for another reason?

Don't get in the elevator! Clancy stumbled back, no longer sure she could trust her instincts. *Take the bike. Get to the resort and call for help.* She turned and fled, racing down the ramp past the pool. She thought she heard a noise behind her but she didn't turn. She reached the railing and grabbed her bike.

"No, Clancy," a voice behind her said calmly. "That's not the plan."

Clancy turned slowly, expecting to see Helen at the edge of the deck in her wheelchair. The last thing she expected was to see her standing with the deputy's gun pointed at Clancy's heart.

THE WIND HAD PICKED UP as they neared the island. Waves hammered the bow and spilled into the boat, drenching them both. Jake didn't slow down. A million thoughts raced around in his brain. All the things he wanted to do with Clancy when they got out of this mess. Ahead he could see the dock. They were almost there. *Hang on, Clancy,* he cried. *I'm coming!*

"YOU CAN WALK!" Clancy cried, unable to take her eyes off a Helen she'd never seen before. "You were never paralyzed!"

"I was for a while." Helen moved closer, leveling the gun at Clancy's chest. "But after a few weeks I started to get some feeling back in my legs. The doctors said I might, but Johnny worried that I never would."

"He doesn't know?"

Helen cocked an eyebrow at her that implied Clancy was smarter than to ask a silly question like that. Of course he didn't know. Helen motioned with the gun for Clancy to start moving up the ramp toward the house. "Let's go out on the deck where we can see when Jake and Johnny get here."

"You stayed in a wheelchair all these years to keep Johnny?" Clancy asked in amazement as she stood staring at Helen.

"With Johnny fishing most of the time, it wasn't hard to keep up the charade. I learned from the master," Helen said. "I watched how Lola entrapped Johnny with her helplessness. Did he want a woman who was strong and resourceful? No, he wanted one who was inept, dependent, hopeless. Someone he'd have to spend his life's energy taking care of." Helen's gaze turned hard. "All I did was pattern myself after Lola. She was what he wanted. So I became her. Totally dependent on him for my very existence."

"You killed Lola!"

"I had no choice," Helen said, seeming surprised by Clancy's reaction. "I didn't know Johnny had gone to the resort that night to break it off with her. But it's probably just as well. I wanted her out of our lives forever and at any price. Unfortunately, for Lola the price was death." She motioned for Clancy to get moving.

Clancy started up the ramp. "And Dex? Was that his price, too?"

"He was just like his mother," Helen said. "He wanted something that didn't belong to him. In his case, it was my money. He thought I'd pay for his silence."

Helen shook her head as if the whole thing saddened her. "He called to say he had something of mine. I didn't believe him at first. He said he had proof. I told him to leave it under a bait can on the dock. Dex just figured Johnny would pick it up for me. He couldn't know that I'd come myself."

The message the cabin girl had taken to the dock. It had been for Helen.

"It was a drawing of the necklace and a demand for money," Helen said.

"How did Dex get the necklace?" Clancy asked, wondering how Helen's necklace had ended up in Lola's belongings after the fire.

"I had it on the night I went to the resort to deal with Lola. She tore it from my neck in the struggle."

That's when the clasp was broken, Clancy thought as she tried to walk more slowly, stalling for time, for Jake.

"I just assumed it had burned in the fire," Helen continued, sounding distant, as if the past no longer mattered. "The police must have found it and, thinking it was Lola's, given it to the family. It was the only proof that I'd been at the resort the night Lola was murdered.''

Clancy felt a chill race across her skin and turned to look at Helen. ''That night at the café. Dex saw something in the pines. It was you. Out of your wheelchair. Walking. No wonder he'd looked so frightened.''

Helen smiled. ''I enjoyed playing with him. Later I surprised him and his girlfriend at his cabin. I was in my wheelchair and convinced Dex he'd only imagined seeing me standing in the pines.''

That would explain why Dex was killed sans underwear.

''You agreed to pay him off?'' Clancy asked, remembering what Kiki had told her about Dex's mood.

Helen nodded distractedly.

''Then, how did the beads get broken at your house?'' Clancy asked.

Helen looked up in surprise as if the question had pulled her from other thoughts.

''I found the beads from the necklace caught in your deck,'' Clancy said.

Helen smiled. ''How very observant of you. Dex made me so angry, coming to the house when I told him not to. It was a good thing I'd given Johnny something to help him sleep. I grabbed the beads and...'' She looked across the pool, her eyes suddenly full of tears. ''The necklace broke. Johnny made it for me while we were in high school. He gave it to me the night he asked me to marry him.''

Clancy thought she heard the roar of a boat on the wind. Helen must have heard it, too. She motioned with the gun for Clancy to head up the last ramp to the top deck.

Clancy felt sick inside. Jake would be here soon. But soon enough? ''How did you get Dex into my garret?''

''Dex thought Lola had embezzled the money from the resort and hidden it somewhere. I just told him it was in your garret and where you kept a key, over the front door.''

Jake had been right; everyone in the world knew about the key.

"And Dex believed you that *I* had the money at the lodge?"

They reached the top deck, and Clancy felt time running out as quickly as beach sand poured from between her fingers.

"Dex was like his mother. Greedy, but not particularly bright," Helen said, not unkindly. "I followed him to your lodge. I didn't know you would come sleepwalking in and pick up the sculpture I'd used to kill him. I remember your mother saying what a sound sleeper you always were. She thought that was one reason you sleepwalked."

Helen had always known about her sleepwalking. "Weren't you worried that I'd remember seeing you?" Clancy asked.

"Of course not, dear, I'd seen you sleepwalk before, the night I killed Lola. I passed you on the dock and you looked right at me."

Clancy turned to stare at her, realizing Helen had spared her that night on the dock only because Clancy had been walking in her sleep. "Then, why did you frame me with Dex's murder if you felt you had nothing to fear from me?"

"I was just buying time, dear." She frowned. "But then you came over asking about the necklace and I knew, as badly as I didn't want to, I'd have to stop you."

Clancy's eyes widened in horror as she realized this soft-spoken, caring woman she'd known most of her life had become a cold-blooded killer. "You tried to kill me." Even now, Clancy found it hard to believe.

Helen wagged her head. "It grieved me terribly, dear. You were the last person I ever wanted to hurt."

Clancy felt repulsed as she noticed the silver bracelet on Helen's slim wrist. "It wasn't a watch that scraped my ankle but your bracelet. After I told you I thought it was a watch, you planted the watch off the end of my dock to make it look like Frank Ames did it." Clancy stared at her in abhorrence. "You couldn't have been the person who ran me off the trail on the motorbike," Clancy said, thinking Helen had to have had an accomplice. Frank?

"I'm quite capable of riding a motorbike, dear," Helen said, sounding offended. "I used to be an athlete, remember?"

Yes, and Clancy had forgotten what excellent shape Helen had kept herself in all these years. She remembered seeing Helen hoist herself into the wheelchair. The woman had incredible strength for her age. And Clancy realized Helen Branson was capable of anything. Including another murder.

"Frank figured out that you were the one framing him," Clancy said.

Helen seemed not to be listening. "That young waitress saw me take Frank's bike and thought to cash in on my misfortune." Helen tsked to herself. "So unfortunate. But it doesn't matter now, does it, dear? Time has run out."

Clancy had reached the edge of the top deck. The wind whistled across the mountain, whipping her hair into her eyes. She backed the last few feet to the railing as Helen indicated her to do, intensely aware of the gun pointed at her heart, but thinking more of the cliff behind her.

"Helen, you can't expect to get away with this," Clancy cried.

"Oh, I don't dear. I'm just cleaning up a few loose ends. Tidying up." Helen stepped around Clancy to look down the cliff, but the gun never wavered. "Don't do anything foolish, will you, dear." She smiled as she glanced up. "I always thought you and Jake Hawkins would make a fine couple."

Clancy could hear a boat motor growing louder over the howl of the wind. She felt tears sting her eyes.

"They're almost here. It's almost over." Helen looked up at Clancy. "Johnny's dying of cancer. He thinks I don't

know." She smiled sadly, her eyes bright with tears. "I'd
hoped for just a little more time with him."

Clancy glanced past Helen in shock. Frank Ames was no
longer sprawled in the living-room doorway. He stood behind Helen, blood running down into his left eye as he
reached out a hand.

JAKE WAS OUT OF THE BOAT the moment they reached the
dock. He didn't bother with the elevator but took the stairs,
two at a time. Below him Johnny stumbled from the boat.
Jake heard him try the elevator. It groaned but didn't move.
Helen had locked it on top to slow them down. Behind
him, he heard Johnny running up the stairs. Jake ran faster.

HELEN SMILED AS SHE SAW the startled expression on Clancy's face. "You really don't think that old ploy is going to
work, do you, dear? I'm suppose to see that look on your
face and then turn around so you can jump me and take
the gun away. Really, Clancy, I thought you were more
intelligent than that."

Frank laid a hand on Helen's shoulder. Surprise, then
fright, registered in her eyes. She started to wheel around.
Clancy lunged for the gun and, grabbing Helen's wrist,
fought to wrestle the pistol away. Helen swung her body
to catch Frank in the face with her elbow; he fell backward,
hitting the deck hard. The gun went off, the shot echoing
across the deck.

JAKE HAD NEARED THE TOP of the stairs when he heard the
shot. His heart in his throat, he drew his .38 from the holster
at his ribs and bounded up the steps, fear racing him up
the last few.

Clancy still wrestled with Helen for the pistol, but her
concentration broke when she spotted Jake. Helen
wrenched the gun from Clancy's grasp and was raising the

barrel to point it at Clancy when his foot came down on the last step.

"Drop it!" he yelled over the wind, ready to fire if Helen hesitated for an instant.

The gun dropped from Helen's hand and hit the deck with a thud.

Jake rushed over to scoop it up. Then pulled Clancy to him. "Are you all right?" His heart slammed against his ribs, making each breath a labor.

She nodded.

Helen smiled as she saw Johnny lumber up the last of the stairs. She ran to him. He took her in his arms and held her, seeming only mildly surprised that she could walk. Jake looked into the big man's face and saw the pain. And the silent plea. "Let me take her in."

Jake nodded.

"It's all over, Helen," he said to his wife, hugging her to him.

She nodded and turned to look back at Jake and Clancy. "Yes," she said. "It's all over."

"Shall we take the elevator down?" Johnny asked Helen.

She looked up at him, her face full of love. "Yes. That's exactly what I thought we'd do."

They walked arm in arm to the elevator.

"Jake," Clancy cried softly. "No, you can't let them—"

Jake pulled her closer. "Let them go, Clancy," he whispered.

Johnny helped Helen into the elevator and stepped in after her, closing the door behind them. He turned to look at Jake, tears in his eyes. Then he pushed the button. The elevator dropped like a rock.

Epilogue

The wind whipped Clancy's hair as she watched the Galveston skyline grow smaller behind the boat. She brushed her hair back and breathed in the smell of the gulf, letting it fill her lungs as she looked at her husband.

Jake stood on the bridge of the thirty-six-foot trawler steering them toward the endless horizon, his Astros baseball cap cocked back, his tanned hands strong and sure on the wheel.

Her husband, she thought, and smiled as she joined him.

"What are you smiling about, Mrs. Hawkins?" Jake asked as he pulled her closer.

She liked the sound of that, loved the feel of him. "You," she answered. For so long, Clancy thought she'd never smile again.

The days after Helen and Johnny's deaths had been as dark as the days after the resort fire and the loss of her parents. But unlike then, Jake helped her through those early summer days, piecing together what had started ten years before and finally ended on the Bransons' deck.

Some of the answers died with Helen and Johnny. Others were locked in Clancy's subconscious. Had she really walked along the cliffs all the way to Helen's in her sleep to return with a single blue bead, not once, but twice? Had part of her known all along it was Helen? Is that why she'd continued to walk down the beach each night?

Whatever the reason, the sleepwalking had stopped as abruptly as it had started. She knew that as long as she could curl up with Jake each night, she would have no reason to walk anywhere in her sleep again.

Frank had lived and become a hero, taking credit for saving Clancy's life, although Clancy knew now that Helen had never intended to harm her or Jake at the end. But Frank seemed happier than he had in years. Maybe he'd finally gotten rid of that chip on his shoulder. Or maybe he'd just finally laid Lola's ghost to rest.

With Tadd's help, Warren Hawkins's case was reopened. He got out of prison in time for their wedding and stood next to his son as Jake promised to love, honor and cherish.

Their lives had been different as they'd left Hawk Island. Like Johnny, she and Jake had once seen the world in blacks and whites, rights and wrongs. Now they could see the grays.

It had been Jake's idea to marry as soon as possible. "Life is too short," he'd said. "We've already lost enough time. Let's not lose any more."

"Aunt Kiki isn't going to like it," Clancy had pointed out.

"Oh, you might be surprised. I think I finally figured out why she hired me to investigate your case."

Kiki had cried at the wedding, then presented them with the thirty-six-foot trawler. "Go see the world, and when you get back, I'll have the nursery ready at the lodge." Clancy had assured her that wouldn't be necessary. Not yet, anyway.

Clancy snuggled against her husband and looked back to see the Galveston skyline disappear behind them. When she turned back, Jake was gazing down at her as if just looking at her brought him joy.

"Did I ever tell you about these hunches that I sometimes get?" Jake asked.

She shook her head and grinned up at him. "I don't believe you ever have."

He rubbed at the back of his neck. "How do you feel about twins?"

"Twins?" Clancy cried.

"Twin boys. Born nine months from now."

She laughed. "You really don't put any stock in these hunches of yours, do you?"

"Nah," he said as he put the boat on automatic pilot and led her down to their cabin. "None at all."